What I Really Learned in College

The With Honors Series
Book One

Addison Winters

2nd Edition

Cover Design by Greg Simanson

Edited by Katrina M. Randall

This is a work of fiction. Names, characters, places, brands, media, and incidents are either the product of the author's imagination or are used fictitiously. Any resemblance to similarly named places or to persons living or deceased is unintentional.

PRINT ISBN 978-1-948143-01-1

EPUB ISBN 978-1-948143-05-9

Library of Congress Control Number: 2014944997

Acknowledgments

A big thank you to my fabulous team led by our fearless leader, Jesse James, followed by the glorious and extremely talented Katrina Randall, who understands rambling gibberish, and our elegant proofer Lydia Johnson, who polishes the manuscript to a high shine. I cannot thank each of you enough for all your support, hard work, and talent. Plus, my "conscience," Liang Ang whose extraordinary feedback helped to shape my words. None of this would be possible without all of you! And finally, I cannot forget the one who inspired this series and his willingness to participate in testing my hypotheses . . . what a fabulous time! He he.

For D. C. R.; the man who haunts my dreams …

Chapter 1

THE BUTTERFLIES IN my stomach had grown to the size of buzzards tearing apart my insides. My palms were sweaty, and my hands were grasping the steering wheel to keep from shaking. The mid-July heat was sticky, the humidity on full blast. The music blaring from my car stereo was more of an annoyance than anything else. I hastily smacked the knob turning it off. "This is stupid . . .," I muttered to myself.

I turned the next corner into a parking lot full of cars. I had no clue where I was and an even lesser clue as to why I was even here in the first place. "You are so lost," I said aloud to the empty car. I sat idling, looking for some sort of landmark that would tell me where I was. To my right was a hulking black man with an armload of books walking confidently across the lot. I slowly eased my car up beside him feeling more stalkerish than anything else.

"Excuse me. Can you tell me where student orientation is, please?" The early morning sunlight was blinding me, and I couldn't get a clear view of his face.

"First time on campus?" he said, rather than asked, with a full-hearted chuckle, leaning into my car.

"Yes," I stuttered in return.

"And you're lost, right? Well . . ." He stood upright and looked around. "Hell, it'd be quicker to show you." And with that, he opened my door and climbed into my little car.

*   *   *

Fast forward three weeks and I found myself in a similar situation except this time, it was the first day of school...my first day of college and I was scared out of my mind.

I was thirty-two years old, a divorced mother with two sons and a victim of my own making. I had always dreamed of going to college, earning my bachelor's degree, and getting myself out of a stream of dead-end jobs. I had finally convinced myself that now was the time to chase after that dream. I knew it was going to be challenging at best, but now that my youngest was in school full time I decided I could do it.

What the hell was I thinking?

So here I was, turning down the wrong way on a one-way street on campus, hearing a wave of horns blasting at me. My eyes searched for a place to turn off safely when my cell phone started ringing.

"Yeah . . ." I hit the speaker button.

"God, I hate the first day of school. Some asshole in a green car is driving down the wrong way on a one-way street. I hate freshman." Isaac's deep voice echoed through my car.

"Sorry, that's me," I stated with frustration, pulling into a parking lot on the east side of campus.

"Seriously? That's you?" He laughed. "Figures."

"Oh, shut up!" I pulled my little car into a vacant spot. "I hate this campus."

"You'll get used to it. By next week you'll know it better than your own backyard." A car horn blasted twice behind me. "Turn around."

"Oh, sorry." I glanced into my rearview mirror and watched him pull into the spot next to mine. I turned off my car and gathered my backpack and keys.

Isaac was already standing beside my car before I even got my car door shut. "You're slow." He smiled.

"No, I'm terrified," I muttered.

"Here. This will help." He handed me a travel size bottle of orange juice.

I was parched so I gladly accepted his offer and took a small swig. "Argh." I almost dropped the bottle. "What is this?"

"Orange juice," he said innocently.

"What's in it?"

"Just a little vodka."

"I think I need some coffee before class," I laughed, shaking my head slowly.

"This way." Isaac gestured towards the building across the street.

Isaac was a pre-med student in his fourth year of college. The day of our first meeting he had kindly showed me all around campus, walking me to each of my classes just to ease my anxiety in anticipation of this day. He was in his mid-twenties, also considered an adult returning student, and was hoping to someday become a surgeon. He was an easy-going man who was quick to laugh, easily over six and a half feet tall, and he weighed at least three hundred pounds.

*   *   *

I sat in the second row feeling completely out of place and casually looking around at my classmates. Almost all of them appeared closer to my eldest son's age than my own. I fiddled with my pen and notebook, wondering once again if I'd made a huge mistake thinking I could do this.

A tiny little woman entered the class toting a bag that probably outweighed her easily by a note. She made her way up to the front of the class and let her bag drop heavily on the floor. This was our teacher… *Damn, she looks barely old enough to drink.* She was a petite girl with a mousey appearance. She stepped up to the podium with an obvious nervousness about her. She cleared her throat loudly and spoke to her feet.

"Welcome everyone to Psychology 104, Psychology as a Social Science. My name is Professor Medea, and I will be your instructor this semester." Her voice was barely above a whisper.

She droned on for the remaining hour of class, never raising her eyes beyond the floor or speaking loudly enough for the people in the back to hear her. The girl seated beside me muttered, "This is ridiculous" several times while rolling her eyes, yet she continued working on the doodles she was creating in her notebook. I was struggling to stay awake.

I am not sure exactly what I expected on that first day, but it was nothing like what occurred. For some reason I thought of colleges with long lecture halls, stereotypical professors with tweed jackets and leather patches on the elbows, plain notebooks and crisp textbooks that had never been read. I thought of the smell of coffee, study groups, and ivy halls. This reality, however, had never entered my thoughts.

*   *   *

I wish I could say that it was easy or that college was everything I had dreamed about, and that first semester went off without a hiccup. I could say that, but I'd be lying. It was hard. So, freaking damn hard. There were times when all I wanted to do was quit and return to my mind-numbing day job. Some nights I would stare at my assignments and cry because I was never going to understand the material no matter how many times I read it.

There were times that I truly hated the younger students in my classes who picked up the material easily, who never opened a book and aced every exam without ever studying. It didn't seem fair. I busted my ass late at night after I'd cooked and cleaned up dinner and helped my boys with their homework. There were more sleepless nights than I cared to count.

But I hung in there, if only for the fact that I wanted better for my children. I wanted them to be able to say that their mother was a college graduate and had a meaningful job that earned more than peanuts. I would look at them after they'd fallen asleep and think to myself that they deserved better than this . . . better than what I was providing for them.

And it got easier . . . eventually. By mid-semester I found my groove and my brain had started working again. I honestly thought I would feel so out of place on a campus where ninety percent or more of the students were in their late teens to early twenties, but I didn't. They seemed to embrace me as one of their peers and thankfully, never made me feel like I didn't belong there with them. For that, I was eternally grateful.

Our home fell into a rhythm as well and soon we were functioning in unison with the shift in dynamics. My six-year-old son, Henry, adjusted the best. My eldest wasn't quite so easy. Max was ten and a die-hard sports fanatic, stubborn and angry. Ever since their dad, Danny, had moved to Arizona three years ago because of a job promotion, Max found it necessary to be as difficult as possible. Their dad and I had been divorced for five years, but Max never let go of the dream of his parents getting back together. When Danny moved Max finally had to let go of the dream as well and that was hard. It was a constant battle that many divorced parents had fought before and nothing, but time was going to make it better.

Chapter 2

SECOND SEMESTER: welcome to the big lecture hall. I climbed my way about two-thirds down the steps in a lecture hall that easily held a couple hundred people. It was huge with three large screens behind a podium that literally stood upon a large pedestal. The rows toward the front were empty. It seemed most of my classmates preferred to sit closer to the top and in the back.

I slid into a seat a couple over from a young man who appeared asleep. He was hunched down in his chair with a beanie covering a mess of loose curls that were trying desperately to escape. He had pulled his winter coat over him like a blanket and had his feet up on the back of the seat in front of him. I wasn't sure, but I thought I heard him snoring.

I put my backpack down in the seat beside me and took off my heavy jacket. He was right; it was cold in here. I quickly put it back on. I got out my notebook and pen and tried to get comfortable in the most uncomfortable narrow space the university could provide. The little table that slid out from the side was slanted the wrong way and wobbled when I tried to write the day's date on my paper.

Our professor stepped up to the platform and pulled up a Power Point presentation and started in on his lecture. I had taken sociology thinking that it would be interesting. I was beginning to wonder how I could have been so wrong. Our professor was a drab, chubby man with navy slacks, and a white collared shirt covered by a badly faded red sweater that looked as if it might have fit him twenty pounds ago. His voice was almost like nails on a chalkboard and halfway through the class I decided that if he was the last man on earth I would happily become a lesbian. Given his drab décor and demeanor, I christened him Professor Drab for the remainder of the semester.

The cute boy crouched a couple seats down and somehow managed to sleep through the entire class. *Lucky bastard.*

* * *

The second day of sociology was cold and windy. Several inches of new snow had fallen in the two days since my last class. It was freezing as I walked across the quad listening to the snow crunch beneath my feet. There was a steady flow of students rushing from one building to the next. No one was spending time lingering around except for a small group of smokers huddled in the corner between two walls trying to keep the wind from biting them.

I wandered back to the seat I had previously occupied and was pleased to find the same young man asleep in his usual position. I was beginning to wonder if he was in this class or a leftover from the previous class because he'd failed to wake when it was over. He looked too comfortable for someone who had just wandered out of the snow. His sandy blonde curls were escaping out the ends of his beanie and softened the chiseled line of his scruffy jaw. I caught myself staring at him a moment longer than I should have, wondering what color his eyes were. He was so beautiful.

Professor Drab started in on his lecture once again but tried today to engage the students in his topic, *"Is there any truth in stereotypes?"* He had stumbled onto the topic of sports in high school and the *quintessential jock* we were all so familiar with. Several people spoke up, saying jocks were stupid, class clowns in letterman jackets, or attention whores. All were typical responses. As Professor Drab made his way up the aisle, stopping to address various students, he paused next to a woman who appeared closer to my own age. However, what came out of her mouth next completely threw me.

"Well, I know at my daughter's school, most of the girls who play on the sports teams are lesbians. My husband and I agreed that we did not want our girls to become lesbians, so we made them both quit playing sports by the time they started high school."

Her words almost made me fall out of my seat. I don't believe I had ever heard something so idiotic in my entire life.

At least until the woman a couple rows over from her said, "I understand, the last thing I ever wanted was for my daughter to become a lesbian because of sports. We also made ours quit."

As a former high school athlete, I could not believe my ears. Personally, I had attended two high schools and played on their basketball, volleyball, and softball teams. Never once did it make me turn into a lesbian, nor any of my teammates. Of course, we had some lesbians on the teams, and we all knew their preferred sexuality, but not one of us cared about it. There were also lesbians in the art club, science club, and on the chess team as well. *Oh my God . . . people are so ignorant.*

It was on the tip of my tongue to say something in defense of all female athletes, but I held back. I knew that getting into a verbal confrontation with ignorance never ends well and nothing I could say was going to deter either of these women. Plus, I truly believed that if the parents held these types of beliefs, there was a very good chance they would share them with their children. And the school teams were better off without such bigotry.

Our professor reintegrated into the conversation. "I can understand why, as a parent, you would remove your child from a team for such reasons. While being a female and participating in sports does *not* make you a lesbian, there is the *perception* amongst their peers that if you are a female who plays sports then you must be a lesbian. How you are perceived by your peers in high school is extremely important to most adolescents, so I can understand your reasoning . . . to a certain degree."

I couldn't. These parents weren't concerned with how their daughters were perceived by others; they *believed* that playing sports would turn their little girls into lesbians. They were not only ignorant bigots, but they were also just plain stupid.

I glanced over at my sleeping beanie boy who was almost purring softly. He hadn't moved an inch since this ridiculous lecture had begun. Again, I wondered if he was even in this class.

"Okay, for the remaining thirty minutes of class, I want you all to break up into pairs and make a list of all the stereotypes you can think of. Put both your names on the list and turn it in before you leave today," Professor Drab said as he walked back to the front platform.

The rustle of paper and the sound of low murmurs filled the hall as people turned to those around them and paired up. I looked up and down the row I was seated in and beanie boy was the only one who shared it with me. He stirred. For once, he moved.

His feet dropped to the floor with a small thump and his arms appeared from beneath his winter coat blanket. He looked around sleepily and smiled at me. "I guess you're stuck with me." He had the prettiest sea-blue eyes.

"I was beginning to wonder if I needed to call the coroner, but I decided I'd wait until the end of the semester." I rolled my eyes at him with a smile.

"I was listening with my eyes closed." He picked up his things and moved over to the seat beside mine. "So, what are we supposed to be doing?"

"Listening intently, I see," I teased. I couldn't believe I was casually flirting with this boy . . . yes boy, I reminded myself. *He is still a boy, not a man!*

I scribbled the word stereotype at the top of the page and then my name in the right-hand corner before I slid the paper over to beanie boy.

"Alex. It's nice to meet you Alex, I'm Mason." He extended his hand with a cheesy grin. *My God, he's flirting back.*

Mason and I spent about five minutes at best scribbling down a laundry list of stereotypes and making jabs about others we dared not put on the list. The rest of the time we talked about school in general. I learned he was a business major, in his second year of college, and going to be twenty-one in April.

Dear lord, he's still a baby! But totally edible . . . and legal.

I dismissed the thought quickly and made certain the conversation remained focused on him and that the only personal information I revealed was that I was a double major: psychology and nursing. I told him my goal was to become a nurse practitioner specializing in mental health disorders. He confessed that the only reason he was taking sociology was to fulfill his liberal arts requirement. I admitted the same.

* * *

The following Saturday morning I piled the kids into my little car and drove across town to their elementary school for their basketball games. Both boys played, but at different times, so most of the day was shot for studying.

It was almost seven-thirty when we pulled into the school parking lot. Snow was falling lightly and there was a bite to the air when I opened my car door. Henry sprinted into the gym; positive he was going to be late. He was supposed to be here a half an hour early before his eight o'clock game. Max didn't play until eleven. I was hoping to run out for coffee between games and maybe pick up something to eat.

Max and I huddled close together and fought the wind to the gym door. He was in an exceptionally good mood this morning, which was very rare for him and made me wonder if he was up to something. Typically, Henry was my good morning boy and Max was my night owl. I, too, was not a morning person and both my boys had learned over the years not to bother me before my first cup of coffee if not my second.

The gym was warm and filled with the smell of sweat and old sneakers. Max saw a couple of his friends and took off to sit with them without as much as a goodbye to me. I hardly noticed his rudeness anymore, which was even sadder than his behavior. I removed my scarf and gloves while my eyes scanned over the bleachers, curious as to whether we were the home team or visitors this morning.

I saw my friend Lisa sitting several rows up on the visitors' side, unpacking her tote bag of team goodies and made my way over to her. Her son, Logan, was on Henry's team. They had also been on the same peewee team the previous spring, so she and I had gotten to know each other well.

It was like that in a small town. You made friends with the moms whose kids played in the same league as your own children. Small town social life or lack thereof was pathetic for the most part, especially if you were a single mom. Lisa was also a divorced mom with three kids. Logan was the same age as my Henry, her daughter McKenzie was three and other, daughter Brie was eight. Lisa was only a couple of years older than me and had gone through a nasty divorce the year before.

"Good morning," I said as cheerfully as my frozen lips would allow. "Are we the visitors today?"

"Yeah." She set the juice boxes and a box of granola bars on the bench below us. "Don't forget, next week it's your turn to bring the snacks."

"Oh, right. Thanks for reminding me." I took out my day planner that had become my holy grail for keeping my hectic life semi-organized and marked it down.

"So how is your semester going? You started classes back up this week, right?" she asked.

"They're okay. I think the microbiology class is interesting. Physiology is going to kick my ass and so far, human sexuality class is most entertaining. My sociology class . . . ugh! I hate it. I wish I had chosen anything else to fill my liberal arts quota. It's so freaking boring."

"Huh, I would think that class would be interesting." Lisa shrugged.

"I was hoping so, but it hasn't been so far. Oh, I did learn something though, did you know that you shouldn't let Brie play sports? Apparently, it will make her a lesbian." She looked at me, confused since she was also a fellow former athlete. I went on to explain to her the ridiculous conversation that had transpired in my sociology class. Lisa chuckled and rolled her eyes.

"If it wasn't for the sexy little beanie boy who sits a couple seats over from me, it wouldn't even be worth going to class," I concluded.

"Excuse me, beanie boy?" she laughed.

"He's this sex on a stick kid that sits in my row. I got paired with him on Thursday afternoon to write this stereotypes list. His name is Mason and he's only twenty years old." I told her all about his curls, his eyes and the cute little scruff on his face. "He barely looks old enough to shave, but he's so freaking sexy."

"Who's sexy?" Kim slipped in behind us.

"Alex is lusting over this kid in her sociology class." Lisa laughed.

"He's legal," I jousted back.

"But not old enough to drink," Lisa informed Kim.

"Jesus Alex, how old is he?"

"Twenty. And all I said was he's cute. I mean, come on, there must be some benefits to going to college at our age. Right?" I shook my head with a smile.

"I thought you wanted a man in your life, not someone you'd have to babysit," Kim teased.

"I've already got two men in my life and they are enough for me right now." I nodded towards the area where my sons were.

"Someday you are going to have to get back out there, Alex," Lisa added.

"Just make sure he can take you out for a drink before dinner," Kim remarked.

"I'm already having enough trouble with Max. I can't imagine what he'd be like if there was a man in my life." It was sad, but true. Max was the real reason I had refrained from getting involved with anyone.

"Max will come around. Boys can be difficult." Kim would know, she had four of them. But she also had a dang near perfect husband. He was the coach for our boys' team, worked a fifty-hour week, and adored Kim. She was one of the few people I knew who was happily married.

*   *   *

We got back home shortly before two o'clock. Max was all hyped up from his game and groaned audibly when I forced him to get into the shower. Henry quietly slumped off towards his room. His team had lost by two points while Max's team had demolished their opponents. My heart went out to my little man. He tried so hard to be like his older brother and always felt that he never quite measured up. Henry was good at sports, especially for a six-year-old, but Max . . . Max had a natural flair for sports. He excelled at every sport he played. Therefore, he played them all. He played baseball in the spring and summer and was the best catcher in his division. Fall brought us football where he was the star wide receiver. I hated to admit it, but the kid did have magic hands. He could catch anything out of thin air and I loved watching him play. The winter winds pushed us indoors and to basketball. Max played small forward and loved the fact that he could hit those corner three pointers like no one else. And he should, he spent enough hours outside in the driveway perfecting that shot. Plus, year-round, both boys took Karate lessons. They had started it at the same time, and Henry was still a green belt. Max had pushed forward already and achieved his purple belt.

My poor little Henry. He always felt he was stuck in his brother's shadow no matter how hard he tried.

I put my things down on the table and walked back to Henry's room. I knocked lightly on his bedroom door that was adorned with a big poster of Iron Man. "Henry, can I come in?"

"Yeah," replied a small voice.

I opened the door and found my little man sitting on the side of his bed still wearing his basketball uniform and kicking the bed frame lightly with his foot. "How ya doing?" I sat down beside him.

"I'm okay." His big brown eyes looked so sad, as if it was taking every ounce of his strength not to burst into tears.

"Would you like to help me make some chocolate chip cookies?" I put my arm around him and pulled him close to me.

"No."

"What would you like to do?"

"I don't know."

"What's going on in there?" I leaned over and kissed the top of his head.

"Do you think I will ever be able to make that shot like Max?" We both knew exactly which shot he was referring to.

"Yes, I know you will."

"When?"

"Sweetheart, Max only learned that shot last year and he is four years older than you are. You'll get there. You just have to be patient."

"I'm tired of being the youngest."

"Well, there's not much I can do to help you with that one, I'm afraid. But, you know, I was the youngest too and it's hard having an older sibling. I understand how you feel," I tried to reassure him.

"Max is always better at everything than I am," he pouted.

"Now that's not true. You're much better at school than Max is." Max was an exceptional athlete, but he also had to study hard to keep his grades up. Henry was only six and already knew his multiplication tables up through his sixes. Learning came very easy to Henry and Max was resentful of him for that.

"That's only because first grade is easy," he muttered.

"It's not easy for everyone."

"I want to be the best at sports, like Max."

"I know, and you will get better as you get older, just like Max did." He smiled up at me, seemingly satisfied with that answer.

"Okay."

"Okay." I stood up. "When Max gets out of the shower, it's your turn, Mr. Stinky." I tickled him a bit.

"I know. I know." He squirmed away from me. "And then I'll help you make the cookies," he said, catching his breath.

"Sounds good." I knew he couldn't pass up a chance for cookies.

Chapter 3

BY THE END of February, Mason and I had become old friends. We sat next to each other and chatted casually about silly meaningless things just to make the class more interesting. So far, this semester, sociology was by far my easiest class. The other three were so much more demanding of my time and attention that I spent very little time on any of my sociology material. That realization hit me hard when our professor passed out our study guide for our first exam next week. As I glanced through the three pages of material, I was responsible for knowing, I had to admit I had not read one single chapter in our text book. In fact, it hadn't moved out of its spot on the corner of my desk at home. The information that was necessary for our little quizzes was all located within our notes so reading the assigned material each week was pointless or, so I had thought.

"Damn," Mason muttered, flipping through the same pages as I was. "I haven't even opened my text." He slowly shook his head, realizing the same thing as myself.

"Good. I'm glad I'm not the only one." I sighed heavily.

"Do you have class tomorrow?" he asked.

Fridays were my study days at home. Monday through Thursdays I had classes on campus so on Fridays I typically stayed in my pajamas after I got the boys off to school and spent the day hovering over my books.

"No."

"You wouldn't want to get together and study, would you? I'm gonna need some help if I'm going to pass this test." He blushed.

"I usually don't come to campus on Fridays," I said, more to myself than to him. "But I can. What time?"

"Tenish?"

"Okay. Where do you want to meet?"

"You can come to my dorm room?" Mason offered with a grin I didn't trust.

"Seriously? How about the student center or the library?"

"We can't have any fun at the library."

I wished he'd stop looking at me like that.

"We're not supposed to be having fun. We're supposed to be studying." I tried to laugh off his flirtation.

"Fine. I'll meet you on the second floor of the student center by the coffee house." He rolled his eyes playfully but held his mischievous grin.

*   *   *

That night I couldn't sleep. The house was silent except for the low murmurs coming from the television in my bedroom. Ever since Danny had moved out, I couldn't sleep without the television on. I spent many nights on the couch before I finally broke down and bought one for my bedroom. I had spent my entire adult life as someone's wife and someone's mother and I had only just in the last year or so begun to feel comfortable with being alone. Now the only one in my bed besides me was our shepherd chow lab mix named Billy. My grandfather had given her to Max when he turned four and Henry was only a couple months old. "Cause every little boy needs his own dog," was my grandpa's logic, and it was tragic that Max didn't have one. Max had insisted on naming her himself and despite us telling him repeatedly that his puppy was a girl, he wanted to name her Billy.

Billy had replaced Danny on the other side of the bed. She lifted her head when I climbed out of bed and watched me walk over to the window. I pulled the curtain back and looked out into the backyard. The woods behind our house were dark and the neighborhood beyond it was asleep. I lived in a little ranch style house that Danny and I bought when I was pregnant with Max as a starter home. But our marriage had died before we upgraded to a bigger house. Danny left shortly before Henry's first birthday. I had kicked him out after learning of the affair he was having with a co-worker. I suppose he would say it was worth it, he did eventually get that promotion and his move to

Arizona. It only cost him his wife and sons and, to be honest, he seemed okay with that.

The house was made of brick with forest green shutters, and I'd built gorgeous flowerbeds with my own two hands. Danny and Max had built Billy a doghouse that stood in the corner of our backyard, rarely used. The backyard was littered with toys, a wooden swing set, and a vegetable garden long since forgotten with the arrival of the snow. Our three-bedroom, two bath Ranch was perfect for the three of us. Not too big but not crowded either. I couldn't imagine ever selling it. This was home.

*　*　*

The next morning, I got the boys off to school and jumped into the shower. The music was deafening and filled me with its contagious energy as I sang at the top of my lungs along with Nate Ruess. It was amazingly freeing, and I was thankful no one was there to witness it except Billy. Although I was pretty sure she was laughing on the other side of the shower curtain.

With my hair still in a towel, I slipped into some jeans, a long-sleeved t-shirt, and a thick, hooded sweatshirt. Even though the snow had finally stopped falling, there was still plenty of it on the ground and the temperature clung to the mid-teens. A part of me dreaded agreeing to meet Mason. The last thing I wanted to do was drive to campus. I would rather stay home in my pajamas and study alone. But I didn't have a way to contact him and cancel. I was, however, grateful that he was meeting me at the student center, a public place that was always buzzing with students. I didn't trust myself to be alone with him.

I shook my hair out and let the towel fall to the floor. My reflection stared back at me in the bathroom mirror. I suppose I didn't look too hideous for my age. My thick dark hair hung almost halfway down my back, my eyes were a dark almond color. Danny had always called them doe eyes and said they were my best feature. I turned sideways and studied myself. My body had held up well considering it'd been through two pregnancies. My stomach was flat, my breasts were still full and perky, my legs long and slender leading the way to a nicely rounded ass that I'd spent many hours in Pilates working hard to obtain. "Not too bad." I told my reflection. "Not too bad at all."

I applied a little bit of make up like I did on any other day I went to campus. I was very careful to resist any urge I had to pay a little closer attention to the application like I would have for a date or special occasion. I blew dry my hair and pulled it up in a ponytail like I did most days on campus. I grabbed my coat and study materials and reminded myself once again that Mason was just a kid, not even old enough to drink.

*   *   *

I found an empty couch in the far corner across the area from the coffee counter. I set my backpack down on the coffee table and began to arrange my notes in front of me. It was quarter to ten and Mason was nowhere in sight. A part of me was seriously hoping he wouldn't show. Lisa and Kim both had taken a liking to teasing me about him every week since I had first mentioned him. Of course, they both also reminded me that I was single and maybe having a little *fling* with this guy would be just what I needed to push me back into the dating world. However, they both agreed that if I did, I had to share all the dirty little details with them, so they could live vicariously through me.

Ten after, and still, no Mason.

Okay, if he's not here by ten thirty, I'm going home.

I took a long sip of my coffee from my travel mug and tried to focus my attention back on the chapter I was reading. I managed to get through the first three chapters yesterday and highlighted key points that were mentioned in the study guide. Only three more chapters to go and I'd finally be caught up and, hopefully, prepared for the exam on Thursday.

"Sorry I'm late." Mason plopped down beside me on the couch. "I overslept." His curls were sticking out the bottom of his beanie as usual as he struggled out of his coat. His clothes were all wrinkled and I couldn't tell if he had slept in them or if he didn't know how to use an iron . . . probably both. The stubble on his face was present as always, but never seemed to grow. I had long since decided that he kept it at that length on purpose because he thought it made him look sexy. And he was right, it did.

He pulled his textbook, study guide, and notebook out of his backpack and set them on the coffee table beside mine. "Have you signed up for your twelve hours of community service yet?"

As part of our class requirements, each of us was required to fulfill twelve hours of community service. Only it had to be at a designated location chosen carefully by our professor. We had about eight different options and there was a list and sign-up sheet on our class community page on the school server site.

"No. Have you?"

"Nope." He pulled his laptop out of his backpack and set it on top of his textbook. I sat quietly watching him login to our class page and bring up our list of acceptable locations.

"Want to do this one? We can go together and it's the only one that we can complete our hours in one day."

"Second Chance? I've never heard of it." Mason clicked on the link below it.

"It's a consignment shop. I guess people donate unwanted items and they resale them. The proceeds go to feed and clothe the homeless." He summarized the paragraph that popped up.

"All right, sure. What's available?" Mason clicked a couple more times until the sign-up sheet appeared.

"The only thing left with two vacancies is the first weekend in April."

"Okay, that's fine with me." I took out my day planner and marked it down while Mason filled in our names on the sign-up sheet. "We're set. Seven to seven." He scrunched up his face.

"What's wrong?"

"That's my birthday." He sighed audibly and clicked the submit button. "Oh well."

"You mean, that's your twenty-first birthday," I stated with a grin.

"No big deal. I can go out afterwards." He closed his laptop and put it back in his backpack.

"Are you sure? We can change it."

"No. It's the only one that will only cost us a day instead of a weekend." He opened his textbook. "How far have you gotten?"

"Through the first three chapters. I just started on the fourth. You?"

"Um . . ." Mason blushed beautifully. "I've read most of the first chapter. Well, maybe not most." He dropped his eyes the same way that Max does when he's lying to me about something. I had to laugh at him.

"Really?"

"Okay. I've read the title of the first chapter."

"Seriously?"

"It's boring . . . sorry."

"All right. Here's what I've gotten so far."

By one o'clock Mason and I were making good progress. Thanks to the coffee house we were keeping well fueled on coffee and scones. He picked things up quickly and we finally made it through chapter four and completed all the questions at the end of the chapter as well as those up to that point on our study guide. Apparently, he had paid closer attention in class than I would have thought earlier, despite looking as if he was sleeping through the lectures.

"Hey stranger, there you are?" I looked up and saw Isaac approaching us with a big smile on his face.

"I didn't know I was lost." I stood up and gave him a big hug. "What are you doing here today?"

"Genetics lab. I just came over for a refill." He held up his coffee cup.

"It's not Irish, is it?" I said with a grin.

"Not yet, but it will be." Isaac had a habit of making about all his drinks Irish.

"Are you getting excited yet?"

"About what?" His eyes drifted over to Mason and then back on me.

"Graduation."

"No, not really."

"Are you kidding? I'd be ecstatic. You're almost done with your bachelors." I couldn't believe how blasé he was being.

"No, because that just means I have six weeks before I take my MCATS which will decide if I make it into med school or not and where I'll go."

"You'll do great. I'm sure of it."

Isaac didn't seem to hear me. "Who's this?"

"Oh, I'm sorry. Isaac, this is my friend Mason. Mason this is Isaac." Mason stood and shook Isaac's hand and exchanged pleasantries before Mason sat back down.

Isaac looked at me with raised eyebrows. "Friend?"

"Friend. We're studying for an exam next week in sociology," I explained.

"I was going to say, you aren't shopping in the kiddie section, are you." He laughed and Mason, thank goodness, remained quiet and pretended to be looking up something in our text. Really, he had no choice, he was a dwarf compared to Isaac. Hell, most men were.

"No, we're just friends," I declared a little too loudly.

"Cause you know, if you ever need a man to help you work out some of your frustrations . . . I've told you; I'd gladly volunteer my services." He laughed loudly.

"Get back to your rats, you ass." I smacked him hard against his solid chest, which only made him laugh harder.

"I'll see you later. Call me." He walked away still laughing aloud.

"Bye," I hollered after him.

"Sorry about that," I apologized to Mason as I sat back down beside him.

"You seemed offended when he questioned our friendship." Mason looked at me with a hurt look on his face.

"No, I didn't," I said, denying it, but we both knew better.

"You'd never go out with me? Is it me or my age?"

"Mason . . ." I didn't know what to say.

"I see." He turned back to his notes. "Let's just get back to work."

Thankfully, he let it drop and we got back to working on sociology. However, he wasn't nearly as playful as he was before Isaac's interruption. I felt terrible because I didn't know what to say to him. *Yes, you're too young for me. I'm sorry, but I could never see you as anything other than a temporary plaything and I would just be using you until I decide to return to the dating world where I would be dating men older than me who I have more in common with whereas you most likely have more in common with my sons . . . at least one of them.* Somehow, no matter how I said it, it sounded cruel. So, I remained silent on the subject.

I left campus a little after three, so I could beat the school bus back to the house. I couldn't get the hurt look on Mason's face out of my mind. We had spent the better part of the last five weeks casually flirting without actually flirting. There was an attraction there. I could not deny that. But the voice in the back of my mind was screaming at me that he was too young for me and would be more trouble than what he was worth if I ever got involved with him. Plus, I hated to admit that Lisa and Kim were right, he could never be more than a temporary distraction.

Chapter 4

THANKFULLY, BY TUESDAY, Mason had seemingly forgotten all about the uncomfortable exchange with Isaac and returned to his casual flirtatious self. He was back to teasing me about the silliest little things and making snide remarks throughout Professor Drab's lecture. It was refreshing to joke around with him again.

We went up to the coffee shop over in the student center. I had skipped breakfast and was starving. I ordered a Venti caramel macchiato and a huge blueberry muffin and took a seat over on one of the many couches. Mason got some coffee as well with a chocolate scone before he came over to join me.

"Any big plans for the afternoon, Lexie?" He set his coffee down on the table in front of us.

"Did you just call me Lexie?" I shifted more towards him.

"Yes. I've decided that you should be called Lexie instead of Alex. You're just very feminine and Lexie fits you better."

"But my name is Alex," I retorted.

"It's short for Alexandria, right?

"Yes."

"Well, Lexie is just another nickname for Alexandria. It's a beautiful name for a beautiful lady." He looked at me with the most adoring gaze. I was completely speechless.

"Well, thank you." I blushed unintentionally. "I've got to get home and study. I've got a quiz in my human sexuality class tomorrow morning."

"You have a quiz in sex ed?" He giggled. "Why would you even need to study for that?"

"Because I do. I'm not fluent in sexual dysfunctions and orgasm disorders," I said flatly and watched as his face turned red.

"You guys actually discuss things like that in class?"

"Of course. Why wouldn't we? It's part of the class." I was enjoying watching him squirm.

"Isn't that a tad embarrassing to discuss as an open topic in class? I couldn't do it."

"It's not like we are discussing personal experience or our own sexuality. It's very academic." I laughed. "I hadn't realized you were so frigid."

"I'm not frigid. I just don't broadcast my sex life," he pointed out.

"I don't broadcast mine either. It's an intellectual discussion, not an account of your personal diary."

"Still, I don't believe I'd feel comfortable discussing such topics in a classroom," he admitted.

"I had no idea you were so conservative. Why would such a subject be insulting to your ears?" I teased.

"Some topics should not be discussed in a public forum."

"It's not a public forum. It's a classroom. There's only about thirty of us in there, four guys and the rest are girls. Professor Hanson isn't exactly a typical professor. For one, she looks like a grandmother and has the personality of Betty White. Secondly, she has never asked us to share anything personal, simply to discuss the topics with an open mind. And finally, if I have learned anything from taking this class it is that our high school educational system has severely uneducated your generation on human sexuality. I was floored by some of the things these kids said." I took a long drink of my coffee and rested back a little on the couch.

"Such as?"

"Well, when the class started some of the girls said, 'you can't get pregnant if you're on top, or you douche afterwards or if you're on your period.' They truly thought there was only a window of a couple days when you could get pregnant. This class has been a rude awakening for them." I put my coffee back on the table. "I still cannot believe how naïve some of these kids are. It's no wonder why there are so many teen pregnancies when they are so misinformed."

"A lot of parents feel uncomfortable talking to their kids about sex. I think they feel it's like giving them permission to do it."

"I guess I look at it differently. I think children need to be informed so they don't accidentally get pregnant or an STD. But yes, I know most parents feel uncomfortable discussing such topics with their kids." I agreed with him on that point.

"When I hit puberty, my dad gave me a penthouse forum and a box of condoms. He tossed them on my bed and told me to always wrap it," he said with a grin.

"Shocker!" I laughed. I could picture Danny doing something similar with our boys.

Chapter 5

I ARRIVED AT the consignment shop just before they opened at seven. Mason had beaten me there and was waiting out front for me. He was wearing grey jeans, a black t-shirt, and a maroon sweatshirt that he'd casually left unzipped. His curls were still damp and hung loosely around his face. He looked gorgeous. It was getting harder and harder to ignore my attraction to him.

"Good morning, Lexie. I thought you might enjoy this. It's a caramel macchiato." He smiled and handed me the coffee.

"Oh, you're so sweet. Thank you." It was exactly what I needed. "And happy birthday."

"Thanks. You ready to get this over with?"

"Like I have a choice." I nodded with a smirk.

Mason opened the door for me and we walked in to pay our penance for class. The manager took us to the back area where all the donations were stacked and sorted. The amount of stuff piled from floor to ceiling was ridiculous. There was hardly any room to walk between all the boxes, huge bins on wheels and bags full of assorted cast-offs. Our job was to sort through as many of these donations as possible and put them into these huge bins.

The woman disappeared into her office and Mason, and I got busy. Clothes were separated by gender and size and were piled everywhere. The bags and boxes were endless, and it seemed like every woman on the north side of the city had decided this was the weekend to do spring cleaning, because we had a steady stream of donors dropping off items.

After lunch Mason started talking about his evening out with the guys to celebrate his birthday. They were headed to a pub in the city called Bernie and Clive's. He was the last one of his group to finally turn twenty-one.

"I'm surprised you guys aren't headed to a strip joint," I teased.

"Nah, not my style." He shook his head and tossed another shirt into a bin.

"Really? Why is that?"

"I just have no desire to go to one. I think they're highly overrated."

"Okay," I muttered under my breath.

"What did you do for your twenty-first?" he inquired.

"My girlfriends dragged me to a male strip club."

"Seriously?" Mason paused and gave me an odd look.

"Yes. It was a blast." I recalled how much fun we had that night. "Just make sure if you do something like that, that no one has a camera. Proof of your behavior never sits well with your spouse." I giggled.

"What did you do?" I could tell he was intrigued.

"Had too much to drink and my cousin's wife took pictures. I didn't think she'd ever show them to anyone, but her husband thought they were funny and showed them to Danny. He didn't find them very humorous," I tried to explain.

"What were the pictures of?"

"I'm not going to tell you. It's embarrassing." I threw a shirt at him.

"Ah, come on. Tell me. It can't be that bad."

"I didn't think it was, but apparently Danny would disagree." I smirked.

"Did you sleep with one of the male strippers or give him a blow job?"

"No! I would never do that!" I tossed another shirt his way. "All I did was lick some whip cream off this stripper's stomach and maybe she got a snapshot of me kissing another one on the cheek with my hand on his ass. But in my defense, my best friend was on the other side doing the exact same thing. It was just a lark, but Danny was furious."

"I can't imagine you doing something like that." He gave me an odd look.

"Why is that?" His statement kind of annoyed me. "I used to be young once too."

"I never said you were old. What I meant was I can't picture you doing anything wild. You're always so calm and kind." His words caught me off guard.

"You obviously didn't know me when I was younger. I wasn't exactly an angel." I smirked.

"Why don't you go out with us tonight and help celebrate my birthday?" A devilish grin slid across his lips.

"You want me to go to Bernie and Clive's with you and your buddies? No thank you." I shook my head.

"Ah, come on. It will be fun. Bring a friend with you if it will make you feel more comfortable. We're just gonna have a few drinks. It's no big deal."

"I don't think so."

"Well, we'll be there around nine. If you change your mind and I hope you do, feel free to just show up."

"I'll think about it," I said then quickly changed the subject.

*   *   *

I called Lisa on my way home that evening. I told her about Mason's birthday party at the pub. I should have known better because she thought it was a great idea. Her children were at their dads for the weekend, and she was home alone watching a bad chick flick and eating cookie dough out of the tub. She begged me to go and nagged until I finally relented. Now all I had to do was figure out what to wear and make sure my parents could keep the boys all night.

After I got home and showered, I tried on about a dozen different outfits. It had been forever since I'd been to a club, and I had no clue what to wear. It was still early spring, and the evening temperatures were still in the mid-forties. Despite that, I knew inside the club it was going to be warm, if not hot and sweaty. I finally decided upon a pair of straight legged jeans, ankle boots, a purple tank top and a teal soft crochet tee over it. I spun around in front of my full-length mirror. It was cute, but still casual. I added a couple of bracelets, earrings, and a couple necklaces, one long, one short. Satisfied, I grabbed my purse and slipped my driver's license and credit card into my front pocket with my cell phone. Lisa was already honking her horn from the driveway.

We pulled into the pub's parking lot just before ten o'clock. I was still questioning her logic for even coming. I felt ridiculous. She turned off her car and tucked her keys in her front pocket. "Ready?"

"No," I replied and opened the car door.

"Great attitude," she muttered, sliding out of her car.

Lisa was wearing snug jeans with knee-high black boots. It matched perfectly with a gray, long-sleeved draped top, and black camisole underneath. Her stylishly short blonde hair was cropped just at the back of her neck. The cut was adorable on her and something I would never have the nerve to do.

"I still can't believe you took his Mustang," I said, shutting my door. Her ex loved his car more than life itself.

"I can't believe you let Danny leave with his testicles intact. I wouldn't have." And I believed her.

"Don't worry. He's paying out the ass for alimony and child support."

"And he should. After all, he's the one who got promoted for his affair. I guess sleeping with the boss has its perks. Although, I can't imagine sleeping with my boss *even* for a promotion." She visibly shuddered. Her boss was grossly obese, bald with permanent pit stains. I had only met him once and that was enough. There was a certain odor that clung to him that was not exactly alluring. No promotion would be worth that no matter what the pay scale rose to.

The bar was hardly a bar. Pub would have been a more accurate description or hole in the wall. I had never been here before and walking in, I understood why. Lisa pushed our way through the crowd and over towards the bar. But with every step I took I could feel my shoes sticking to the floor from all the spilt drinks.

"Two crown and cokes," Lisa told the bartender when I finally reached her side.

"I cannot believe we are actually in this place." I leaned over and basically shouted at her.

"Where's your sense of adventure?"

"I think it got stuck to the floor back there." I nodded over my shoulder.

"You're such a snob, Alex." She laughed and paid for our drinks. She pushed my hand away when I tried to give her some cash. "You get the next round."

I nodded and picked up my drink. Lisa turned around and began scanning over the people in the bar. I sipped my drink and watched several people over in the far corner rack up another game on the pool table. One of the girls over there couldn't have been a day over twenty-three and was already staggering between her boyfriend and her friend, spilling her drink along the way. I shook my head and continued looking over the crowd.

"Loser. Loser. Gay. Loser. Thinks he's all that. Gay and won't admit it . . ." Lisa rattled off her opinion in a voice low enough that only I could hear. "Not bad. College boy. Cute . . . Oh, wow. Check him out." She nudged me in the ribs. "I could eat him with a spoon . . . Damn." I giggled.

"Who?" I tried to follow her line of sight. "The one in the blue shirt with the beanie on?" A smile spread across my lips.

"No!"

I nodded.

"You bitch." I laughed at the look on her face. "I hate you." She took another long look at Mason. "Seriously? That's him?"

"Yep. That's him." Then Mason noticed us and began waving to get our attention. I smiled and waved back.

Mason wove his way through the crowd towards us. Lisa was all smiles while I stood there still trying to figure out why I had let her talk me into this.

Mason gave me a big hug. "You made it! I'm so glad you decided to come."

"Mason, this is my friend Lisa. Lisa, this is Mason."

"So, you're the little study buddy." Lisa raised her glass to him. "It's nice to finally meet you."

"You too. Come on. We have a booth over here." Mason took me by the arm and started dragging me off in the direction in which he came. Lisa grinned mischievously and followed us.

The three of us ended up at a booth standing in front of the three boys Lisa had referred to as "not bad, college boy, and cute."

"Alex, Lisa, this is Josiah, Jerad, and Nick." Josiah was "not bad," Jerad was "college boy" and Nick was "cute." Jerad slid out of the booth and gestured for Lisa to sit down. She smiled over at me and slid in beside Nick. "After you." Mason smiled in my direction, so I slid in beside Josiah. Mason squeezed in on my other side.

The booth was clearly intended for four occupants, not six, and we were smashed in like sardines. "So, what are you ladies drinking?" Jared asked. He had sandy brown hair and light blue eyes. Lisa was right; he wasn't bad to look at.

"Crown and coke," she answered. "What about you guys?"

"Jack and coke with lemon drop shots," Nick replied. He was by far the cutest of Mason's friends with his dark brown hair, deep brown eyes, and broad chest and shoulders.

"Lemon drops?" I hadn't heard of those before.

"Yes, lemon drops. They're delicious." Mason said as the waitress arrived and dropped off four more shots.

"Six more please." Josiah ordered. The poor guy looked more like a sidekick compared to the other three and was clearly the comic relief of the group. He was a ginger, not a homely one but also not a comely one either. He had too many freckles to be considered comely.

"Make it twelve." Jerad handed her his card and said, "And run a tab please."

"Sure thing." She smiled and took off again.

Lisa held up her drink to make a toast. "Happy Birthday, Mason."

Everyone raised their glass and the four of us added, "Happy Birthday" in unison and all drank. The four guys followed it with a lusty cheer and downed their lemon drops. Lisa and I laughed. It had been a long time since we'd celebrated our twenty-first birthdays. The waitress came back around and dropped off fresh drinks and shots for the entire table.

"Okay, this is how you do it." Nick took a packet of sugar, ripped it open and emptied the contents on top of his hand. "Lick." He licked. "Shot." He squeaked out the word. "And suck." He quickly picked up a lemon wedge from the bowl in the center of the table and sucked hard on it. "Your turn." He looked over at Lisa with an I-dare-you look on his face. She looked across the table from me, silently telling me he should know better.

I rolled my eyes back at her. "You too." Mason nudged me in the side. "Come on," he urged until I picked up a packet of sugar and handed one to Lisa.

She shook the contents of the packet down to one end keeping her eyes on Nick. "Are you even old enough to be here?" she teased him.

"I'm old enough," he replied with a smirk.

Lisa looked at me and winked. Then she took a hold of Nick's hand, turned it upside down and dumped the sugar on the inside of his wrist. The other three guys chuckled, and Nick smiled nervously. She leaned over him in a seductive manner and gently licked the sugar off Nick's wrist. Nick blushed four shades of red while Lisa took her shot and eagerly sucked on a lemon wedge. I couldn't stop laughing.

"Top that!" Lisa dared me and slid a shot towards me.

"Please . . ." I shifted in my seat towards Mason and ripped the sugar packet open. Mason had a devilish grin on his face. I smiled and shook my head at him. I tilted his head to the side and brushed his curls out of my way, dumping the sugar on the small of his neck. That brought about another holler from the other three guys and Lisa roared. I leaned into Mason, so he could feel my breath against his neck and slowly dragged my tongue over his warm skin, did the shot, and sucked on the lemon. Everyone at the table cheered.

I smiled over at Mason not believing I had just done that to him. From the look on his face, he couldn't believe it either. Each of the guys picked up their shot, toasted Lisa, and I, and downed them.

"Okay, it's on soccer mom." Lisa said with a smirk as the waitress brought around a fresh round of drinks and shots for us all. She playfully pushed Nick's face sideways and scattered the sugar grains along his cheek, ending right next to his lips. Nick was grinning from ear to ear in anticipation. Lisa twisted herself around to where she was nearly sitting on Nick's lap. She caressed his cheek as she slowly dragged her tongue over the sugar, ending with a long passionate kiss. This trick brought about a round of applause and cheers from the guys, who then immediately turned to me to see if I was going to attempt to top her last play.

"Was that supposed to be sexy?" I tossed at her jokingly. "This is sexy." I lifted another sugar packet and gave it a good shake before I turned towards Mason. "Stick out your tongue please." He obliged. I emptied the sugar packet on his tongue. "Forgive me if this is out of line," I whispered softly in his ear when everyone else thought I was just tormenting him. Mason turned towards me cupping my face in his hands and sliding his tongue gently over mine. Then he tightened his hold just a bit and finished the kiss with a passion and fire that I had not felt in years. He literally took my breath away. When he finally broke away from me he buried his face in my neck and whispered softly, "Ditto."

"Damn . . . would you two like to get a room?" Josiah teased.

I resituated myself in my seat as the waitress brought another round. We all started talking and telling silly stories when Lisa leaned over and whispered something to Nick. He grinned and nodded back.

"Okay, we finish these, and we hit the dance floor." She turned forward again.

"Sounds good." Nick agreed. We made a final toast and climbed out of the booth.

As soon as I stood my head began to swim. I was a casual drinker at best and rarely had more than two glasses of wine. This stuff, however, was an entirely different monster. Mason had to steady me a bit until I got my bearings.

"Are you alright?" He leaned in closer still holding onto my arm.

"Yes, thanks."

Mason grinned and pulled me along with him to the dance floor behind Lisa and Nick. Josiah and Jared stayed at the table chattering. I felt kind of bad leaving them there until Mason slipped his arm around my waist and pulled me closer to him on the dance floor.

"I cannot believe you did that." He leaned over and whispered in my ear.

"I know. I'm sorry." It was my turn to blush.

"I'm not. I've been wanting to kiss you since I saw you on the first day of class."

"You have not." I playfully pushed him away. "You were sleeping the first day of class." I tossed my hair out of my face as he pulled me back into his arms.

"No, I wasn't. You only thought I was, but I saw you." He flashed me his naughty grin.

"I don't believe you," I laughed.

"Can I ask you a question?" I nodded. "Why did Lisa call you a soccer mom?"

I looked at him curiously. "Because I am one."

"Are you serious?" He looked almost confused. "You have children?"

"I thought you knew that." I stopped dancing for a moment. "Do you have any idea how old I am?"

"Twenty-five."

"Ah . . . you're so sweet." I stood on my toes and kissed him on the cheek. "Now I really don't want to tell you the truth." I sighed heavily. This small dose of reality was killing my buzz.

"Tell me." Mason pulled me closer and kissed me again. "You act like it is going to change the way I feel about you." He took my face in his hands. "It won't."

I held his eyes with mine for another minute before I could bring the words to my lips. *Why do you have to be so beautiful . . . and so freaking young?* "Mason, I will be thirty-three years old in a couple weeks and I have two boys. Max is ten and Henry is six."

"And their dad?" Worry flashed through his eyes.

"We've been divorced for five years. He lives in Arizona. My boys are spending the night at my parents' house tonight."

"Why didn't you ever tell me?"

"I don't know, I just don't tell people about my personal life." I shrugged, and he pulled me back into his arms kissing me firmly.

"I don't care about your age or that you have a couple kids. It makes me think you're even more amazing now if that's even possible."

I was about to respond when Lisa came up and poked me on the shoulder. She had her arm around Nick's waist and his was draped across her shoulder. Both were grinning like high schoolers.

"Can you give Alex a ride home?" she asked Mason.

I looked between their three faces and then back at Lisa. "Are you okay?" I was hoping she wasn't feeling sick. "We can leave now if you need to go."

"No. Nick and I were going to go." She rolled her eyes at me like I was dense or something. And for a moment, that's how I felt.

"Oh . . . okay." I couldn't help but smile.

"Of course, I'd be happy to." Mason chuckled lightly.

"Call me tomorrow." Lisa leaned in and gave me a hug.

"Be careful," I whispered before she let me go.

"I will. Have fun." She waved as the two of them disappeared into the crowd.

"Nick is in way over his head, isn't he?" Mason looked down at me.

"You have no idea." I shook my head in disbelief. I never would have guessed Lisa would end up taking one of Mason's friends homes.

"Let me guess, she's a divorced mom also?"

"Yep. Except she's a little older than I am and has three kids, two girls and a boy. Her son, Logan, and Henry play on the same basketball team," I informed him.

"Where are her kids tonight?"

"It's their dad's weekend."

"Oh, I see."

Mason and I danced a couple more songs while reality sobered us both up. We moved together in time with the music, and I rested my head against his chest. I could feel his strong heartbeat through his cotton shirt. His muscular arms held me tightly. It felt wonderful to be in his arms. No matter how briefly. It only made me sad that it would soon end, and we would both return to our former reality. A part of me really didn't want to let him go, wanted to throw all caution to the wind and be more like Lisa just for one night. But I couldn't. I hated to even think about what class would be like on Tuesday.

Much to my surprise and delight, Mason drove a new Camaro. It was a smoky gray trimmed in black and absolutely gorgeous. Jared and Josiah were still highly intoxicated. Apparently neither had slowed down on the drinking after the rest of us took off to the dance floor. The two of them climbed into the backseat making every crude joke they could think of.

It wasn't long before I realized that Mason was heading back towards campus and away from my house. "Are you heading to campus?"

"Yes."

"I thought you were going to drop me off first. I live on the west side. If you just take—" He didn't let me finish.

"I know, but I thought I would drop these two off before I take you home."

"Isn't campus way out of your way?" I glanced over at him briefly.

"Would you rather these two boneheads know where you live?" He gave me a look that told me to drop it.

"Geez, Alex, don't you get it. He wants the chance to be alone with you," Josiah slurred from the backseat with his arms gesturing wildly.

Jared leaned up against the back of my seat and stuck his head up next to mine. "He's hoping for a good night poke, sweetheart."

"Yeah, a little birthday slap and tickle." The two idiots in the back rolled with laughter.

"Knock it off you two or I'll let you walk back to campus." Mason's threat only brought about more laughter from behind us. I looked over at Mason and started laughing. I hated to admit it, but the comedy team behind us was funny. They continued their antics all the way back to campus.

*　*　*

Mason and I barely talked after we dropped off the comedy duo and drove seventeen miles to my house. I occasionally pointed out where to turn and he would comply. It was after three in the morning and the streets were almost empty. I waited silently wishing he would break the silence. I kept replaying the night's events over and over in my head.

What the hell were you thinking? You should have never let Lisa goad you into kissing him!

I turned towards the window and looked at the sleeping stores passing by on the wayside.

I hope things aren't weird on Tuesday. I don't want to lose him as a friend. Those kisses, the dances, the intimate exchanges . . . does it have to change everything? Oh, damn it, how can you be so stupid?

"Turn left here. It's the fourth house on your right."

Mason pulled in the driveway slowly and put his car in park, but I noticed he didn't turn it off. Instead, he shifted in his seat to face me. "Strange night, huh?"

"Yes, it was," I agreed.

"I had a great time." He fumbled to find the right words to ease the tension between us.

"So, did I." He ran his fingers through the side of his hair. "Would you like to come in for a night cap? I don't know about you, but I could use one." I tried to keep my voice light.

"Sure. I could use a drink." He turned off his car and we climbed out.

The cold early morning air hit me in the face like a bucket of ice water and my jacket was still in Lisa's car. I began shaking almost immediately and my fingers trembled as I tried to punch in my garage code to open the door.

"You don't use the front door?" Mason rubbed my arms trying to warm me as I shivered waiting for the door to rise enough for us to slip in.

"We rarely use the front door."

"That's odd," he remarked as we bent down under the half-raised door and walked through the garage.

"Why is that odd?" I asked as I opened the door to the house.

"I don't know. It just is." He followed me through the laundry room and into the kitchen. I flipped on the light and turned towards him with open arms.

"Welcome to my home." I gestured wildly and playfully tried to ease the tension.

Mason looked around and absorbed everything he was seeing. I was suddenly grateful I had cleaned up last evening after my dad had picked up the boys.

"Have a seat. Make yourself at home." I pointed at the barstools at the island. "I'll get us that drink."

"I like your house. Have you lived here long?" Mason sat down and looked extremely uncomfortable. His foot kept kicking the bar across the bottom of the stool.

"A little over ten years. We bought it when I was pregnant with Max. It was supposed to be our starter home." I rambled while I fixed us both a double vodka and tonic. I added a slice of lime in each glass and handed one to Mason. "It didn't quite work out the way we'd planned." I smiled and had a long drink.

"Why did you get divorced?" He sipped his drink.

"He had an affair with his boss." I shrugged and took another swig.

"I'm sorry. I can't imagine why he would ever cheat on you."

I smiled. "For a promotion," I stated bluntly.

"Really?"

"I suppose it was a trade-off for him. His wife and kids in exchange for a healthy raise and a corner office in Phoenix." I hated this topic. I still hated Danny for the choices he made. I hated that his love for money and deep desire for success had robbed my boys of their dad.

"He's a stupid man."

"I like to think so." I finished off my drink and started fixing myself another one.

"I hope you took him to the cleaners."

"I got the house and all its contents. I got the new car and most importantly, I got sole custody of my boys. That's all I really wanted anyway. He got the credit card debt and his clothes." I dropped another slice of lime into my fresh drink. "Hell, I just gave him his yearbooks and his bowling ball last summer when he came out to see the boys." I chuckled.

"I would have thrown them out." He finally finished his drink, and I aptly fixed him another.

"No. It bothered him more that I had them. Childish, I know, but that seems to be the first rule in divorce . . . see who can behave the most childish." I rolled my eyes and handed him a fresh drink.

"When I get married, it's going to be for good." He looked at me and smiled sweetly. "For better or for worse, 'til death do us part."

I smiled at his naivety. "That's what I used to think." I raised my glass at him then took another long drink. "Whose death?"

"Excuse me?"

"You said, 'til death do us part.' Whose death? Yours? Hers? Or the long sad death of your marriage? You know, when you decide you can't cook dinner tonight because you know if you get out the pots and pans, the urge to smack your spouse upside the head with the iron skillet is so strong you forgo the temptation altogether by not cooking at all." I laughed.

Mason laughed aloud and slid off the stool. "I think you've had enough of these." He took the glass from my hand and set it on the island. "You're beginning to sound bitter. I've never heard you talk like that." He wrapped his arms around me.

"Sorry. Danny is a poor subject for me to talk about when I'm drinking," I muttered into his chest.

"I'm going to go out on a limb here and say you don't drink very often, do you?"

"Nope."

Mason laughed lightly. "Let's get you to bed." He guided me through the family room and down the hallway. "Which room is yours?" he paused.

"That one." I pointed, not wanting to let him go.

But as we walked through the doorway Mason let go of me. I turned on the light on my nightstand and noticed it was well after four in the morning. I was suddenly very aware that I was in my bedroom and Mason was lingering in the doorway looking lost and uncomfortable. It was a sobering moment.

"You can come in." I stood in front of my mirror and tried to unhook my necklace.

"If you don't mind, I can sleep on your couch. Do you have any extra blankets?" *Sleep on the couch? My God, I must have made a great impression as the bitter, scorned ex-wife!*

"Sure, just a second and I'll get them for you." He saw me still struggling with the tiny lock.

"Here, let me help. You'll be here half the night struggling with that thing." He smiled and walked over to me and gently replaced my hands and unfastened my necklace. He placed it on my dresser and slowly turned me around.

Mason's hand was still on my shoulder. He lightly brushed my hair back and lifted my face to meet his. He held my gaze intently and gently traced my cheek with his finger, down to my lips then under my chin where he lifted my lips up to meet his. He kissed me very softly at first, his lips barely brushing against mine. He paused a moment and looked deep into my eyes. What I saw at that moment literally took my breath away. I knew if I didn't stop this now, there was going to be no turning back . . . for him.

Butterflies churned in my stomach, and I closed my eyes. *If he walks away, it's on him. If he stays, it's on him.*

Mason gently pulled me closer to him and kissed me more firmly. His lips parted slightly, and I felt his tongue searching for mine, discovering it, caressing it hungrily. My arms pulled his body closer to mine. My hands freely explored the muscles that lined his back and his firm rounded buttocks. I could feel them flex beneath my fingertips as he eagerly grasped my body. I grabbed the bottom of his shirt and pulled it up, barely pausing our kiss long enough to yank it over this head. He smiled broadly and nudged me towards my bed. I felt the top of the mattress against my hip of my raised canopy bed. It was much too tall for us to stumble back upon it.

Realizing this minor obstacle, Mason placed his hands firmly, yet tenderly on my hips and lifted me up and placed me gently down upon my sateen duvet. I kept a small, tan suede step stool with iron legs on my side of the bed, but I wasn't about to mention it. Instead, he gracefully lifted himself and was seated beside me and back in my arms so swiftly I had hardly noticed it. He reached out and wrapped my hair in his fingers gently pulling me towards him and kissing me passionately. He slowly lifted my shirt over my head being careful with the delicate material and dropped it to the floor. I was thankful that I had put on my matching silk and lace light pink panties and bra. The dim light on my nightstand cast a flattering glow through the partially closed drapes that hung from my canopy. His face looked radiant and the hue around his curls looked like a halo. Mason pulled me closer to him and gently lowered me back on the bed.

He hovered over me lying partially on top of me, his weight crushing down more heavily than I expected. *He's young and clearly inexperienced.* His kisses were strong and hungry. His lips drifted down to the small of my neck. I tangled my fingers in his hair and arched up to meet his body. Mason's hand cupped my breast firmly then slid up to my shoulder lowering my strap. His lips traced over my collarbone, his tongue trailing the curve to the clasp between my breasts. He took two fingers, trying his best to be smooth, and managed somehow not only to pinch his own fingers in the clasp but also catch a tiny bit of my skin as well. It was so unexpected my instinctual reaction was to scream and jerk upward. In doing so, we collided awkwardly.

The look on his face was one of sheer embarrassment. I fell back against the covers and burst into a fit of laughter. "I'm so sorry." His face was every shade of red on the color wheel. He leaned up on his elbow, lying on his side.

"No, it's okay." I tried my best to pull myself together. "Really . . ."

Mason rolled back over on me, pinning me between him and my bed. He kissed me sweetly, almost as if he was some nervous shy little boy again. *He's young, he's young, he's young . . . but definitely has potential.* I ran my hands over his back and felt his muscles ripple. *Definite potential!*

I wrapped my legs around him and grabbed a handful of his buttocks with a firm grasp. I slightly encouraged him with a nudge and rolled him over. My body took an unnoticeable sigh of relief to have his weight off me. I straddled over him. Mason grinned sheepishly. I placed my hands over his and placed them on my hips, so he could help guide the gentle rhythm of my body against his. He caressed me, tried to lean up to kiss me, but I placed my hand in the center of his bulging chest and pushed him back on the bed.

I smiled at him seductively and aided his hands along my sides until they reached my breasts. I massaged my breasts using his hands then I slipped a finger between them, unclasping my bra and letting it drift down my arms, my back. I flipped it lightly with my hand, letting it fall gracefully to the floor.

Mason eagerly devoured my breasts . . . a little too roughly. I tried to slow him down, guide him, nudge him, sort of instruct him without words. Thankfully, he was eager to learn and had a desire to please. I edged back just enough down Mason's lap to reveal the top of his jeans. I unfastened the button and skimmed my fingers up the barely noticeable trail of light brown hair to his naval. I teased him playfully, bent down over him and took his nipple in my mouth. I sucked on it lightly and tormented it with my tongue.

Mason let out this small, enchanting moan from somewhere deep inside him. I could feel him harden against me as he groped for me. I brushed his hands away with a sly grin as I slid down his thighs and unzipped his pants. Lying in a prone position over him, gliding down his body until my toes touched the floor. I pulled his jeans down his legs and off completely, dropping them purposely and carefully on the floor. I stood over him lying there on my bed in his navy-blue boxer briefs, his chest, stomach, arms, and legs muscled and well-toned, his curls in an array. I had never seen a man look so sexy.

The hair on his legs was there, not too little of it and not too much of it. He had just the right amount and it was soft with a hint of coarseness. Mason had a sleepy dreamlike look on his face. I absentmindedly pulled his socks off, one with each hand while my eyes held his. He sat up and wrapped his arms around me, crushing his lips upon mine with a fever that left me breathless. His hands reached down and pulled the button open on my pants. I took a step back and gently pushed him back down on the bed.

I leaned over him and grabbed the waistband on his boxer briefs. I raised my eyebrows at him with a knowing look. Mason placed his hands behind his head and grinned from ear to ear. The head of his cock was peeking out the top of his briefs. It throbbed and twitched as I brushed the fabric over it. I was pleasantly surprised by the size and girth of it.

I climbed up on my bed with slow, enticing, deliberate motions. My breasts brushed lightly against his thighs, and I watched his beautiful cock throb with anticipation. I brushed my tongue lightly along the base and moved along the shaft with a pent-up desire. My long thin fingers enveloped his cock, bringing it to my lips. The light gleamed off the head as a drop of pre-cum ran down onto my index finger. I leisurely lapped it up, bringing the head fully into my mouth.

Mason moaned and brushed my hair away from my face. I accepted his quivering member fully down my throat for several strokes. Mason moaned a little more loudly and arched his hips towards me. Seconds later, most unexpectedly, he came down my throat. He took me totally by surprise, off guard and without time to react.

You have got to be kidding me!

"Oh, my God! I am so sorry!" Mason covered his face.

I sat back up and wiped off the corner of my mouth before I removed Mason's hands from his face. "Mason," I whispered. "It's okay. It happens." I glanced over at the clock on the nightstand. It was after five. "We're both tired and have been drinking all night. It's no big deal."

It was easier to tell a little white lie than to add insult to injury. Mason was humiliated and there was no reason to make him feel worse. I rubbed my hand over his chest tenderly. "Hey sweetie, I'm going to jump in the shower really quick."

"Mind if I join you?" he asked before I could climb off the bed.

"Not at all." I smiled and took his hand.

I turned on the shower to let the water warm up. Mason stood awkwardly in the doorway. I picked up my toothbrush and applied the toothpaste.

"Can I use some of your toothpaste?" It was obvious he was going to do the generic finger brush.

"I can do better than that." I reached into the linen closet and gave him a new toothbrush.

"Thank you." He smiled and unwrapped it.

"I always keep extra in the house because of the boys," I remarked and started brushing my teeth.

The steam from the shower was starting to warm up the bathroom. I stood with my jeans undone, the soft pink lace barely visible, and nothing on from the waist up. I hesitated a moment. No one had seen me nude except Danny in the last twelve years. I couldn't believe how nervous I was. I had nothing to be ashamed of. The only evidence that I'd even given birth were two tiny stretch marks on my right hip from Max and those had almost completely faded away. I had a slender waist and fit into a size five comfortably, three in some cases. I shaved my legs and everything else important. But I still hesitated. The lighting in the bathroom was much brighter than the soft hues left behind in the bedroom. I took a deep breath and slipped out of my jeans and panties and kicked them aside. Mason was watching me very closely. I smiled nonchalantly and climbed into the shower.

The hot water washed over me like a warm blanket. I hadn't realized how exhausted I was. I had been up for twenty-four hours, and a thirty-two-year-old body doesn't handle that as well as a twenty-one-year-old body, nor does it recuperate at fast. I closed my eyes and brushed my hair away from my face. When I opened my eyes again Mason was standing in front of me smiling.

"You look so beautiful." He placed his hands on my hips drawing me to him. "I love watching the water run down on you. You're so incredibly sexy.

"Thank you. So are you." I placed my hands on his biceps.

"About before . . ." he began, but I placed a finger on his lips and shook my head.

"Don't give it a second thought."

"I didn't mean to."

"I know."

"Please don't think . . ."

"Don't worry, I don't." I stood on my toes and kissed him fully.

We washed each other thoroughly, laughing and playing around in a way that I hadn't done in years. We helped each other dry off and even tried to snap each other with our towels, chasing one another around my bedroom. It was goofy, and silly, and I chalked it up to sleep deprivation. By the time we calmed down and stopped laughing, I was ready to fall over and sleep for the next twelve hours. I stepped into a pair of white lace panties and slid into a cotton nightie that clung loosely to me and flattered my curves.

I used my little step stool and climbed up on my bed. Mason looked at me like he wasn't sure what to do. He picked up his boxer briefs and started to put them on.

"Are you leaving?" I pulled the covers up around me.

"I wasn't sure if you wanted me to stay."

I patted the empty spot beside me. "Please stay."

Mason dropped his briefs back on the floor and climbed into bed beside me. I reached over and turned off the lamp. By the time I rolled back over, he was lying on his back with the covers pulled up to his chest. *Damn, he is beautiful . . . and edible.* I scooted closer to him and lay down with my head on his chest, arm and leg casually draped over him. He kissed me on the top of my head and wrapped his arm protectively around me. I listened to the steady beat of his heart and drifted off into a deep sleep.

Chapter 6

MY CELL PHONE rang at one-thirty, waking me abruptly. My head was in a deep fog and it took me a minute to realize where the noise was coming from. Mason was spooned up behind me, still holding me in his arms. I carefully wiggled away from him and grabbed my phone off the nightstand.

"Hello." My voice came out sounding raspy.

"Hi, Momma. Did I wake you?" Henry sounded hyped up on sugar.

"It's okay, sweetheart. What are you doing?" I climbed out of bed trying not to wake Mason and crept out of my room.

"I was playing baseball with Max and grandpa. I was practicing batting. I'm getting better. I got several hits too." I sat down on the couch curling my feet under me and listened to him ramble on about Max hitting the ball out past my parents' barn, about Billy chasing the ball after Max hit it, and then how both boys chased Billy to try and get the ball back. "Grandpa said that soon I'll be hitting as well as Max!" he exclaimed.

"That's great, Henry, I'm so glad you're having a good time. Did you remember to brush your teeth this morning?" He hated brushing his teeth and I had to constantly remind him.

"Yes, grandma made me." I heard my mother's voice in the background. "She wants to talk to you. I'll see you later Momma. Bye."

"Okay, bye sweetheart." But he was already gone.

"Hi, Alex. How are you doing? Did you have fun last night?"

"Hey, Mom. Yeah, I had a good time. I was still sleeping." I tried to stifle back a yawn.

"You do realize what time it is?"

"Yes, Mom."

"Well, get your homework done. We'll be bringing the boys back after dinner. Max wants me to fix him some chicken, cheese, and rice."

"That sounds good." It was my grandma's recipe and Max's favorite meal.

"I'll bring you a doggie bag." I could hear the smile in her voice. "Enjoy your afternoon, Al. We'll see you around seven."

"You too, Mom. Thanks again for keeping the boys. I love you guys."

"Love you too, honey." She hung up the phone.

I set my phone down on the coffee table, leaned back and closed my eyes. "Is everything all right?"

I turned in the direction of Mason's voice coming from the hallway. He was standing in his boxer briefs looking half asleep. "Yeah, that was my parents. They're going to drop the boys off around seven."

I crawled off the couch and went to him. He greeted me with open arms and a small, sweet kiss.

"Sorry, morning breath." He smiled. "Just a sec." He let go of me and disappeared back into my bathroom. I tagged along behind him needing to brush my teeth as well.

"Are you hungry?" I asked when we finished.

"Only for you." Mason had a devilish grin on his lips. He picked me up and carried me over to my bed.

He lay me down gently and climbed up beside me. I wrapped my arms around him and pulled him down to me. I kissed him passionately with a fire that had been burning in me since the first time I had laid eyes on him. His mouth devoured me, his tongue lapping hungrily at mine. I raked my nails over his buttocks and wrapped my legs around him arching into him. He moved his lips down to my neck firmly and his hand slid under my tee. His touch was warm, his fingers deliberate. He lifted my shirt over my head and tossed it aside.

Definite potential!

Mason brought his lips down and grazed them over my breast. His tongue playfully teased my nipple making it stand fully erect. I intertwined my fingers in his hair and moved my body to the rhythm of his. He slid his hand down into my panties and pulled them off with ease. I could feel his dick throbbing hard against my thigh. My body ached for it. I was dying to feel him inside me.

Mason worked his way down my body, kissing and caressing as

he went. His hand slid in between my legs, parting my lips, searching, discovering. His tongue grazed my stomach and toyed with my bright pink belly button ring. His fingers pushed up inside me a little too roughly. I shifted a little trying to ease his pressure without being too obvious. Thankfully, he eased up a little and I began to move my hips in rhythm with him.

He continued along his journey, stopping upon his desired destination. I closed my eyes and leaned into him. His lips felt amazing as he moved slowly, teasing me. His tongue reached out and parted my lips with a single stroke . . . and then continued and continued. He fingers followed suit . . . in out in out. *What the hell is he doing? Am I being weather proofed for the winter? Oh my God . . . this is pathetic!*

For the mere sake of his ego, I let out a low moan, but really it was in exasperation. He was driving me insane with frustration. I finally tugged on his arms and shoulder, bringing him back up to me.

I yanked at his boxer briefs but despite my efforts, my arms weren't positioned in a way I could get them off. Mason obliged my wishes and aided my efforts. He kicked them off the end of his foot and discarded them without a second thought. He shifted himself gracefully to position himself between my legs. His kisses became breathless and probing with anticipation. I placed my hand firmly in the middle of his chest and edged myself up and away from him.

"Hold on a second," I said breathlessly.

"What? What's wrong?" His cheeks were red, and his lips were full.

I squirmed a little away from him reaching for the nightstand drawer. There was a box of condoms in there although I couldn't exactly remember what year I had gotten them. My sister, Samantha, had put them in a gift basket she had given me for my birthday a few years back as an incentive to start dating again. I could only hope it didn't break when I opened it. I grabbed one out of the box and shut the drawer. "We need one of these." I held it up and nudged Mason over on his back and straddled his thighs.

"Oh, right."

I ripped the condom open and hoped I would remember how to put one on correctly. I couldn't even recall the last time Danny and I had used one. Before we were married, that was for sure. There was simply no way to make putting on a condom sexy. Strangely enough, putting on a condom really was much like riding a bike, you never forget how.

I climbed back over Mason and lowered myself onto him. There was a delicious scream of pain and desire that escaped from deep inside me. My body exploded with pleasure as I slid down his hard cock. It ripped me apart and filled me up. *God, I missed this . . .*

Mason placed his hands on my hips and moved his body expertly with mine as we became one. My hands gripped his chest, my nails slightly digging in. He arched his hips and drove hard into me before leaning up and wrapping me in a full embrace. His lips devoured my neck roughly. His whiskers felt harsh against my smooth skin. I grabbed his face and brought his lips to mine, crushing our mouths together. His tongue tangled hungrily with mine as I pumped my pelvis against his.

With his arms holding me tight in a firm embrace, he placed his hands on the back of my shoulders and thrust firmly into me, burying his face in my chest. He moaned loudly and tightened his grip as our bodies exploded in perfect rhythm. His breath was coming out in hot bursts as he kissed my neck so softly and sweetly. I held him in my arms until our breathing slowed down a beat or two.

Mason collapsed back upon the bed and stared up at the ceiling. I slid off him, curled up to him and rested my head upon his chest, listening to his heartbeat. I was surprised by how comfortable I was with him, like this was where I was supposed to be. He wrapped his arm around me and leaned down, kissing the top of my head. I gazed up at him and smiled. "Come on lazy butt, let's get in the shower."

We jumped into the shower and let the hot water rain down upon us. I stood with my eyes closed wondering if I had just made a huge mistake taking this guy into my bed. *What must he be thinking of me? Does he think I'm some kind of slut who sleeps around? I hope not. He's a nice guy, but too young, nonetheless.*

"Are you all right?" Mason took me in his arms under the water and forced me to look him in the eye.

"Yes, of course." I smiled and leaned up, kissing him lightly. "I'm fine."

"Regardless of what you might think of me, I honestly don't sleep around. In fact, you are only the third girl I have ever slept with," he confessed.

"Seriously?" I laughed aloud. "You're my third."

"Okay, and this is where we have the awkward ex conversation, right?" He picked up the shampoo and began to lather up my hair.

"Well, you already know about my ex-husband, Danny, who now lives in Arizona. And before him, was my high school boyfriend." He tilted my head back and rinsed the suds from my hair. "You?"

"Um, high school girlfriend and then a girl I dated last year for a while." We switched places.

"Was it serious?" I couldn't help but be curious.

"For all of three months or three minutes." He shrugged. "She got drunk at a party and slept with someone else. Nick and Jerad saw her and told me about it. When I asked her she fessed up. She apologized and blamed it on the alcohol, but I couldn't get past it."

"Yeah, I couldn't swallow that one either. Of course, Danny wasn't nearly as apologetic because his affair was going to benefit our entire family." I smirked.

"Unbelievable," Mason muttered while I rinsed the shampoo from his hair. "Wait a second. Are you telling me the last time you had sex, it was with your husband?"

"Yes." I turned around and picked up the conditioner trying to ignore the look on his face.

"I thought you'd said you've been divorced over five years."

"I have." I rubbed some conditioner through his hair.

"So, you haven't had sex in five years?"

"Nope." Mason smiled in a weird way. "Don't look at me like that." I playfully smacked him on the chest.

"But how . . ."

"I own stock in Duracell," I stated without cracking a smile.

Mason roared with laughter and kissed me again. "You amaze me."

*   *   *

I put the boys down a little before nine. My dad had completely worn them out and they were both tired and cranky. I barely got them through their nightly routine before they dropped off to sleep. Mason had headed back to campus a little before six. I wanted to make sure there was no chance of him running into my parents or my boys. He really wanted to meet the boys, but I insisted that it wasn't a good idea. I assured him it had nothing to do with him, but that Max was giving me enough problems and them meeting would only make my life more difficult right now.

I put on a pair of pajama bottoms and a sweatshirt and curled up on the couch with a blanket. I flipped on the television to a rerun of *Criminal Minds*, one of my favorite shows. The last thing I wanted to do was study even though I knew I needed to catch up on some reading. I snuggled in with my blanket and got comfortable. Visions of Mason kept haunting me and I could only pray that I hadn't made a big mistake.

My cell phone buzzed, bringing me out of the fog. It was Lisa.

"Hey, what's going on?"

"I just got the kids down, finally. McKenzie did not want to go to sleep tonight. I fight with them every time they come back from their dad's," she complained.

"Luckily, my dad wore the boys out today. They barely stayed awake long enough to take their showers. I put them down just a little bit ago. They're already asleep."

"So, how did things go with beanie boy? I've been dying to call you all day."

"Me? What about you and Nick? I cannot believe you took Nick home with you." I laughed.

"Nick," she laughed. "Nick is built like a hamster."

"What? You're kidding me. He's so cute," I exclaimed.

"Yes, beautiful, young, built like a brick shithouse, Nick is hamster boy. You got sex on a stick beanie boy. I got hamster boy. How freaking fair is that?" Lisa complained.

"I'm so sorry." I couldn't stop laughing. "Please, tell me he at least knew what he was doing?"

"Ten second hamster boy? Are you kidding? It took longer to get undressed than have sex. It was horrible."

"Oh, I'm so sorry." I tried my best to stop laughing but I couldn't.

"I would have been better off taking Jared home or even the little ginger headed boy." Her voice was dripping in sarcasm.

"So, I am guessing you won't be seeing him again?"

"He's twenty-one years old, I don't need another child," she remarked.

"This coming from the woman who's encouraged me for the last three months to ravish beanie boy?" I teased.

"That's different."

"How's that?"

"Because you've spent two days a week with him every week for the last several months. Because you two have been playing this flirty little game since you've met. Because you need to return to a world where men exist, and sex is fabulous and curls your toes and makes you scream. Because he's good for you." Her explanation surprised me a little.

"Do I need to remind you that he's the same age as Nick?"

"Do I need to remind you that you're five years younger than me?" she shot back.

"I am twelve years older than him. He's a kid!"

"You need someone young to bring you back to life. Like I said, he's good for you."

"You keep saying that. I'm not so sure."

"So . . .," she said, edging me to further explain.

"So, what?"

"Oh, come on, Alex. Did you pop the boy's cherry or not?" Lisa laughed.

"That ship sailed long before I got my hands on him." *Not long before.*

"Please, tell me he was better than hamster boy?"

"I would have to say he's definitely not hamster boy. Not at all."

"I knew it, you slut! How was he?"

"He's a little rough around the edges, but he's got potential." I wasn't about to tell her about our first encounter last night. I'd sooner forget about it myself.

"His performance was a six, a high six, and there was definite potential for growth. No pun intended, but his pregame needs a lot of work!"

"How bad was it?" I knew she was fishing.

"Let's just say I've been weather proofed."

"Oh, my God!" she roared with laughter.

"It was bad, really bad. I mean I could have propped my feet up on his shoulders and given myself a perfect pedicure. The boy had one stroke." I couldn't keep from laughing at myself. "I mean I could have given him a roadmap, a GPS, put up neon signs and he couldn't find my clitoris. I don't think he even knows what one is let alone where it is. And don't even get me started on his poking . . . Ahhhhhh!" I playfully screamed into the phone but not loud enough to wake my boys, before I burst into laughter with her.

"We're so terrible," she said out of breath.

"Why? Because we're honest? Thank God he's got a huge cock, or I think I would have cried." She roared through the phone. "I'm serious."

"How big was he?"

"It was nine, easy. I wanted to measure it. And it was so beautiful. Or maybe it's just been that long cause I swear I almost came as soon as I climbed on it."

"Lucky bitch," Lisa said, her voice heavy with envy.

"I don't know. I think it may have been a big mistake. I probably shouldn't have slept with him."

"You think too much, Alex. Just have fun and enjoy yourself for a change. Live life a little."

"You're insane." I sighed heavily. "I'm gonna go. I am exhausted."

"I bet you are!"

"Night."

Chapter 7

TUESDAY MORNING, I turned the car off and sat in the campus parking lot. I had twenty minutes to get to class and I was terrified to go. Mason had called me twice yesterday and I didn't answer either call, nor did I call him back. I still wasn't sure what to say to him. I knew the affair could never last, but a part of me wanted to listen to Lisa's advice and live life a little. There certainly was no harm in having a good time. And maybe it was safer to have a good time with someone whom I knew was never going to last than with someone whom I believed could possibly stand the test of time.

"Fuck it!" I grabbed my things and locked my car. It was now or never.

I sat down in the same chair I'd always sat in, beside Mason. He looked delicious. *Why does he have to be so damn edible?* He was doodling on the corner of his notebook, but he smiled when he saw me arrive.

"Good morning," I said casually.

"Hi, I wasn't sure if you were going to be here today or not."

"Why wouldn't I be?"

"I tried to call you twice yesterday and you never called me back." I could tell he was a little annoyed.

"I'm sorry. I had classes yesterday morning and spent the afternoon trying to sign up for my summer class. And then Henry had practice last night. I wasn't trying to avoid you I was just exhausted by the time I got them to bed," I apologized.

"I didn't know you were planning on taking a summer class. I've been debating it. What did you sign up for?" He shifted slightly in his seat towards me. I could see the anger melt away from his face.

"Sexuality and society."

"I haven't heard of that class, but it sounds interesting. Maybe I'll take it with you." He gave me a devilish grin.

"Have you taken human sexuality? It's the prerequisite." I raised one eyebrow. *Judging by your performance, I'd say no.*

"No. I'm a business major. Remember?"

"What's that have to do with anything?"

"It's not required for my major." Mason looked at me as if that explained everything.

"It's not required for mine either, but it is interesting and counts as a humanities credit."

Professor Drab started his lecture, cutting off our conversation. He was droning on about pluralist and elite models of political government. To say it was dull was a mild understatement, but Mason seemed to be paying close attention to it. I took notes accordingly. I watched Mason more carefully than I heeded the professor. I couldn't understand his fascination with the subject when I was struggling with staying awake.

Class finally ended. I put my things back into my backpack and got ready to leave. Mason and I began ascending the steps of the lecture hall. However, today, Mason slipped his arm around my waist and pulled me a little closer to him in a sweet protective sort of way. I didn't say anything to him, he seemed so happy.

"Would you like to get something to eat?" he asked me once outside.

It was a warm day, and the late morning sun was flirting with the clouds. We walked over the little flower garden in the middle of the concrete campus. The tulips and Easter lilies were starting to awaken and added some color and life back into this previously gray world.

"I should probably head home. I've got some studying to do before the boys get there." I set my backpack on a bench.

"Lexie, did I do something wrong?" He set his down beside mine.

"No, why do you ask?"

"Because it seems like you're avoiding me." He put his arm gently around me.

"No, I'm not. I'm sorry if you think so." I gestured at the bench. "Have a seat, Mason." We sat down beside one another.

"So here it comes." He looked as if I had just slapped him in the face.

"Mason, you've got to understand something. Your only responsibility is going to class and getting good grades. I live in an entirely different world than you do. I have two sons to care for, a household to run, bills to pay and all my sons' sports activities. All of that on top of studying, papers, and exams. It's a lot and it's not easy. I just don't see how this," I gestured between us, "could possibly work."

"Do we have to figure it all out now? Isn't it a little soon for this conversation?" He laughed.

He had a good point. I felt kind of foolish for being so concerned at this stage in the game. Perhaps Lisa was right. Maybe I needed to live life a little.

"Yes, I suppose you're right. I'm sorry. I guess I'm so used to planning for tomorrow I forgot how to enjoy today."

Mason smiled and leaned in and gave me a quick kiss. I smiled slightly and kissed him again with a little more heat. I wrapped my arms around his neck and pulled him a little closer to me.

"You do realize my house is empty for the next three hours." I gave him a devilish grin. "Do you have another class this afternoon?"

"Nope, but I do have a dorm room that's a lot closer than your house," he offered.

"Are you kidding?" He shook his head with a cocky grin. "No, I am not, nor will I ever, have sex with you in a dorm room." I laughed. "Come on."

Mason followed me home in his beautiful Camaro. He pulled into my driveway right behind me while I parked in the garage. He was out of his car before I was. I tried not to laugh out loud at his enthusiasm. I was just as eager to be with him but wasn't about to let him know how strongly I desired him. He walked into the garage and took my hand. I kissed him teasingly and led him into the house.

I found myself in his arms before we even got through the kitchen. Our kisses came quick and heated, our arms embracing, our hands groping. I could not get enough of him. I wanted him so badly, but I had to slow down. I didn't want another debauched sexual escapade as before. I could only hope that his stamina would improve with time and experience. And perhaps with a few pointed lessons, his ability to give head would improve as well. I did not believe I could stand another episode like before without screaming at him for being so bad at oral.

A trail of clothes littered the way towards my bedroom. He lifted me up and placed me on the bed in my bra and panties. Unlike last Saturday, when I was more cautious and was wearing my cute little matching set of undergarments, today I was sporting a relatively plain white lace bra and a pair of royal blue boy boxer briefs made for ladies. It was cute and casual and sexy in a soccer mom sort of way.

Still, that did not seem to faze him in the slightest bit. In fact, he loved them even more than the lace silky ones I was previously wearing and stated as much. I just smiled and removed them without haste. He rolled me over and moved his lips down to my breast, teasing my nipples with his fingers and tongue. I arched my back with a low moan. I could feel the heat rising within me and burning in my thighs. I wanted him in me. I didn't want to play with his miserable attempts at being seductive.

He slid his tongue down, grazing it against my skin and dancing it around my stomach. As he continued his way downward, my body filled with dread and immediately tensed up. His tongue traced across the waistline of my panties in a playful manner. Mason felt me tense and looked up at me, concern written all over his face.

"What's wrong?"

"Nothing. Why did you stop?" I tried to sound as innocent as possible.

"Let's start by being honest with each other." He sighed heavily. "Your entire body tensed up the further down I went. Why is that?"

"It's nothing." *How can I possibly explain this one? Nerves?*

"Don't you enjoy it?" He was already looking like a chastised little puppy.

I took a deep breath and decided to go for broke. I leaned up on my elbows and looked down at him as he rested his chin on my stomach.

"Normally, yes." His face looked as if I'd slapped him. "No, Mason. Let me explain. Every woman is different. We're not like men. Men are universal in foreplay. It's not that difficult to please a man. Women are much different. Each of us is different and it takes time for a man to figure out exactly how to please a woman in that way." It was the gentlest way I could put it.

"So, teach me." A sly smile spread across his lips. "I'm your eager student. I want to make you happy." He edged his way back up to me, kissed me gently and whispered, "I want to make you scream."

"Have you ever made a woman scream doing that?" Curiosity got the best of me.

"A couple times but I would put money on it she was faking it just to make me feel better." We laughed. "Come on. Teach me. I don't want you to feel like you must fake it."

"Oh, don't worry. I won't. I'll just take care of myself after you've left," I teased.

"Oh, will you now." He leapt up on his knees and began tickling me.

We wrestled around like a couple of kids, tickling and teasing and behaving as immaturely as possible. It felt wonderful. I couldn't recall the last time I had felt so free.

"Okay. Okay. I give. Please stop." I was breathless and not in the way I had anticipated when I left campus that afternoon.

"You're pretty great, you know that?" He leaned back on my pillow.

"I don't know about that, but I do enjoy spending time with you." I brushed his curls away from his face.

"So, are you going to teach me or not?" He leaned up on his elbow.

"If you're willing to learn, I'll teach you a few things."

"Are you really going to take that sex class this summer?" he inquired with a smirk.

"I signed up for it. Why?"

"Why would you sign up for a class about sex?"

"It's not just about sex. It's called sex and society. And I think it'd be interesting."

"Sounds kind of weird. I mean sex is basic." He shrugged.

"This coming from the man who thirty seconds ago was asking me to teach him how to go down on a woman." I laughed at the irony.

"That's different. You said every woman is different and I want you to show me what you like." He tried to back himself out of the corner he'd put himself in.

"First off, sex is never basic. There's so much more to it than that. Secondly, every woman is different, but if you know what you're doing you can adapt quickly by reading her body language in how she responds to your touch. Thirdly, and I'm not saying this to be mean, but you have no clue what you're doing down there."

"Yes, I do. I . . ."

"No. You don't. Trust me," I cut him off.

"But . . ." I placed my finger over his lips and shook my head.

"Can I tell you something without upsetting you? And it's not a personal blow to your male ego. It's merely a lack of knowledge and experience. But do you want to know what I told Lisa about it?"

"Okay, amuse me." A smirk formed on his shapely lips and his tone got all cocky.

Initially, I was going to be gentle and sugar coat his inability to give head, but since he thought so highly of his talent, I figured I'd give it to him straight.

"Truthfully, I told her I could have given myself a perfect pedicure." I left out the GPS part so as not to crush him completely.

"You're kidding. Women don't talk that way." He scrunched up his face a bit.

"Please tell me you're joking, right? Of course, we do. Why would you think we don't?"

"I just never really thought they did. Did she say anything about Nick?" I could feel the blood rushing to my face recalling what Lisa had said.

"Maybe she did, maybe she didn't," I giggled.

"Oh, come on. Tell me." He started tickling me again. "I'm not going to stop until you tell me." He pinned me down.

"Okay. Okay. But you're not going to like it." I tried to squirm my way from underneath him, but it was hopeless. He was so much stronger than I. "Or maybe you will. But you can't tell him." I laughed. "You have to promise me you won't say anything."

"I promise," he straddled me, grinning down. "I won't say anything."

"She told me he was built like a hamster and that it took longer to get undressed than to have sex with him," I stated bluntly.

"Oh, my God! Nick would die if he heard that!"

"I know. That's why you can't ever tell him," I pleaded.

"He would freak if he heard that. He said their night was amazing."

"Yeah. For him, maybe," I pointed out, trying not to giggle.

"Have they spoken since?" I already knew they hadn't. She had told me as much at the boys' practice last night.

"I don't believe so. She pretty much blew him off the next morning when she took him back to campus." I had already heard her rendition of the awkward morning after.

"I know Lisa isn't looking to get involved with anyone right now." *Anyone so young anyway.*

"Yeah, he mentioned that." He shrugged. "I was afraid after I couldn't reach you that you were going to give me the same speech." He kissed me sweetly. "You sort of did."

I kissed him again and then I saw my alarm clock on my nightstand out of the corner of my eyes. "Oh, my God. Is that the time?" It was just after three. "My boys will be here in about a half hour." We had managed to talk through our small window of opportunity. I slipped off the bed and went in search of my clothes.

"What?" Disappointment was written all over his face.

"I'm so sorry." I tossed him his boxer briefs. "You'll have to go." I took off down the hallway.

"Are you serious?" I heard him call after me.

I gathered my clothes and dressed as I walked back into my bedroom. "Yes, I'm so sorry things didn't go exactly as we expected this afternoon." I handed him his clothes and kissed him again. "I promise I will make it up to you."

"I'm going to hold you to that." He wrapped his arms around me and kissed me fiercely. I felt myself relenting. I wanted him so badly.

"Please do."

"Do you really want me to leave?" The hurt look crossed his face again.

"My boys will be here shortly, and I don't think it's a good idea if you're here."

"I'd love to meet them." His eyes implored. "We can just say we're studying for our exam next week. I have my backpack and stuff in my car."

I held his gaze for what felt like an eternity. My mind was racing with all the cons of introducing him to my boys. I couldn't think of one single pro. It terrified me to my very core. I had never introduced my boys to anyone, any man anyway. Of course, I hadn't dated anyone, so it hadn't exactly been a problem until this moment. *But the age difference . . .*

"I don't think it's a good idea. Please don't be mad at me. Maybe some other time," I tried to explain.

Mason sat down on the corner of my bed and took my hands in his. "Hey, I like you. And I think you like me too. I have known you for over four months and we just shared an extremely intimate afternoon without even having sex. I don't care if you only introduce me to them as a friend from class."

"Oh, all right." I cringed inside. "Go get your books."

Max and Henry were heard before they were seen. Their voices echoed from the bus stop two doors down and only grew louder as they tramped across the lawn to our front door. Mason and I were sitting at the table surrounded by laptops, papers, and textbooks.

"Hey, Mom, what's going on?" Max came to a screeching halt when he saw Mason sitting in the kitchen.

"Studying. This is Mason, a friend of mine from sociology class. He came over to help me prepare for our exam next week. Mason, this is my son, Max and lingering in the doorway is my son, Henry."

"Hi." Henry sort of waved and Max just glared at Mason for a moment then chose to ignore him.

"How was school?" I asked as Max started rummaging through the refrigerator.

"I got an A plus on my spelling test." Henry handed me his paper.

"That's fantastic." I gave him a big hug. "Why don't you hang it up on the fridge?"

"Okay." He beamed.

"How was your day, Max? Anything exciting happen?"

"No." He stood there for a moment eating a handful of grapes glaring at Mason, watching him carefully. "I'm gonna shoot some hoops." He started to walk away.

"Hey," I hollered after him. "Do you have any homework?"

"Yeah," Max yelled back.

"Don't you think you should get it done before practice?" I called back.

His "Later" was followed by the front door slamming.

I looked over at Mason and smiled. "He's delightful, isn't he?"

"He's ten."

"Yes, he is." I rolled my eyes.

"I don't have any homework, Momma." Henry climbed up on my lap.

"I wish I didn't." I kissed him on the cheek. "Are you hungry?"

"Can I have some grapes?" Henry's big brown eyes looked at me sweetly. His brown hair was messed up and needed to be cut.

"Of course, you can." He smiled, hopped down and scurried over to the refrigerator.

"He looks a lot like you," Mason remarked.

"Yeah, he's my sweetheart," I said full of pride.

Henry left shortly thereafter to join his brother. I got up and started fixing dinner while Mason quizzed me on some of the material that was going to be on our next test. He drilled me over various concepts while I chopped potatoes and fried the chicken. He even razzed me about making homemade gravy and biscuits. Apparently, the *mom* in me was showing through.

I asked Mason to join us for dinner.

*   *   *

Saturday was filled with baseball games at the town park. The rain had finally ended, and the air was filled with the sweet aroma of freshly cut grass and spring flowers. The sun was finally getting some of its strength back and it warmed us up nicely. Max was invited to spend the night at his friend, Aaron's, and the two of them were talking with some of their classmates over by the concession stand waiting for Henry's game to be over. I joined Lisa in the stands to watch our boys. She had confessed that when she signed Logan up for baseball that she had written on his form that he needed to be on the same team as Henry due to carpooling. I had to admit I was thrilled. She and I had become such good friends. It made attending all Henry's sporting events even more enjoyable since I had a friend there. When I sat down beside Lisa and told her Max was staying with Aaron for the night, she immediately invited Henry to stay with Logan, so I could have a free evening with Mason. I loved her for it. She was such a wonderful friend. I eagerly took out my cell and sent Mason a text telling him I was child-free for the night.

Almost immediately, I got a return text asking what time he should meet me at my house. I showed Lisa and she laughed. "Anxious little man, isn't he?"

"He's not the only one." I smiled. "I don't know what it is about him, but he's . . ." I didn't know how to finish the sentence.

Lisa only grinned. "I know." She nudged me playfully. "It's good to see you happy again."

"It feels good to be happy again."

* * *

Mason arrived around seven. He was wearing faded jeans, a dark blue T-shirt, and an unbuttoned white casual dress shirt. His loose curls blew gently in the breeze and the stubble along his jaw only enhanced his looks. I watched him walk from his car to my front porch. I stood in the front doorway smiling happily as he approached.

"Aren't you a welcome sight?" He took me in his arms and kissed me.

"You saw me two days ago." I couldn't stop grinning.

"I wasn't sure if I was going to see you this weekend." He kissed me again and gently pushed me backward over the threshold of my house.

Mason kicked the door closed with his foot and we stumbled in each other's arms, locked together in an obsessive kiss down the hallway into my bedroom. We tugged and pulled each other's clothes off, dropping them along the way. My desire for him was overwhelming. My heart was pounding in my chest. My muscles tightened in anticipation. My breath quickened. My hands were grabbing him, tearing at his clothes, longing for him to be inside me.

We scrambled up on my bed still grasping at each other. He lay over on top of me, his lips firm upon mine, his tongue fervently stroking mine. My arms and legs wrapped around him with a fevered desire. I firmly rolled him over and straddled him. I sat up and looked down into his bright blue eyes. I leaned forward slightly and helped guide him inside me. I could feel the world around me explode as I slid down his hard shaft and rocked my hips gently back and forth on it. He lifted his hips guiding my rhythm with his hands. I leaned back loving the way his cock filled me as I exploded into a screaming orgasm.

Mason rolled over on top of me and wrapped my legs around his neck. Our bodies moved together as if we were made for each other. I took a firm hold of his ass and dug my nails in, arched my hips into him. I loved the way his body moved with mine. He moaned loudly and quickly pulled out of me and removed his condom to cum across my stomach and breasts.

Mason collapsed down upon me, breathless. I slipped my legs off his shoulders and stroked his hair while he regained his steady breathing. His curls were a sweaty tangle from our desire. His skin was hot and smooth with a gleam of shine to it. I never wanted to let him go. I loved the feel of him in my arms, the weight of him on top of me and the way his big thick cock filled me up.

We lay wrapped in each other's arms, spent but still filled with desire. Mason finally rolled off me and took me by the hand. "Come on. Join me in the shower."

"Shower?" I giggled and followed him willingly.

"Yes, shower." Mason turned on my shower before taking me back in his arms. "Then we'll get something to eat, and then I'm going to ravish you again. I believe you still owe me for the other day." A devilish grin spread across his shapely lips.

After a playful shower, Mason got dressed and I disappeared into my walk-in. When I emerged again several minutes later, I was adorned with a simple black strapless dress that was perfect for the late spring evening. Underneath I had hidden black lacy undergarments, stockings, and a garter for later. Once finally ready, we went out to a restaurant in the heart of the city. We had a nice dinner, a couple of drinks and teased each other with sexual innuendos. We shared an oversized piece of cheesecake dripping in hot caramel for dessert.

It was such a beautiful warm evening without a hint of humidity. The stars were twinkling brightly overhead in the clear sky and the streets were alive with people taking advantage of the weather. We strolled hand in hand down to the canal and followed the stone pathway around the art museum. We chatted about the various sculptures scattered across the vast lawns, our families, and what we wanted to do after graduation. I learned that Mason was from a very large family and was, in fact, the second oldest of eight children. He only had one brother and the rest were all girls, the youngest was even younger than my Henry. That left me with a very odd sensation in the pit of my stomach.

It was the perfect romantic evening. Mason draped his arm around me as we started back towards his car and the temperature dropped just enough to remind us that summer had not yet fully arrived in the Midwest. I leaned in against him as we walked, completely thankful that I hadn't decided to end this after our first night together.

*   *   *

Since we had already devoured each other with our desire, I was ready to take a step back and begin our lessons. I took his hand and guided him down the hallway to my bedroom. Mason followed me willingly with a sheepish grin. I stopped him just inside my bedroom door. He started to speak but before he could utter a word, I placed a finger up to his lips and slowly shook my head. I left him standing there while I lit several small candles on each of my nightstands and a couple on my dresser. It added a soft erotic hue to the room with the light sent of jasmine. I proceeded to undress him slowly, lingering on every motion and drawing on his desire. I could feel his heart racing under his shirt and his body trembling. Once naked, I led him over to the bed and with a single finger in the middle of his chest, pushed him back against it. Then I proceeded to carefully remove my dress but left on my stockings, heels, garter, and undergarments. His eyes followed my every move like a long-drawn-out dance of seduction.

I stood on my toes and kissed him softly. He tried to put his arms around me, but again, I shook my head and placed them back at his side. "You wanted me to give you a few pointers on pleasing a woman," I said coyly.

"No. I wanted you to show me how to please you and only you." Mason smirked.

"Don't get cocky." I playfully smacked him on his ass.

"Yes, ma'am." I smacked him again a little harder causing him to smile wider.

"Let your actions speak for themselves. Eye contact can speak volumes." I nudged him backward indicating I wanted him to climb up on the bed, and he complied.

I followed and pushed him back gently with a finger indicating that I wanted him to lie down. "Sex for women is a totally different experience than it is for men." I straddled over him and put his arms up, holding him down with no pressure. "For women, sex is most often an expression of deep emotion or love. For men, it is an act of lust, a deep-seated desire. Men can be angry and still have sex. Women cannot. We have to be relaxed, aroused, in order to receive, and it is the man's job to get us there."

Mason tried to gently rock his hips beneath me, still grinning. I reached back and smacked his thigh while shaking my head at him. He immediately stopped but the grin remained. "Kissing, on the other hand, is an entirely different entity. Whereas, sex conveys an act of love, kissing says, I like you. Kissing someone is so much more personal and intimate than sex. Meaningful passionate kissing is a sure-fire way of arousing a lady." I leaned down and touched my lips softly to his. Then with more pressure and demand.

I pulled away with some reluctance and held his gaze. His beautiful blue eyes were full of thirst and hunger. I took a deep breath and tried to squash my own desire for him. I could feel my heart racing, my palms were sweaty, my toes tingling. I lost myself in his eyes trying to recompose myself. I had to know I was going to educate him properly. And I was determined to do so.

I slid back off him pulling him into a seated position and poised myself on the bed between his thighs. I took his hand and placed it between my breasts. I put my hand on his sternum and held his gaze. "Feel my heartbeat. Slow your breathing to match mine." My eyes embraced his as he slowed his breathing down. "Feel the warmth of my hand on your chest and draw the heat into your body. Feel my desire for you."

"Sex is an awakening of the senses. The body is a playground to explore, with each of the senses. Sight, touch, smells, sounds and tastes are tantalizing and need to be shown attention." I gently pushed him back against the pillows with a single finger.

"It's an exploration of desire." My voice was barely a whisper. I traced my fingertips lightly up each of his arms, lingering on his shoulders, across to his neck. I could see the goose-bumps rising on his chest, his arms and down his legs. He shuddered noticeably, and his erection throbbed. I ran my fingers over his stomach around his belly button and teased the small trail of hair across his sculpted abdomen. I kissed the small of his stomach and played lightly with his inner thighs and all along his pelvic region, swirling my fingers around but never touching his cock. Mason eased into it and moaned softly with desire. I could almost feel an electrical spark passing between his skin and flowing through my fingers.

I climbed back up to his face, my body hovering over his, and kissed him fully. My lips devoured his, my tongue stroking his. I loved the taste of him, the heat that passed between us and burned throughout my body. Mason caressed my buttocks and ran his hands over my back and through my hair. He rolled me over and for once, kept his weight directly off me. *He is a quick learner!*

Mason moved his full lips down my neck to my collarbone, his tongue just barely tracing against my skin. I placed my hand on his shoulder, and he paused for a moment and brought his gaze to meet mine. "Slow down. This is not a time to hurry to the finish line. This is where we enjoy the journey." I eased him up into a seated position and kissed him once more.

I interlocked our hands together then placed his beneath mine, on my shoulders. I removed mine and let them fall to my sides. Mason slipped his fingers under the straps of my bra and eased them down my arms massaging them as he went. He gracefully unhooked it and let it fall off the corner of the bed. My breasts stood fully exposed with my nipples erect. He paused in a moment to drink in the vision in front of him.

Mason leaned forward to kiss me again and I could feel the hunger raging forth. I tore myself away enough to catch my breath. I had to remind myself to slow down. It was so easy to get carried away with him. He was so freaking sexy, desirable, edible, and everything I had ever fantasized about.

I lay back against the pile of pillows at the head of my bed with Mason sitting on his heels between my legs. He lifted my legs and stretched them over his thighs. With my hips raised several inches off the bedding, Mason easily slid my black lace panties down over my garter and stockings. He tossed them aside casually and kissed the top of my pelvic bone.

"All right, you wanted to teach me how to please you, and I am your most eager student. So, teach me," Mason whispered in a sultry voice.

"Okay," I began with a satisfied smile. "With your index finger on your right-hand place it on my clitoris."

He tried, missed the mark. *That explains a lot.*

"No, sweetheart." I moved his hand. "Here."

"There . . ." He added a little too much pressure.

"Not so hard." I instinctively jerked back a bit.

"Oh, sorry." He blushed.

"Now slide your finger back slowly and slip it into me." He desperately needed some lubrication. "But don't jam it in there," I quickly added.

Mason smiled slightly and if I'd hurt his feelings, he didn't show it. Instead, he followed my instructions and tenderly slipped his finger between my lips and up inside me. I let out a small gasp. "Now gently, push up a little higher." He complied, and I had to bite down on a moan. "Move your finger towards the front of my body. Now, feel that little spongy ridge?"

"That?" He found it. My entire body quivered.

"Yes," I said breathlessly. "That is a lady's G-spot. If you take . . ." But Mason had already moved on.

He slipped his legs out from under him to lay on his stomach, his head appropriately between my thighs. His tongue promptly landed at my desired location. After one long stroke, I immediately stopped him before I felt the all too familiar urge to scream at him. "Stop, stop. Please, stop!" I pulled away slightly. "Sweetheart, not like that." I propped myself up on my elbows. "Please, do not ever do that. It feels like you're weather proofing me for the winter."

Mason chuckled. "Wow, what a creative insult."

"I'm sorry." I tried not to laugh. "I know it isn't funny. But your technique is mind numbing, not mind blowing," I explained.

"Ouch!" He propped his chin on his fist." "Okay, tell me what I'm doing wrong."

"It's a clitoris, not a cream filled donut. You need to play, flirt, tease, suck and yes, lick it, but not with one long monotonous stroke. Have fun with it. React to my reactions, my body language, listen to the sounds I make and follow my lead." I smiled coyly at his big blue eyes.

A devilish grin formed on his shapely lips. His eyes danced with mischievousness. "Yes, my lady." He ran his tongue across the inside of my thigh. Then he began to tease me with his tongue. He parted my inner lips and tormented me blissfully before sliding two of his fingers deep inside me. He toyed with his new discovery of my G-spot and soon I was shaking and screaming in pleasure. My nails raked across his back as I tried to escape him, but he locked his arms around my thighs and hips and wouldn't let me go. I begged for mercy, but he refused.

I finally collapsed against the pillows, spent and numb. My body was torn between tingling and trembling in a state of pure unbridled ecstasy. My breathing was labored, my body sweaty. All I could think about was having him inside me.

"Take me." I pulled him to me. "Take me, now!"

And he did. Twice!

Chapter 8

WE SPENT THE NEXT several weeks until the end of the semester continuing our naughty little tryst on the afternoons after class. We would disappear to my house four days a week and play for hours. I had turned into the instructor and Mason my willing and eager student. And as time went by, he stayed later and later, under the guise of studying. At least until mid-May, when he mentioned to Max that he had played on his high school baseball team as catcher also. After that, Max was sold. As soon as he'd come home after school, he'd have Mason outside practicing. It wasn't long before Max had invited him to watch his practices which, of course, led to Saturday morning games.

Lisa and Kim had gotten used to his presence and had stopped teasing me about my beanie boy, at least when he was around. However, the other moms . . . they were a problem. It was bad enough, in general, I was an easy ten years younger than most of them. Most were successful career women or die-hard stay at home moms. They viewed Lisa and me as social pariahs and a threat to their happy little lives. The married ones felt threatened that we'd flirt with their husbands and the divorced crones hated us for having something akin to a social life. The sidelines at any junior league sporting event reminded me of being back in high school it was so cliquey.

And most of these women were vicious. If their husbands so much as spoke to us, their claws came out. It was common to see any one of these women casually waltz over to her husband's side, place a hand on his arm—a clear claim of ownership, and smile through her fangs as a warning. It was pathetic how sad these women were. They might as well pee a little circle all around their husbands cause that was exactly what they were doing. And the divorced ones were even worse. They truly considered us their competition if not their enemy. They envied our energy and our age. There was an invisible line drawn on every set of bleachers regardless of the sport.

Now, they wanted to begrudge me Mason. I could hear the whispers behind my back about his age, how they called me a cougar when they thought I couldn't hear them, or the looks of disapproval they would glare at me whenever I looked their direction. I knew they were jealous. There was no way in hell these ladies could ever have a twenty-one-year-old cabana boy as sexy as Mason.

And it didn't take long for word to spread. On Memorial weekend, I was getting breakfast ready while the boys, Mason included, were playing X-box when my cell phone rang.

"Hello," I answered without looking first at the number and immediately regretting it.

"Good morning, doll. How are you?" A familiar voice greeted me.

"What do you want Danny?" Annoyance immediately took over. "You know I got Max a cell phone, so we don't have to have these pleasant conversations."

"I called to talk to you. I have been hearing some interesting things about you lately and I was curious. After all, I am concerned about my boys."

"Good grief, Danny. What do you want?" I flipped the blueberry pancakes and leaned against the counter.

"I heard you were having a naughty little affair with the paper boy," he said, trying not to laugh.

"What? Who told you that?" That was the very last thing I expected to come out of his mouth.

"A little birdie told me."

"Imagine that." Max must have told him about Mason helping him with baseball and how much time he was spending over here, even after our class was done.

"So, how old is this kid anyway?"

"What I do or who I do is none of your business, Danny." I tapped my fingers on the counter.

"It's my business when he's spending so much time with my sons," he countered.

"You gave up that right when you gave me sole custody and decided to move across the country. You have no right to say anything about what I do. I would never do anything inappropriate around them, in front of them, or anywhere near them. You know I wouldn't. Don't you give me any shit! God only knows what you're doing down there." I walked out onto the back deck, so no one would hear me.

"Geez, Alex, don't get your panties in a bunch. I was just teasing you." He laughed. "Seriously, though, how old is this kid?"

"That's none of your damn business." *He's such an ass.*

"Oh, come on, I'm only playing. What happened to your sense of humor? You used to have one." He chuckled.

"I don't know, maybe it went away when my low-life of a husband cheated on me?" I stated flatly.

"Ouch, you might want to get that checked soon, Alex or you could turn into a real bitter bitch." His laughter made me wish I could slap him across his smug face.

"I'm hanging up now."

"Wait, Alex. Seriously, Max told me you were happy." His laughter died away. "He said you try to play off that you two are only friends, but he knows there's something going on between you two. He said he can tell by the way Mason looks at you that he's in love with you."

"Max told you that?" I turned around and looked at my back door half expecting Mason or Max to be standing there.

"Yes, he told me that last night. So why are you trying to hide your relationship from the boys? You obviously like this man," Danny inquired.

"Jesus, Danny. Really? Why do you think? Mason is younger than me." I sighed audibly. "Okay, a lot younger than me. He's twenty-one." I closed my eyes and waited for that to sink in.

"Good Lord, Alex. He's a child! What the hell are you thinking?" He laughed again. "When Max said younger than you, I was thinking he was twenty-six or twenty-eight, not twenty-one!"

"It's just a fling, Danny. That's all."

"Does he know that?"

"I don't know," I answered honestly.

"You may want to tell him before this kid gets too attached to you or the boys to him," he pointed out. I hated him for acting like the responsible adult when I should have been.

"I know," I whispered. "I will."

I hung up the phone and sat down on the porch swing staring out over the backyard and the woods surrounding it. The grass was finally green once more and starting to grow again. It wouldn't be long before I would need to mow. The sun was flirting with a few clouds that passed overhead as it rose higher in the sky. I loved this place. This was our home and where we belonged. But somehow, in my heart, I knew Mason did too.

"Who was on the phone?" Max's voice startled me from the doorway.

"What? Oh, it was your dad." I wiped away a tear I hadn't realized had escaped.

"Is everything all right?" He came over and sat down beside me.

"Yes, of course. Breakfast is almost ready." I got up and took a step towards the door when Max spoke again.

"Are you mad at me?" His voice was lower.

I turned towards him. "No. Why would I be upset with you?"

"Because I told Dad about Mason?" he confessed.

"Ah, Max. I'm not upset with you for talking to your dad about Mason." I returned to the swing and sat down. "I would never tell you that you can't talk to your dad about anything. He's your dad and you don't have to keep secrets from him." I put my arm around his shoulders. "Mason is a part of our lives and he's been helping you with baseball."

"And he's your boyfriend," Max said it more as a statement than a question.

"I suppose he is. We haven't really discussed it," I confided in my eldest son.

"He really likes you."

"You think so?" Max nodded his head.

"Do you love him?" he innocently asked.

"I don't know, maybe. I do like him a lot," I answered him honestly. "Come on. Let's eat." We rose together and headed in. "You can set the table for me." I smiled and messed up his hair.

"Great," he muttered but smiled back at me.

* * *

Isaac graduated with high honors and disappeared for the next few weeks studying for his MCAT's. I couldn't imagine the pressure he was under. I had spoken with his girlfriend, Heather, earlier last week and she said he was a complete mess. I had gotten to know her through Isaac and we had become fast friends. She was sweet and had also recently graduated with a business degree. They had been dating for a couple of years and she knew Isaac was a tremendous flirt—with everyone. Thankfully, she was secure enough in their relationship and in herself that she never let it bother her that he was that way. She always just laughed it off or joined in just to get a reaction out of the other girl.

My neighbor across the street, Debbie, was a divorced mother of three unruly teenagers and a big drinker. Over the years she and I had become good friends and spent many an evening hanging out on her sun porch discussing pretty much everything from our ex's, our children, and anything else we could think of. Debbie was notorious for two things: her holiday parties and her famous punch that she served at them. She had a large in-ground pool in her backyard that we had adopted pretty much as our own. I had become close with her children as well and had spent countless hours lounging poolside with her two daughters soaking up the sun and listening to them complain about the men in their lives. I had even gotten so comfortable with their family that Debbie's parents referred to me as another daughter and I called them Mom and Dad when they visited.

Debbie was sweeping off her front sidewalk when we pulled into our driveway, returning home from the boys' Saturday baseball games. It was a sunny, hot and humid afternoon and I could think of nothing better than slipping into my suit and taking a swim. She waved at us as we got out of the car.

"How'd it go?" she hollered.

"We won," Max shouted on his way into the house.

"We didn't." Henry slouched, smacking his glove against the tree in the front yard.

"I'm sorry, little man. Why don't you put on your shorts and come on over?" Debbie offered with a grin.

Henry looked over at me and I nodded. "Okay." His spirit immediately uplifted, he trotted into the house.

"We'll be over in a few. Thanks," I hollered back with a wave.

*   *   *

The boys splashed around in the cool water while Debbie and I soaked up some sun. She was in a good mood and enjoying the peace and quiet. Her kids had gone to Florida with their dad for the next two weeks, giving her a well-deserved break. By six o'clock we were drinking strawberry daiquiris and grilling steaks poolside. It was the perfect afternoon.

Shortly after we finished eating, my parents came by and picked up the boys for a sleepover. I met my parents over at my house and gathered up the boys' things. I chatted with my folks for a bit then kissed the boy's goodbye, telling them to behave themselves. As they left, I made my way back over to Debbie's for a nice relaxing evening.

Debbie's boyfriend, Mark, had arrived during my absence and was helping himself to a plate of food. I fixed myself another daiquiri and rejoined Debbie beside the pool. We were enjoying the sunset and sipping our drinks when my phone buzzed. It was Mason.

"Hey sweet ass," I teased. "How are you?"

"Are you drinking?" he laughed.

"A little. I'm on my third one."

"Where are you?" he inquired.

"Poolside at Debbie's." She gave me a coy grin and shook her head.

"Get your cute little hiney over here," Debbie hollered loud enough for Mason to hear.

"Where are the boys?"

"My parents picked them up a while ago for a sleepover. You should come on over." I was dying to see him.

"Okay. I'll be there in a few."

"See ya soon." I put my phone back on the little table between us. "He's on his way." I smiled over at Debbie.

"You know you should be ashamed of yourself, Alex. He's a child." Debbie shook her head with a grin.

"You're just jealous." I smirked. "And trust me, he's no child." I laughed and took another drink.

Mark came over with a beer and took the lounge chair on the other side of Debbie. "Who's no child?"

"Alex's little boy toy." She turned towards me. "How old is he? Twenty-four? Twenty-five?"

"Twenty-one." I flashed them a devilish grin.

"Dear Lord." Debbie laughed.

"And you're . . .?" Mark fished.

"Just turned thirty-three."

"So, he's closer to your son's age than yours?" He pointed out the obvious.

"And your point?" I questioned.

"No point. Just an observation," he remarked.

"He's just jealous," Debbie said. "He'd trade me in for a twenty-one-year-old in a heartbeat if he had the opportunity."

"I would not. You're more than enough for me." Mark leaned over and kissed her cheek.

"Yeah, right." Debbie playfully smacked him away.

Mark laughed and went over to turn the music up a bit then disappeared into the house to make more daiquiris. The evening air was still hot, and the humidity was thick. I got up and went over to sit on the steps with my feet in the water and a drink in my hand. The water felt so refreshing and the daiquiri was helping to melt the stress of my first year of college away.

I could not believe I had managed to complete my first year. Several days ago, I received an official award from the university for making the Dean's List for the spring semester. I framed it along with the one I had gotten for the fall semester and hung them both proudly in my dining room. It had not been easy, not by a long shot, but the boys and I had adjusted somewhat smoothly into this new life and had even found room in it for Mason. I knew in my heart the relationship between us would never endure college, but despite that knowledge, I was determined to enjoy what time I was given with him.

"Hey, Lexie," Mason's head popped over the top of Debbie's privacy fence. "Care to unlock the gate?"

"Sure." I walked over and let him in.

"Wow." he pulled me to him and gave me a quick kiss. "You look fabulous in that bikini."

"Thanks. Glad you made it."

I returned to the steps while Mason walked over to the chairs, slipped off his shoes and shirt and put his keys and phone down on the little table beside mine. Mark offered him a beer and the two of them struck up a conversation about something. Debbie came over and sat down beside me on the steps.

"Okay, I understand." She smiled and nodded in Mason's direction. "He's certainly edible. I see why it would be so hard to part with that."

I shrugged with a grin. "Ah, I think I'll keep him for now."

"Well, if you ever get tired of him, send him my way," she whispered with a cheesy grin.

"I'm sure Mark would appreciate that." I gave her a playful shove.

"But I would." She smiled and took another drink of her daiquiri.

The four of us swam for a while, and they teased us relentlessly about our age difference. Eventually, we gathered on the sun porch with our drinks to play Euchre. Mason and I teamed off against them. He had never played before and they beat us the first two games. By the third game Mason started getting the hang of it, but we got interrupted by my phone.

"Hey." I recognized Isaac's number when I picked up my phone.

"Alex?" Heather replied. "This is Heather. Are you home?"

"Sort of. I'm across the street. What's up?"

"Isaac and I were out running around, and he wanted to stop by. Is that all right?" Her voice sounded a little off.

"Sure. I'm across the street at my neighbor's house. I'll keep an eye out for you guys."

"Okay, thanks. We'll be there in about ten minutes or so."

I set the phone aside and went back to the game. Within five minutes we heard the screeching of tires out front. The four of us rose and hurried to the gate. Sure enough, it was Isaac and Heather. They were arguing back and forth until he tried to step out of the car and fell in the street. Despite ourselves, the four of us couldn't help but laugh. Isaac was not merely a tall man. He was a ridiculously large man in size and volume. He was also clearly drunk.

By the time the four of us made it over to them, Heather was trying desperately to get Isaac off the ground. And as large of a man as he was, Heather was one of the most petite women I'd ever met. She was barely over five feet tall and couldn't have weighed more than ninety pounds soaking wet. I always referred to them as the Great Dane dating the Chihuahua. It was almost humorous trying to figure out how the two of them ever had sex.

"Get up," Heather growled between gritted teeth at Isaac who was still lying in the street laughing. Heather looked up and blushed as she saw us approaching. "I'm so sorry. He's been drinking since he finished his MCAT's, and I couldn't get him to go home. Your house was the closest. I was trying to get him off the road before he killed us both."

"I'm not drinking. I'm celebrating," Isaac slurred and climbed awkwardly to his feet. He tried to balance himself against his car and then seemed to notice the four of us standing there for the first time. "Hey, Alex! How are you?" He grabbed me in a clumsy bear hug. "I didn't know you were here." He paused and looked at the others. "And your little study buddy is with you. Hey man." He reached for Mason and hugged him as well. "I need a drink. Is there anything to drink around here?"

Luckily, Mark and Debbie both thought Isaac's antics were entertaining and steered him across the street to the back, trying to make sure he did not falter. It wasn't easy, but they managed it. Heather grabbed my arm and repeatedly apologized for Isaac's behavior.

Mark helped Isaac sit down on the edge of the pool and put his feet in the water thinking the cool water would help sober him up a bit. But Isaac didn't want to sit still. He leaned forward and fell into the water. Luckily, he was in the shallow end, and he stood up immediately laughing before stumbling up the steps.

"Wow, that's some cold water there!" He shook his head like a dog and grabbed a towel off the nearest chair. He half-assed dried himself off and flopped down into the lounge chair. There was a loud crack and popping sound as the chair gave way to Isaac's hulking frame. Before any of us could do anything, Isaac was on his ass with his feet sticking straight up in the air.

Debbie, Heather, and I stared with our jaws hanging down while Isaac struggled to his feet. Mark and Mason quickly rushed to help him.

"Oops!" Isaac laughed and pointed down on the rubble. "That chair is dangerous. Someone could get hurt." He stumbled a bit forward and Mark steadied him. "Sorry, about your chair."

"Don't worry about the chair. Are you all right?" Debbie said.

"Yeah, I'm fine." Isaac dusted off his rear. "Ouch!" He spun around, and we could all see a little piece of the wooden chair embedded in his backside.

"Oh, Jesus," Heather muttered under her breath and took Isaac by the arm. "Don't move. You're bleeding."

"I've got some bandages and Neosporin in the house," Debbie said before heading inside.

Mason was still holding onto Isaac's arm trying to hold him steady. Heather had turned Isaac around trying to get a clear view of his injury, but Isaac wasn't making it easy for her.

"Would you stand still? I can't get a good look at this," Heather chastised him.

"You want a look? Fine." Isaac dropped his trousers.

"Damn it, Isaac," Heather said in a voice filled with anger, but he just laughed it off.

Mark reached for a towel and offered it to Isaac who didn't even acknowledge it. Despite myself, I couldn't help but let out a small giggle at the comical scene in front of me.

"Oh." Debbie returned and came to an abrupt halt by my side. "What is he doing?"

"I have no idea." I shook my head. "Apparently he's making it easier for Heather to view his injury."

Debbie handed the supplies to Heather who looked completely mortified. "I'm so sorry," she repeated once again.

"Not a problem," Debbie assured her. I knew she'd seen more bizarre things than this at her poolside. So, had I for that matter.

Heather finally got Isaac stable enough to get a good look at his injury. There was about a three-inch piece of wood embedded in Isaac's right butt cheek. From where I was standing it looked to be in there fairly deep especially since he didn't dislodge it when he yanked his shorts and boxers off.

Heather tilted his backside towards the light on the outside of the sunroom and tried to pull the long sliver out. Isaac let out a scream that startled us all. Then he jerked away from her and Mason, stumbling backwards a few steps.

"Damn woman! What the hell! That hurt!" he shouted.

"Don't be such a baby. I've got to get it all out. Come here!" Heather demanded.

"I don't think so." Isaac bolted towards the gate, flipped the latch, and took off at a stumbling run down the middle of our street.

"Oh, my God!" Debbie exclaimed and the five of us took off running after him.

Thankfully, it was almost ten at night. Still, there was a full moon shining down on Isaac's naked body as he tried to evade us hollering and laughing at the same time as this was truly the best game ever. It didn't take long before various porch lights up and down our street sprang to life. Several of our neighbors even stepped out on their porch to find out what the ruckus was about.

Just a large naked black man streaking down the avenue screaming like a loon. No need for alarm . . .

Mark, Mason, and Heather finally managed to get Isaac calmed down and back behind the confines of Debbie's privacy fence. Debbie and I tried to pacify our self-righteous neighbor who lived beside her and was threatening to call the police on Isaac for indecent exposure.

Mrs. Pious-Airs and her holier-than-thou husband were standing on their porch screaming at us. She looked ridiculous spouting about morals and values in her fuzzy robe all red-faced and puffed up. I wanted so badly to tell her where to stick it. We listened to her lecture for a good twenty minutes to calm her down enough and convinced her not to call the police. Plus, the look on her face when Debbie told her Isaac was celebrating his MCAT's and in fact, was well on his way to becoming a surgeon was priceless.

"That's probably the only cock that old bat has seen in twenty years," Debbie stated as we walked down the sidewalk. "And she wouldn't even know what to do with it if we told her."

"She would benefit immensely from a hard drink and a hard dick." I laughed and opened her back gate.

Heather had managed somehow to bandage Isaac's ass, and he was lying on his stomach on a floatie in the middle of the pool. The other three had fixed themselves another drink and were betting on how long it would be before Isaac rolled over and fell into the water. Mark had started a little bonfire in the pit on the patio and the smell of the wood burning was so relaxing. Debbie and I fixed ourselves another daiquiri and rejoined the others at the fire.

* * *

Mason left the following Thursday morning for a three-day weekend end-of-semester blow-out with Jared, Nick, and Josiah. The four of them headed north to Cedar Point in Mason's Camaro. That evening after I got the boys down for the night I curled up with a blanket on the couch and flipped on the television. The house felt strange without Mason. It was too quiet. I had gotten so accustomed to his presence in such a short time, his absence was an oddity.

I scrolled through the channels and settled on *The Avengers* simply because of the number of delicious men starring in it. Then I pondered who was better looking: Robert Downey Jr. or Chris Hemsworth. It was a toss-up. Each had their own edible attributes.

I picked up a copy of *Doctor Sleep* by Stephen King that my father had given me for my birthday in April. My dad, an avid Stephan King reader, introduced me to the man who exploited everyone's darkest nightmares when I was thirteen years old. He started with his favorite, *The Shining*. I dove headfirst into it and it scared the hell out of me. I was addicted from that moment on. Since then, every year on my birthday, my dad would buy me another novel written by King. Thankfully, King's ghoulish imagination worked on overdrive, and it didn't appear my father would ever run out of material any time soon.

Chapter 9

I ABSOLUTELY LOVED my sex and society class. My professor, Dr. Wilson, was fabulous and unlike any professor I'd had thus far. He was humorous, renown in his field as a *Sexpert* and had gotten his doctorate at the Kinsey Institute at Indiana University. To say he was knowledgeable on sex was a mild understatement. Our accelerated summer course ran for six weeks instead of the traditional fourteen. My morning classes were two and a half hours long on Tuesday and Thursdays. My mom initially helped by watching the boys for me while I was in class, but Mason started staying over, and the more he was around, the boys seem to prefer to spend their mornings under his more relaxed style of babysitting.

Dr. Wilson told us he was going to be passing around the sign-up sheet for the hour-long speech we were all responsible for giving in the next three weeks. I listened to him start his discussion on homosexual bathhouses, something up until five minutes ago, I didn't even know existed. He wanted us to watch a short film that he and his assistant had made at a bathhouse in New Orleans that consisted of various interviews with the patrons.

The sheet finally made it to my desk. I glanced over the topics others had chosen trying to keep the shocked look from showing across my face. Pony play, bestiality, tantric sex, bondage, sadomasochism . . . the list went on and on. I sat there for a moment before writing my topic down on the line beside my name. Ever since we had been told about this assignment on the first day of class I had been milling over what topic I truly wanted to research. Finally, I scribbled down "female domination" and quickly passed the paper to the person behind me.

When class let out I gathered my things and started out with my classmates when Dr. Wilson called after me.

"Oh, Ms. Rose, may I speak with you a moment please?" Dr. Wilson was standing at his desk sorting through papers.

I made my way back to the front of the class. "Yes, Dr. Wilson?"

"I was looking through the sign-up sheet and noticed that you decided to present female domination. Have you begun your research yet?" he inquired.

"No, not really."

"Well, I have a couple books in my office that I believe would be very useful if you would like to borrow them," he offered.

"Yes, thank you. I would appreciate that." I felt a sigh of relief and tried not to show it.

I followed Dr. Wilson across the campus quad to his office in the communications building. He chatted about research studies conducted on the subject and I was honestly surprised by almost everything he said. I always knew sex was a powerful tool both physically and emotionally, but I had no inkling how it could be used as a complete and total control mechanism over a person. My mind immediately went to Mason. *This could really be fun.*

We climbed up to his office on the third floor. It was a crowded little office covered in books and papers. I couldn't imagine being able to find anything in here. But Dr. Wilson knew his office and went straight to the bookshelf behind his desk and located the books he wanted me to read. He handed me down four paperback books written by various experienced mistresses that gave similar accounts of the art of seduction and how to be a dominatrix.

Some of the things Dr. Wilson discussed on our walk kept running through my mind on my drive home. I wondered to what extent female domination could be explored. The more Dr. Wilson had told me about research studies done on sexual behavior and dominance, the more intrigued I had become. I considered what I had learned last fall regarding classical and operant conditioning. I found myself anxious to get home, so I could pull out my old textbook from psychology class.

* * *

After I got the boys down for the night, I finally got the opportunity to thumb through the books for my presentation. The first one covered a large range of topics such as bondage, cross-dressing, fetish wear, and role-playing to water sports. None of which I planned to include in my speech, so I tossed it aside. The second one was much more helpful for my report and my own little personal experiment I wanted to try with Mason. It was more of a step-by-step instruction manual on how to become a mistress, establishing authority, asserting, planning, and enacting it and how to become a goddess in your own right. I found it fascinating.

I quickly became engrossed and read the entire one hundred and sixty-seven-page manual until three in the morning. I took extensive notes and marked pages of all the important passages I thought would come in handy for my report. My bed was scattered with papers, notes, and books. Billy grunted at me and kicked some papers on to the floor, so she could lie down.

After I turned off the light, the soft glow from the television was an odd comfort. My mind was whirling in a thousand different directions. *Was any of this possible? Could a woman really have such a strong sexual control over a man that he would devote his love to her entirely?* I seriously had my doubts. Danny and I had had a very active sex life and that hadn't deterred him from cheating on me.

*   *   *

The next day Mason came over before lunch. He was dressed casually in light cream shorts with blue and grey plaid design on them and a cotton blue t-shirt that enriched the color of his eyes. The boys ran out to greet him as soon as he pulled in the driveway. Both began tugging on him, wanting his undivided attention. I stood in the front door and smiled, happy that they had accepted Mason and welcomed him into their lives, yet a part of me was saddened by the realization that they were in desperate need of a father figure because of Danny's absence and instead of a man, they were looking up to this twenty-one-year-old kid. Thank God, he was a good and decent young man who cared dearly for them.

Mason walked up to me and kissed me lightly then turned back to my sons. "Give me just a moment to speak with your mom and then I'll come back out and practice with you."

"Hello, I thought you'd come by yesterday." My hand lingered in his.

"I didn't want to bother you. You said you were going to be doing research for your speech." He followed me inside.

"I was up until after three reading and the boys were kind enough to let me sleep in until ten this morning." *An extreme rarity for them.*

"So, it was a good thing I left you alone." He paused in the family room and kissed me again.

"If you say so," I teased.

"Did you learn anything?" He walked over to my desk.

I walked up behind him and wrapped my arm around his neck and whispered, "You have no idea."

Mason picked up one of Dr. Wilson's books and his eyes widened. "Is this what you've been reading?" I nodded. "What kind of kinky class is this?"

"It's an exploration of various sexual expressions," I explained, taking the book out of his hands, and placing it back on my desk. "It's intriguing." I kissed him lightly on the back of his neck before I let him go.

"Really?" He leaned back on my desk looking irresistible. "How so?"

"I'll have to show you later." I trailed my finger across his chest with a seductive smile. "Right now, I have research to do, and you have baseball practice."

Mason disappeared back outside with my sons. I sat down at my desk and watched the three of them through the front window and opened my old psychology textbook from last fall. I turned to the chapter on associative learning and dug around until I found the section on classical and operant conditioning. I leaned back in my chair and reviewed what I had previously highlighted. The classical conditioning section covered the Nobel Prize-winning Russian physiologist Ivan Pavlov and his experiment from 1906 with drooling dogs and how they learned to associate the ringing of a bell to feeding time. Of course, it was a little more in-depth covering terms such as unconditioned stimulus, unconditioned response, neutral stimulus, conditioned stimulus, and conditioned response and how each was related to the next. I remembered when we initially started this in class how confused I was. It took sitting down and creating a flowchart on paper to get it all straight in my head how one affected the other.

I took out a blank sheet of paper and created a similar flowchart as before except this time I would be using sexual components rather than mapping out the causes of dog drool. After reading so much information on female sexual dominance, I realized that I couldn't ever be the type of dominatrix covered in those books. They specialized in bondage and sadomasochism. Something I could never do or become. I simply wasn't the leather and whips type of lady. I was more of the fashion of silks and lace. I could never inflect pain and humiliation under the guise of sexual gratification. I have always maintained a firm sexual belief of if it feels good, do it. It was beyond me to comprehend how some individuals could ever believe that pain equals pleasure. I have never been a prude, and I always held to the belief that whatever two consenting adults did in the privacy of their own bedroom was no one's business but their own. Still, there were certain things that were just beyond my realm of understanding.

I wanted to find a way to utilize my newfound knowledge of female domination and combine it with the tools of classical and operant conditioning and the sensual eloquence of tantric sex. I wanted to control and dominate Mason utilizing the processes of acquisition, stimulus generalization, stimulus discrimination, overshadowing, as well as higher-order conditioning and test extinction and spontaneous recovery in practice. I drew out the flowchart on the paper in front of me leaving the blocks empty but mapping the before, during, and after conditioning maps. I scribbled in the terms in their right places and leaned back in my chair considering exactly how I wanted to approach this little project. I knew where I was starting and where I wanted to go but filling in the "how to get there" was the tricky piece of the puzzle.

The unconditioned stimulus and unconditioned response were obvious as were the conditioned stimulus and conditioned response. Achieving the neutral stimulus for the desired response would be a slow and steady pleasurable journey. Given that the unconditioned response to the unconditioned stimulus was natural response, the key to connecting them with a neutral stimulus. Once I linked the neutral stimulus with the unconditioned stimulus to elicit the desired unconditioned response, I was in business.

I chewed on the end of my pen staring at the flowchart in front of me. At the top under the heading 'Before Conditioning,' the unconditioned stimulus was listed as arousal, which elicits the unconditioned response of an orgasm. The middle column or the 'During Conditioning,' included the introduction of the neutral stimulus of a non-sexual touch coinciding with the unconditioned stimulus to create the desired result of the unconditioned response of an orgasm. Near the bottom of the page, I had written in the final category, the 'After Conditioning,' which included the desired results of a conditioned stimulus or rather the non-sexual touch bringing about the conditioned response, an orgasm.

I wanted to have fun with the various aspects of operant conditioning such as the law of effect, the positive and negative effects of reinforcement and the schedules of them. Most dominatrixes used pain and humiliation to achieve their desired conditioned response. I, however, was adamant that I could achieve my goal using sensual touch, pleasure, and positive reinforcements for desired behavior.

Creating the flowchart helped a great deal as did the book on Tantric sex. Some of the elements of the dominatrix books were very useful for my presentation but very little for my own home project. I jotted down a few more notes and passages from my psychology book before tossing it aside. I picked up the female dominance book and began scanning over various pages hunting for key points for my paper. I could understand the basic psychology behind most of techniques and how it made them affective on a submissive personality and revered by a dominant one.

I finally put that one aside and opened the final book given to me by Dr. Wilson. It strictly covered bizarre fetishes and I seriously doubted I'd find much information in here that I could use. It was divided into four sections, animal transformation, objects, taboo, and growth. Among the pages were scores of colored pictures of fetishes I could never have possibly fathomed. I giggled at most of what I saw and was astonished by the others. I would never in my wildest dreams have imagined that pony play, furverts, a person that apparently finds anthropomorphic art sexual, robots/dolls, infantilism, crush freaks, fat admiration, and people who loved body inflation even existed let alone ever brought it into the sexual realm. It was a whole new level of weird and peculiar that couldn't penetrate my brain on that connection.

I didn't even bother to write anything from that book down before I hid it under a pile of other books and papers and safely out of the eyes of my sons. Thankfully, they were both very respectful of my desk and never bothered about anything on it.

*   *   *

By the time we'd finished dinner, the dishes, and gotten both boys showered, it was almost ten o'clock before they fell asleep. Mason and I curled up on the couch together under a blanket. The windows were open, and the cool early summer air had just enough of a chill to make snuggling a pleasant choice. I flipped on the television and began scrolling through the channels. I finally settled on the *Bourne Identity* playing on cable. I tossed the remote aside and curled into the nook under Mason's arm, resting my head against his chest.

My eyes drifted over to my desk and the flowchart I had stashed under my textbooks. I kept running over the steps in my mind and how I could go about executing my little home experiment. I traced my fingers lightly over Mason's thigh absentmindedly, lost in my own thoughts of various ways I could begin his training. With the boys being gone for the next several weeks, I had the perfect window of opportunity. I couldn't help but smile to myself just thinking about how much I was going to enjoy this.

Chapter 10

MY CELL PHONE woke me early on Sunday morning. I crawled out of bed, quickly grabbing it off the night table and snuck out of my room hoping the noise wouldn't awaken Mason.

"Hello," I whispered, glancing into both boys' rooms. They were still sound asleep. Both were up late the night before because of the bonfire cookout we all attended at Lisa's.

"Good morning doll, did I wake you?" Danny's voice sounded a little too cheerful.

"Yes, what are you doing up so early?"

"It's almost seven here. Tee time," he explained. "Last game before the boys come out."

"Oh." I went into the kitchen and started the coffee maker.

"Are you still going to pick me up on Tuesday?"

"I thought you were going to rent a car." It was too early to deal with him, and I was not awake enough yet.

"I was hoping I wouldn't have to." I could hear various voices hollering at him to get off the phone.

"Don't you think it would be easier?" I sat down on the couch curling my feet beneath me.

"No. I want to spend my time there with the boys. I'm going to be there for less than three days. I figured it would be easier if I just stayed with you."

"No! Out of the question. There are numerous hotels in the area, and you can stay at any one of them." His audacity never ceased to amaze me.

"Why? It makes sense if I just crash out on the couch or with one of the boys. It's only for a couple days," Danny pleaded.

"You want to stay here? In my house? Are you serious?"

"Yes. We're adults. I can control myself. Are you worried you can't?" He laughed.

"Hardly," I muttered. "I just do not think it's a good idea."

"Oh, I get it. The paper boy will be upset if you have a real man in your house." He laughed harder.

"Danny? Seriously? You want to go there?"

"I am being serious. If I stay in a hotel room I'll be running back and forth several times a day, cutting into time I could be spending with my sons," he reasoned.

"You're going to have the boys for the next five weeks. I'm sure they'll survive only spending part time with you while you're here," I pointed out.

"Fine, I'll tell them I can't spend as much time with them as I want because their mommy's boy toy might get jealous." He laughed again.

"Book your hotel room and rental car because you're going to need them!" I said angrily before hanging up my phone.

"That was a pleasant conversation." Mason's voice spoke up from behind me. "When's your ex arriving?"

"Tuesday evening." He came over and joined me on the couch. "He's here to spend the Fourth of July with the boys. Then he's taking them to Disney World, so they can visit Hogwarts and Pirates of the Caribbean before they head to his place in Arizona for the rest of the summer. It's part of his visitation rights."

"And he wants to stay here?" He put his arm around me. "You know I don't care if he does. I trust you completely."

"I know. It's not that. If I let him stay here, he's just going to irritate me any way he can. Danny loves to make himself a nuisance," I tried to explain.

"I suppose he wants to meet me?"

"Yes, I suppose he does. You do not have to meet him if you don't want to." I couldn't imagine being in his shoes.

"I guess I'll have to meet him eventually anyway because I love you and I love your boys." Mason leaned down and kissed me softly. "And I'm not going anywhere. This is not a fling for me."

I stared deep into his blue eyes and saw so much love there. And it hit me that this was more than a fling to me too. I'd been trying so hard to convince myself that it was simply a pleasurable tryst and Mason could never be more to me than just a transition back into the dating world that I had been completely blind to the man that was sitting beside me.

"Oh, Mason." I placed my hand gently on the side of his face. "I love you too."

"So, I get you alone for the rest of summer? This could be fun," he declared.

"Yes, it will be." I kissed him once again and retreated to the kitchen to fix myself a cup of coffee.

*   *   *

Tuesday evening, I cleared the dishes off the table and stacked them in the dishwasher. The clock on the stove informed me it was a little past five. Danny's plane had landed forty-five minutes ago, and Henry had tee-ball practice at six. I honestly expected Danny to be here by now.

No sooner had the thought crossed my mind than I heard a car door shut and the boys slam the front screen door. I set the dishtowel on the counter and took a deep breath before walking back into the family room to greet my ex-husband.

"Hello doll, how are you?" Danny walked through the front door with both boys hanging on him jabbering away.

"Danny," I acknowledged. "How was your flight?"

He stood in the foyer all smiles trying to listen to both boys at once. He was wearing khaki shorts and a maroon polo shirt that accented his golden tan. His dark brown hair had a few wisps of grey around his temples, but his smile and brown eyes were as vibrant as ever. Danny held a commanding presence with his six-foot-five stature and broad shoulders. It was hard to deny his good looks and charming nature.

"Fine, fine." He walked over and kissed me on the cheek. "You look good, doll." His hand lingered on my arm.

I backed away from him with a half-smile. "Henry has tee-ball practice at six, so we need to get going." I announced turning to my son. "Get your glove and bat and put your stuff in the car."

"Put them in my car, son. I'll drive." He patted Henry on the shoulder.

"Great," I muttered and went to fetch my purse.

I sat next to Lisa during practice while Danny hung out with Max next to the fence along the diamond. Max looked so happy to see his dad as he hung on to every word Danny uttered. It made me sick to think of my boys getting on a plane and leaving me for the next five weeks. I was going to be lost without them.

"Danny still looks good," Lisa commented. "Don't you hate that?" She smirked.

"Yes, I guess an industrial accident was too much to ask for," I replied.

"Where's Mason?"

"Back on campus. I didn't think it would be a good idea for the two of them to meet on Danny's first night here, especially with having to be here." I gestured around us. "He wasn't happy about it."

"I'm sure he wasn't." Lisa chuckled. "Has Mason ever seen Danny?"

"Not that I'm aware of. I took down all the photos of him in the house when he moved out."

"So, he has no idea what he's in for? Boy, I wish I could be a fly on the wall when those two meets." She was enjoying this a little too much.

"I'd honestly rather just skip that part. Danny is never going to let me forget how old Mason is." I sighed heavily. "He'd be perfect if he was at least in his late twenties."

"Oh, my God! You're falling for the kid, aren't you? Good Lord, Alex. What are you thinking?" She looked astonished.

"I know. I know. It's ridiculous. He's far too young and should be with someone closer to his own age."

"I think it might be time to cut your losses on this one and move on. He was supposed to be a fling just to get you back into the dating world. Remember?" She pointed out the obvious.

"I know I should, but Danny's taking the boys back to Arizona for the rest of summer and I'll have all the freedom in the world to do whatever I want." I flashed her a sly smile.

"I see." Lisa shook her head slightly. "I can see the wheels turning in your head. You're up to something."

"Let's just say I plan on enjoying Mason's company a lot while the boys are gone," I said coolly.

"You are bad." She giggled before turning her attention back to the boys on the field.

* * *

Danny helped me get the boys showered and settled down for the evening after we returned home. He turned out the light in Max's bedroom and took a seat on the couch. I was sitting on the loveseat watching a rerun of *The Big Bang Theory* when he joined me.

"I miss this." He made himself comfortable. "All of this. The boys, watching them play ball, getting them ready for bed, tucking them in . . . you."

"Really?" I refocused my attention back on the television.

"I'm serious, Alex. Don't you miss me at all?" He almost sounded sincere.

"Nope."

Danny laughed heartily and moved over to the loveseat beside me. "You're such a stubborn woman. It's one of the many things I love about you."

I tried my best to ignore him.

"Why don't you come to Arizona with us? I know you'd love it down there. And there is a great university not too far from my house if you insist on continuing with your college degree." He traced his finger lightly down my arm, which I promptly jerked away with an angry look in his direction.

"What is that supposed to mean?"

"I don't know why you're bothering. If you and the boys joined me in Arizona, then you wouldn't need a degree. I could give you anything you want." He reached over and put his hand on my bare thigh.

"I think it's time you left, Danny." I stood up and walked over to the front door opening it for him.

He chuckled. "What? Don't tell me the paper boy is coming by with a late delivery?" He came over and stood in front of me. "I know I was an ass to you, Alex. I know I hurt you. Can't you give me a chance to make it up to you?" He spoke so sweetly I almost believed him. Almost.

"Good night, Danny." I took a step back still holding the door open for him. He leaned down and kissed me lightly on the cheek.

"Just think about it," he whispered softly in my ear and left.

*   *   *

Mason arrived first thing in the morning before me or the boys had even gotten dressed. We had just finished breakfast and were lounging around the family room watching reruns of *Supernatural*. He knocked lightly on the front door then let himself in.

"Good morning." He was all smiles.

The boys hollered greetings and turned back to their show. It was one of their favorites.

"Hello, sweetheart." I got up and gave him a kiss. "It's nice to see you. Would you like some coffee?"

"Sure." I took him by the hand and led him into the kitchen.

Mason sat down at the island while I fixed each of us a mug. "What did you do yesterday?"

"Not much. Played X-box with Josiah and Nick. It was pretty boring." I set the coffee down next to him and climbed up on the stool beside him. "How did it go with your ex?"

"The boys were happy to see him. He arrived right before Henry's practice, so he went with us."

"Where is he staying?" Mason looked around almost as if he was expecting Danny to walk in on us.

"Not here." I smiled. "I'm not sure which hotel he's staying at. I didn't ask."

"What time's he supposed to be here today?" Just as the last word rolled off his tongue, I heard Danny walk through the front door. Funny, I never heard him knock.

Suddenly, the house was alive, and the boys' voices carried to the roof. Henry was begging for something or other while Max was trying to tell him about something else. I heard Danny ask them where I was hiding, and Max told him I was in the kitchen with Mason. Before I could utter anything to the young man seated beside me, my ex-husband appeared in my kitchen doorway flanked by each of our sons.

"Hello. Danny Rose," my ex said and extended his hand towards Mason.

Mason climbed off the stool and accepted his hand with a firm grasp. "Mason Brooks. Nice to meet you."

An awkward silence filled the room. The boys stood quietly on either side of their dad looking between the three adults as if we knew what to do next.

"Danny, would you like a cup of coffee? I just made a fresh pot." I slid off the bar stool and walked over to the counter.

"Sure. Thanks." He walked over and leaned against the island.

I fixed his mug, just like I used to and handed it over to him. He took a sip, smiled, and set it back down. "Perfect. Thanks, Alex." He slapped his hand on the island heartily. "So . . . what's on the agenda today?"

We all looked at each other having no clue how to respond. There simply was no correct response. The last thing I wanted to do was spend the day with Mason *and* my ex-husband.

"Why don't you take the boys to the zoo or something?" I suggested looking at Danny.

"Yeah," Henry hollered excitedly.

"Boring . . .," Max moaned.

"Okay. What do you want to do?" Danny asked him.

"Hurricane Mountain!" Max eagerly suggested.

Hurricane Mountain was an oversized overpriced water park on the north side of the city. It fit Max's thrill-seeking nature to a tee, but poor little Henry's gentle nature shied away from it and then suffered the torment from his older brother for it. I looked down at my youngest son and saw the fear in his eyes at the mere mention of the place.

"How about a compromise? Max, you can go to Hurricane Mountain with your dad and Mason, and I will take Henry to the zoo," I offered.

Danny was the only one who didn't look relieved. "Separate activities. I wanted us to do something as a family."

Now everyone looked even more uncomfortable.

"I think this would be best. Max doesn't care much for the zoo and Henry doesn't enjoy Hurricane Mountain," I explained without pointing out the obvious response to his remark.

"Fine." Danny turned towards Max. "Go get changed."

*   *   *

Danny arrived first thing the next morning I am certain just to verify the fact that Mason spent the night. He walked in unannounced once again. Mason, the boys, and I were all seated around the table enjoying what was a peaceful breakfast. Henry was telling Max about riding an elephant with Mason when I heard the front door open. I quickly excused myself to confront Danny before he could interrupt our morning.

"Good morning," he greeted me with a smile. "I brought donuts." He held out a box that I didn't bother taking.

"What are you doing? Haven't you ever heard of knocking? This is *my* house!" I tried to keep my voice down.

"I pay for it." He smirked.

"You will respect the fact that this is *my* house, and you will *not* just barge in here uninvited." I purposely ignored his previous comments. I was too upset to participate in his games.

"Don't give me any crap, Alex. It's too early in the morning." He took a deep breath, leaned against the wall, and ran his fingers through his hair. "Look, doll. I only get to see my sons once a year. Is it too much to ask that we at least try to get along while I'm here? Is it that difficult for you? You used to love me. We used to be a family. Can't you just pretend for a couple days?"

"Don't you dare make me the bad guy here, Danny. You're the one who cheated on me. You're the one who moved across the country. You left to play golf and attend business dinners. I stayed to raise two kids," I whispered in a harsh voice.

"I have apologized to you a hundred times for the mistakes I've made. I've begged you to give me another chance. If you would just let go of your pride for five minutes and let go of the past. I know I can make you happy again." His confidence was most irritating.

"You are unbelievable. You know that?" I shook my head at him and looked down at the donuts. "And your sons have already eaten a healthy breakfast. I don't let them fill up on junk first thing in the morning."

"Geez, you really should try and remove that stick out of your ass before you choke on it, Alex. I figured if you were getting laid you might be in a better mood. But then again, that's a man's job, not a little boys." He lowered his voice just enough so the other three couldn't hear his remark and I knew it was not for Mason's sake.

"You're an ass," I muttered and walked back into the kitchen with Danny chuckling behind me.

*   *   *

By nine in the morning, the sun was blazing down upon us. The humidity had risen to an almost unbearable level. Merely stepping outside from the air-conditioning felt like walking into a steam bath. It was miserable and only going to get worse as the day progressed.

The three of us dropped the boys off with their teammates and coaches in the high school parking lot where all the baseball and softball teams were lining up for the annual Fourth of July parade. Each team had a pick-up truck decorated with homemade signs and filled with children hanging off the sides and tailgates. They all loved the parade and tossed candy along the way to the people in our community lined along the parade route. Max had participated for four years but this was Henry's first time. He was so excited, not to just watch on the sidelines this year, but to be in it.

Lisa was already there with Logan waiting suspiciously just to get a glimpse of the awkwardness oozing from our little trio. She balanced McKenzie on her hip and kept glancing over at the two men, so drastically opposite of each other, and trying not to comment. I knew it must be killing her. Remaining silent was never one of her strongest attributes.

"Mind if we watch the parade with you all. I really don't want to have to join . . ." She nodded in the direction of her ex-husband casually talking with mine.

"Why not? I have to." I rolled my eyes.

We could hear their laughter from where we were standing. Poor Mason looked so uncomfortable. He casually strolled over to where Lisa and I were standing.

He leaned in-between us and whispered, "Is it me or is this just weird?"

"It's not you," Lisa responded.

With a final wave to our boys the six of us walked a little way down the parade route. Since both our exes were engaged in conversation, Lisa's ex seemingly joined our bizarre little group. The exes lagged along behind us discussing Danny's expedition in Arizona since he took up residency there. I tried hard to ignore the two of them walking a short distance behind us. But it wasn't easy considering how loudly the two of them were talking. Danny was putting a lot of emphasis on the glorious climate in comparison to the Midwest. He knew how much I hated winters and wished the spring would arrive immediately after the Christmas holidays. He was trying to tempt me and from the look on Lisa's and Mason's faces, they knew it too.

We found a small gap along the sidelines and stood there in the blistering heat waiting for the parade to start. I was already sweating through my shorts and tank top. Soon I was sticky and uncomfortable along with every person standing out there.

Finally, the parade started and the Shriner Brothers, our community Veterans, and town council, were the first to stroll past. The high school marching band and the trucks directly followed them full of the girls' softball teams. We got a small glimpse of Lisa's daughter Brie, who waved franticly from the tailgate of a silver pick-up surrounded by her friends. She tossed a handful of candy to her little sister standing in front of us. Brie's teammates followed suit and bombarded us with suckers, tootsie rolls, and gumballs. McKenzie squealed in delight and began gathering up her loot.

The boys little league team trailed behind the girls, and it wasn't difficult to locate Logan and Henry. They were bouncing up and down in the bed of the truck tossing candy in every direction. Henry hollered at us when he noticed and waved. I snapped a couple quick pictures of him and Logan with my phone. Once again, McKenzie received a landslide of treats that had grown increasingly sticky due to the humidity. Several minutes later Max's team went by. He was on the opposite side of the truck so I couldn't get a decent snapshot of him. He was so caught up with the people on the other side that he never noticed us.

It was past noon by the time we all returned home. I hurried back to my room and literally peeled off my sweaty clothes. Mason knocked softly before entering and caught me standing there in my bra and panties.

"Are you all right?" He took a seat on the edge of the bed. "You've been quiet all morning."

"I'm fine." I climbed out of my under garments and put on my bright pink bikini. I stood in the mirror tying the strings and looked back at

Mason. "I hate it that my boys are leaving, but I am anxious to put Danny on a plane . . . to China preferably."

"I heard what he said this morning when he was trying to whisper."

"I'm sorry. I told you he was an ass." I went over and sat down beside him. "Did the boys hear?"

"Max did. He looked at me kind of weird. Henry heard it too, but I could tell he didn't understand it."

"Well, thank God for that at least." I leaned over and kissed him. "And yes, you do satisfy me, very well I might add." That at least got a smile from him.

*   *   *

Debbie had invited us over for a cookout and swimming. I brought over some steaks for the grill, a homemade potato salad, and some brownies to share. I hadn't even set everything down on the sun porch before my boys were in the water. I couldn't blame them. I was dying to get in myself. Mark was standing by the grill wearing a "kiss the cook" apron with his swim shorts and flip-flops. Mason handed him the steaks and Mark, in return, handed him a beer from the cooler.

Danny set his own cooler of beer down and helped himself to one. He popped the cap and took a long drink. "How are you doing, cheater?" Debbie lifted her drink with a playful sneer in Danny's direction.

"Doing fine, lush, doing fine," he teased back.

"Play nice you two." I picked up a frozen mug filled with Debbie's special punch and headed out to join my family.

Several of our other neighbors joined us as well. It wasn't long before there was a bustle of kids everywhere, parents with their cocktails and the grill was sizzling away. My boys were having a blast with the other kids and it didn't take long for most of the parents to join them in the pool. The sweltering heat demanded it.

Twice, I made the boys come out of the water to apply more sunscreen. Henry didn't care, but by the second application, Max scowled at me. "Would you stop embarrassing me?"

Danny, who was standing a short distance away, grabbed Max by the arm and took him off to the side and gave him a firm talking to. They returned a few minutes later and neither looked so happy.

"I'm sorry." Max stood in front of me with his arms crossed and a scowl on his face.

"I just don't want you to get sunburned, Max."

"I know." He shifted his weight from one foot to the other impatiently.

"Okay, go play." I took a deep breath and let it go. It really wasn't worth the argument.

After everyone was full and waterlogged it was almost eight. The adults started pulling out the lawn chairs to the front yard for the big firework show that we held every year. All the neighbors on our street pitched in and we had piles of assorted fireworks to play with. I stayed behind and helped Debbie clean up some of the piles of used paper plates and cups left around the pool area by the kids.

By the time we got around front they were just about ready to start the fireworks. Most of the men were a little more than slightly intoxicated, just like every Fourth of July. Apparently, you have to be in order to play with fireworks or, so they believed. Mason had set up a chair for me next to his and unfortunately, Danny had decided to join us as well. The two of them were chatting like old friends, and I hated to consider exactly what they were discussing.

"Hey, you two," I hollered when I saw them together. "Knock that crap off." I pointed at them with a smile.

"We're comparing notes," Danny said with a cocky grin as I took a seat beside Mason.

"I'm sure you were."

Overall, I don't believe I could have asked for things to go more smoothly. It wasn't the best holiday I'd ever had, but it was far from the worst. I gave Mason a great deal of credit. Most men twice his age couldn't have been so graceful when forced to spend a day with their lover's ex-spouse. But Mason never faltered. Granted, I'd never seen him drink quite so much, but it was understandable.

Chapter 11

AFTER A LONG and tearful good-bye, I watched my sons disappear beyond the security gates with Danny. Mason wrapped his arms around me and held me tight. As much as I longed for a respite from my parental duties, I hated being separated from my boys.

It was barely nine in the morning by the time we returned home. I told Mason I was tired and was going to lie down for a while. I hadn't slept well the night before. I usually didn't in anticipation of their travels. I slipped out of my shorts and crawled back under the covers. My bed felt so warm and welcoming after such an emotionally draining morning. I put my cell phone next to my pillow knowing that Danny would call me as soon as they landed. I closed my eyes and tried to relax. I just wanted to drift away for a while.

*   *   *

The loud buzzing from my phone awoke me abruptly shortly before two o'clock. I reached over and grabbed my cell.

"Hello." I sat up on my pillows.

"Hi, doll. It's me. We just landed in Orlando." For once his voice was like a breath of fresh air.

"Good. How was your flight? How are the boys?" I anxiously inquired.

"Fine. Everything's fine."

"Ok, thanks." I felt relieved.

"We'll call you later. I've got to go find up our bags."

"All right. Thanks for calling. I'll talk with you soon." I leaned back feeling much better now that my sons had their feet back on the ground.

"Bye," Danny muttered quickly and then was gone.

I set the phone back on my night table and stretched my arms and legs. I could hear the soft voices drifting down the hallway from the television in the family room. Mason was watching something, but I couldn't make out what it was. I climbed out of bed and headed to the bathroom.

After I cleaned myself up and splashed some cool water on my face, I headed into the family room. I found Mason lying on my couch dozing softly. He had one arm crooked behind his head and his prominently long eyelashes curved in an angelic sway. His hair had grown out a little since he'd gotten it cut at the beginning of summer and little curls poked up here and there along the arm tucked behind his head.

I straddled over him careful to keep all my weight on the couch. I brought my lips to his and brushed against them lightly. Mason's lips responded eagerly. He parted his and grazed his tongue along mine, slowly and then hungrily. His arms came up around me trying to pull me to him. But I locked my arms and kept my distance.

I hovered over his body while his hands explored mine. My lips found his neck, his collarbone. I reached down, untucked his shirt and slipped my hands beneath it. Moving slowly, pulling it up as my hands explored the muscles of his abdomen, the sculpted structure of his chest. I swiftly lifted it over his head in a smooth motion. I could feel the heat radiating off his skin against mine.

Mason reached for me again, trying to pull me down to him. I looked longingly at him then shook my head slowly. I held his gaze while my fingers gracefully unfastened his khaki shorts. With a devilish grin, I reached in and took hold of his throbbing manhood. Mason let out a low moan and raised his hips towards me. I straddled a little higher ensuring his pelvis never contacted mine. He squirmed with a little more determination.

"No," I whispered in a sultry tone.

"Please . . ." He replied with a sexy grin.

I placed my hand in the center of his chest. "In the past, we have had problems with you getting too excited, too fast. Now I love that I turn you on so much, but you're going to have to learn how to control that."

"And how do I do that?"

"You're going to learn how to use your cremaster muscle." I reached down between his legs and took a gentle yet firm hold of his scrotum. "You're only going to be allowed to cum when I say so. Understand?"

"I think you enjoyed your summer class a little too much," Mason remarked.

I squeezed a little harder. "Do you understand?"

"Yes."

"Good."

I slid down his legs and positioned myself between his thighs. I stroked his cock lovingly and bent to give it a long, sweet kiss, carefully taking the head into my mouth and rubbing my tongue firmly across the upside of the head. Mason let out a long moan and his cock quivered. "Easy," I whispered and began stroking him once more, starting at the base and caressing my way upwards.

Every time I could feel him getting too excited, I'd pause and loosen my grip. Once he relaxed again, I'd give his beautiful thick cock another long kiss of approval before I continued with his education and torment.

After thirty minutes Mason couldn't take it anymore and exploded over my hand, his chest, and stomach. I shook my head at him as I licked my fingers seductively. "You did not have my permission to do that."

"I'm sorry. I couldn't help it." He squirmed a little. "I held out as long as I could."

I leaned over his abdomen and lapped up his semen with my tongue. But there were still little splatters across his chest. I wiped one up with my index finger and sucked it longingly off while holding Mason's eye. He smiled. So, I did the same with the last little droplets, but this time held my finger up to his lips.

"Try it," I offered in a whisper.

"Um . . . No." He edged back a bit but with a smile.

"Why not? You kiss me after you've cum in my mouth before?"

"That's different," he declared.

"How so?"

"It just is. It's not still in your mouth."

"Don't be so dramatic. Try it." I moved my finger a little closer to his lips.

"What's it tastes like?"

"Yours is sweet." I grinned.

"Mine's sweet? Don't all men's cum taste the same?"

"No. Do all women?" I countered simply for reaction.

"No." his smile returned. "Oh, all right."

His lips parted just enough for him to stick out the tip of his tongue. I lightly touched my finger to his tongue then traced it around his lips as his smile broadened. I leaned forward and kissed him passionately, hungrily, devouring him.

"It is sweet." He laughed.

"I know."

Mason made like he was about to get up when I placed my hand back on his chest. With a slight nudge, he rested back on the couch.

"Where do you think you're going?"

"Nowhere," he quickly replied.

"You're learning." I rewarded him with another passionate kiss before commencing once again with my previous torment.

"You're going to drive me insane if you don't stop that." He placed his hands behind his head making himself comfortable, so he could watch me work.

"No. I'm trying to build your endurance and increase your stamina, your tolerance and teach you how to control your ejaculation," I explained.

Mason crinkled his forehead. "Don't you mean orgasm?"

"No, ejaculation. They are two separate things. You can experience an orgasm without ejaculating," I informed him.

"Really?" Mason responded eagerly.

"Yes, and I'm going to teach you how. But first we need to build up your tolerance and sensitivity."

"Okay." Mason relaxed once more with a contented smile resting on the corners of his shapely lips.

I spent the next several hours tormenting Mason in the same fashion. His tolerance did increase with each session, but he had a long way to go before he learned how to adequately control his ejaculation. It took a great deal of restraint on both our parts to continue. As much as I desired him, I kept myself collected so he could not see how much I wanted to take him. He asserted much less control and tried on numerous occasions to tempt me. He was making it very difficult although I maintained my composure. I wanted desperately to ravish him.

Chapter 12

I ARRIVED AT my parents' house shortly before noon. My mother had insisted that I join them for lunch. I knew she was worried about how I was coping with the boys being gone. They even insisted I bring Mason with me. Apparently, my boys didn't just rat me out to my ex, they also ratted me out to my parents.

My folks lived on the outskirts of town on seven acres of wooded property. Their house sat in a small clearing a good distance from the road. They really had no neighbors close to them, making it a very peaceful place to spend time. My dad was fiddling around under the hood of his classic Mustang. I parked the car off to the side and looked over at Mason.

"Are you sure you want to do this?" I asked him one more time.

"It'll be fine." He smiled cheerfully.

"You don't know my mom," I muttered half under my breath and climbed out of the car.

My dad was already heading towards us before Mason got his door closed, and my mother was eyeing him through the front window. My dad extended his hand to Mason, his expression not the friendliest.

"Jack Carlton." Mason shook his hand firmly. "So, you're the young man my daughter's been hiding from us."

"Mason Brooks," he responded without missing a beat. "Beautiful Mustang, sir. Is that a 69' or 70'?"

My dad and Mason started walking towards the garage. "That, son, is a 70's, Mach I, Cobra Jet with a 428 engine in it. Alex steals it every chance she gets," my dad informed him.

"Where's Mom?" I inquired, already knowing the answer.

"In the kitchen," he replied.

"I'm going to see if she needs a hand." I leaned up and kissed my dad on the cheek. "Play nice," I whispered softly in his ear.

My mother was standing over the island dicing tomatoes. "It smells good in here," I observed. "What are you fixing?"

"Fried chicken, mashed potatoes, gravy, corn on the cob, and a salad." she answered, barely looking up.

"I thought this was going to be a light brunch. That's what you said on the phone."

"Your dad wanted fried chicken. You take it up with him," she said, knowing full well I wouldn't.

"What can I do to help?"

"Set the table for me, will ya? I'm trying to get this salad put together."

"Sure." I got the plates out of the cupboard and began setting the table.

"He's a lot younger than I thought," my mom casually remarked, adding the tomatoes on top of the greens.

"Please don't start. I'm not looking for a serious relationship right now!" I snapped at her.

"I just think this is a bit inappropriate. Especially having him around your boys." She paused and gave me that look like she always did when she disapproved of something I was doing.

"It's not like I have a parade of men through my bedroom, Mom. He's the only man who's ever met them. And the boys like Mason. He's great with them," I pointed out.

"Man?" she scoffed. "You're using that term rather loosely, don't you think?"

"Mom . . ."

"Well, he should get along with them. He's closer to their age than yours," she stated, chopping some hard-boiled eggs.

"Mom! Really!" I set the forks in their place a little harder than I normally would have and turned towards her. "Can't you just be happy that I'm happy?"

"He's just a child, Alex. You should be dating men around your own age who—"

The door to the garage opened and silenced her.

"Dinner ready?" Dad asked as he stepped through the door.

"Yes. All I must do is put it on the table. Go wash up first." Mom tossed the eggs in the salad and mixed it well before setting it on the table.

"Mom, this is Mason. Mason, my mother, Connie." I made quick and easy introductions.

"Nice to meet you, Mason. My grandsons have told me a great deal about you." Mom smiled in his direction and continued putting food on the table.

"They're great boys," Mason commented, clearly uncomfortable.

"What would you like to drink? Coke? Lemonade? Tea? Beer?" I offered him a chair at the table.

"Tea is fine. Thanks. Can I help with anything?" he offered.

"Nope. Just have a seat and relax. Everything's ready." Mom put a platter of chicken on the table.

I fixed everyone's drink and set them on the table keeping a close eye on my mother. She had a bad habit of being blunt to the point of rudeness. I could only hope and cross my fingers that she'd behave herself this afternoon.

Once everyone was seated and food passed around, there was an awkward silence while we all just ate. It was extremely uncomfortable, and I felt so bad for even subjecting Mason to my parents, particularly my mother.

"So, Mason, my grandsons told me you go to college with Alex," my dad started.

"Yes, we met in our sociology class," Mason said between bites.

"What year are you in?" Dad asked.

"I'll be starting my third year in the fall," Mason informed him.

"I see. And what's your major?"

"Business marketing."

"What made you choose that?" my dad asked while buttering another roll.

"Really, Dad? This is not an inquisition." I gave my dad a stern look, which he ignored.

"It's okay," Mason put his hand over mine. "My dad owns a marketing firm in Chicago. He wants me to someday take it over for him."

"And what do your parents think of you getting involved with someone so much older than yourself with two sons half your age?" My mother couldn't resist.

"Mom!" I shot back at her with a dirty look.

"What? I'm just curious how his parents are taking this nonsense," she explained.

"They were surprised and not exactly thrilled about it." Mason looked over at me with sad eyes. He'd never told me he had mentioned me to his parents. "But they ultimately want me to be happy and I assured them that I am very happy with Alex."

"But you must realize that this will never last," my mother added to my horror.

"Connie . . ." My father shook his head slowly at her.

"No, I don't know that." Mason squeezed my hand again. "And I believe that is between us, Mrs. Carlton."

"But you cannot think . . ." Mom began.

"Connie, let it go." My dad silenced her.

An uncomfortable silence fell over the table. I kept my eyes down just to keep my fuming glare off my mother only out of simple respect for my father. I was so mad at her. I moved the food around on my plate, but my appetite was completely gone, and I hadn't had much to begin with. I knew my dad was embarrassed by my mom's behavior. She was notorious for it. I knew this was a bad idea.

*　*　*

After we returned to my house, we sat out on my back deck and watched the sun set behind the woods at the edge of my property. The sky was littered with vibrant oranges, purples, and pinks shining brilliantly through the trees. Mason slipped his arm around my shoulders and pulled me closer to him. I rested my head against his shoulder and placed my hand over his. The air was warm, and the humidity was low. It was as close to picturesque as I could imagine.

"I'm so sorry about my mom," I said for the hundredth time. "I was hoping she would behave. I should have known she wouldn't't."

"It's okay. Don't worry about it." He squeezed my shoulder.

"You never told me you told your parents about me?" I leaned my head back on his shoulder.

"Honestly, I haven't. I just said that to appease your mom."

"And why haven't you?" I asked out of curiosity.

"To tell you the truth, I don't know. My family is close and can be suffocating at times. It's kind of nice being away from them and having my own life for the first time. I finally have some privacy and can do what I want without them looking over my shoulder judging everything I do," he explained.

"I thought you were close with your family. The way you always talked about them, that was the impression I got."

"Don't get me wrong, I love my family dearly. It's just that sometimes they can be a little overwhelming."

"And you don't think they would approve of me?" I asked.

"I don't believe my mother will ever approve of anyone. She is very old school Catholic. As is my dad and well . . ."

"I see . . ."

I didn't know what else to say. It seemed that everyone thought this little fling or whatever it was, was a bad idea. I'm not sure why, well I did actually. But at this moment I couldn't have cared less what everyone else thought. I glanced up at Mason's silhouette and was in awe of his angelic features against the sunset. For the first time in years, I was happy. I had forgotten how good it felt to be happy and if everyone else had a problem with it then it was their problem.

After we showered, Mason made himself comfortable in the family room watching television and surfing on his laptop. I took the opportunity to slip into something sexy. I browsed through my lingerie and settled on a pale pink silk nightie. It had spaghetti straps, came down about mid-thigh, and slit up both sides to my hips. My golden tan accented it perfectly.

I sat down at my vanity and brushed out my hair. It fell gracefully across my shoulder and parted a way down my back. I applied a little bit of lipstick and mascara to emphasize my facial features just a notch without being overly obvious. It was a subtle application and sensual in the soft hues of the candles I'd carefully placed around my bedroom.

I picked up the matching delicate robe off the edge of my bed and headed out into the family room to find Mason. I paused at the end of the hallway and watched him unnoticed for several moments. He looked so comfortable in my house, like he was truly at home himself. Even though we had never actually discussed it, he had unofficially moved in. His clothes were here, I was now doing his laundry every week, he had managed to take over a small but substantial section of my closet and he hadn't been back to his dorm room in weeks.

Mason was watching reruns of *The Big Bang Theory* and browsing through Facebook. Every now and then he would chuckle to himself at a posting from a friend. It made him look even more adorable as I watched him type out a comment quickly before scrolling on again. Somehow, he fit in here, in our lives, in my life and in my bed.

"Who are you IMing with?" I leaned casually against the wall.

"Nick." He typed a response quickly before looking up. "He wanted to know if I was alive or if he should call the police to file kidnapping charges against you."

"And should I be expecting a swat team to arrive?" I inquired with a sexy leer.

"No. I assured him that you have me tied up but that I love it and would be totally pissed off if we were abruptly interrupted by the police." He flashed me a shit-eating grin.

"Good. I would hate to have my playtime ruined by them. They are so old-fashioned about how handcuffs are supposed to be used," I remarked with a wink.

"Handcuffs?" Mason raised an eyebrow. "You don't like handcuffs, too cold and impersonal."

"Good boy." I slowly approached him. "There is hope for your education yet." Mason quickly closed his laptop and slid it off his lap as I slowly climbed on the couch and gracefully straddled him.

"I've always been a quick learner," he whispered, sliding his hands lightly over my thighs.

"And we're only just beginning . . ." I leaned down and kissed him hungrily.

I slithered elegantly back off his lap, taking him by the hand and leading him back to my bedroom. We approached the side of my bed, and I brought my lips to his with a little more intensity than before. Reluctantly, I pulled myself back and placed a finger in the center of his chest, giving him a gentle nudge. Mason eagerly scrambled into my bed and lay himself out in the prone position with a grin plastered on his shapely lips.

I climbed up beside him and lifted his shirt up over his head. I tossed it aside to the floor before I began working his pants off. Once those were discarded as well, I reached behind the pillow beneath his head and pulled out a couple of white silk scarves. The smile on Mason's face broadened as he willingly raised both arms above his head.

I tied the scarves round his wrists to each of the posts at the head of my bed. Mason struggled playfully against his bindings. I traced my fingers lightly over his arms and he settled down immediately. I kissed his lips softly and grazed his neck and chest with my tongue. My hands explored his torso gently but firmly. He closed his eyes, relaxing and losing himself to the soft caresses of my fingertips.

I enjoyed tormenting him, enticing him, and making his squirm beneath my touch. His skin was hot and glowing with anticipation. I massaged his thighs, his calves and maneuvered myself between his legs. His cock was throbbing with eagerness and standing at full attention. I traced my tongue over it, feeling it twitch involuntarily. His hips rocked slowly with the rhythm of my tongue playfully lapping at his big, thick member.

Mason was learning how to control himself. His stamina had increased tenfold since our first sexual encounter. He was also now able to control his ejaculation almost every time, even after I played with him for hours. I would bring him right on the edge of an orgasm and then deny him the release. Then as soon as he regained his composure, I would start over once more. I tried various levels of distraction. The principle of classical conditioning was working beautifully. Combining it with the positive reinforcement techniques of operant conditioning only strengthened Mason's desire to please me.

Now I was ready to step up my game and push Mason to the next level of sexual intensity. I reached under the pillow beneath his head and pulled out the last and final scarf. I straddled over him and smiled mischievously.

"What are you doing?" He lazily looked at me.

"Placing this over your eyes so that you can focus solely on your other senses." I carefully wrapped the black silk scarf snuggly over his eyes.

"Should I be nervous?" His voice cracked a bit.

"Yes," I said in a sultry voice.

I took out the massage oil and tilted the bottle just enough to watch a few drops drip down the head of his dick. I rubbed it all over to spread it evenly, stroking him firmly and slowly. A low moan escaped from Mason as he twisted his hips with each stroke. He struggled against his bindings and tried desperately to free himself. But much to his dismay, I knew how to tie a good bowline knot that would never fail me.

"Okay, I give," Mason pleaded.

"Hush," I gripped him a little stronger and raised a finger with my other hand to his lips. "I'm just raising your intensity and sensitivity. Don't be such a baby," I chastised him.

"Lexie . . . Please? I'm begging you."

I smiled to myself fully enjoying the extent of Mason's tormented pleasure. His face held an expression torn between pure ecstasy and torture. I couldn't have been happier with his progress. He had proven himself a very eager student.

"Relax, darling," I whispered and poured a little more oil on him and spread it over his groin area and scrotum.

"Aw . . . Lexie," Mason groaned deeply as I massaged his testes, and pulled on them gently.

"Are you familiar with the prostate gland?" I leaned up and whispered in his ear.

"Somewhat. I mean . . . I know where it is. Why?"

"From what I have learned, applying pressure to a man's prostate during sexual arousal is mind blowing," I educated him. "I decided it was time we gave it a try."

"I put my faith in you, my love." His smile returned. "Just don't hurt me."

"Never, my darling," I promised.

I applied some more oil and stroked him deeply. Mason was so lost in his own little world of pure heaven I don't even think he realized I was there any longer. He was moaning and groaning with an expression of pure delight. I nudged his legs a little farther apart and firmly rubbed his scrotum. Mason moaned a little louder. I lightly rubbed the outside of his anus, teasing him. I could tell he was torn between curiosity and fear.

I made sure my fingers were completely saturated in oil. I slowly and gently slipped my finger inside him. Mason moaned a little louder. I applied a little pressure to his prostate, and he surprised me a little by leaning into it. I pressed a little harder against his prostate and he groaned a little louder and came immediately, shaking uncontrollably.

"Oh my God!" Mason shrieked. The look on his face was of sheer terror.

I wiped my hands off on a hand towel I'd left on the foot of the bed before I leaned up and untied the black silk scarf from around his eyes. Mason blinked a couple times as his eyes adjusted to the soft hues from the candlelight. He had a few beads of sweat glistening on his forehead. He looked astonished and embarrassed at the same time.

I smiled softly and kissed him deeply. I could tell by the look in his eyes he was close to tears. His eyes silently pleaded with me to release his bonds. I reached over him and loosened the scarfs enough for him to slip both his hands out. He immediately rubbed them both absentmindedly while holding eye contact with me. Neither of us spoke. There were no words to say. We had reached a new level of intimacy and trust and it had brought us closer than we ever imagined.

Mason reached up and took me in his arms. For the first time in a very long time, I tossed my sexual rulebook with him aside and let him take the lead. Something inside me told me that he needed to and that I would be the one to benefit overall by letting him do so now.

He kissed me hungrily and rolled over on me. He entered me with such a force it literally took my breath away.

Chapter 13

HEATHER AND ISAAC came over for a cookout at Debbie and Mark's on our last Saturday of freedom before the boys came home. Isaac had called me earlier, very excited, and said he needed to see me right away, but he wouldn't tell me what it was about. Mason and I already had plans to lounge across the street. We'd been doing a lot of that recently, so I just invited them to join us. I knew Debbie wouldn't care. She lived firmly by the belief "the more the merrier."

Mason had taken a liking, or so he said, to landscaping and gardening. We had gotten up early, eaten, and decided to get some work done outside. I put on a bikini top and a pair of old shorts and walked out to the shed to get my gardening tools. It was a beautiful morning. The grass was still just a little damp with dew and the sun was already telling me it was going to be hot and humid before noon.

I took my little tool caddy around the front and started weeding the gardens. Mason pushed the lawnmower from the shed around to the driveway. He filled it up with gasoline and fired it up. He looked so cute cutting my lawn. I didn't mind doing it myself. It wasn't my favorite chore, but it was far from the worst. Still, sometime around the end of July, Mason took it over. I think he was trying to find ways of helping me out around the house. He wasn't much on the actual cleaning, but he would vacuum occasionally.

We finished the yard shortly before eleven. Mason was in the backyard trying to put everything back in the shed, so I took a moment to sweep the walkways free of the grass leavings. I paused for a moment on the sidewalk in front of my house and looked around. Our street was particularly quiet this morning. A couple of my neighbors were out working on their yards but not nearly as many as there usually were.

My house was a little brick ranch with mossy green shutters. There was a large porch that ran almost the length of my house. Danny and I carefully designed the landscaping the first year we lived here. I remembered sitting at the kitchen island with Danny milling over different trees, shrubs, and flowers, what we wanted and where to put it. It was a painstaking process, making sure it turned out exactly as we envisioned it. I loved the big blue cypress pine that sat on the other side of the driveway. It was barely four feet tall when we planted it, now it is taller than the house. And the birch tree that sat just off the end of the porch on the side of the house was now a gorgeous focal accent that looked incredible behind the flowering white dogwood on the front bump of the bed. It was surrounded by huge hastas' that had been carefully cultivated.

The colors, the design, the carefully placed Japanese maple next to the yellow and green shrubs made the front of my house pop. The rows of violets, daisies and of course my favorites, lilies of all varieties, acted as a front row audience to the activities up and down our street. It was hard to forget the time and fun Danny and I had built the gorgeous gardens that surrounded what was now my home.

I smiled to myself, recalling when we had planted the garden down the side of the house. It was our first summer in the house and Max was barely crawling. It was a cloudy and humid day and Danny and I had removed the top layer of sod. We were trying to get the plants in before the rain started, and we were running out of time. Danny had finished digging the final hole for the many plants we were putting in that day and I was carefully placing each plant and covering it with topsoil and peat moss.

As the first few drops of rain fell, Danny made some smart remarks to me, and I tossed a handful of black soil at him. Before I knew it, we were chasing each other around the yard throwing and smearing soil on each other. Our neighbors, whom we hadn't met at the time, were curiously watching our juvenile behavior. By the time I called a truce, I was covered in mud, soaking wet and laughing so hard I could barely breathe. The memory felt like a lifetime ago. Mason rounded the corner from the backyard and brought me back to reality. I brushed away a lone tear that rested on my cheek.

Looking back never does anyone any good.

"I am so ready to jump in the pool," Mason said as he approached. "It's so muggy today."

"Yes, it is. Let me just put this in the garage." I started walking towards the house.

"Are you alright?" He reached out and touched my arm.

"Yeah, I'm fine." I forced a smile.

"You looked so sad when I came around the corner."

"I was just thinking about my boys. I miss them."

"They'll be home tomorrow." He tried to cheer me up.

"I know. I just can't wait to see them." I held his eyes for a moment then walked over to the garage.

*   *   *

Debbie and I spent the afternoon floating around the pool, soaking up the sun. I told her about Heather and Isaac joining us later with some big news and she was as curious as I about what it was. We speculated back and forth about what it could possibly be. We both felt certain that they were going to announce they were engaged.

Mason and Mark had joined us in the pool for a while but were now resting in lounge chairs on the side drinking beers. The two of them had become good friends over the summer and I think Mark in a way had become a sort of mentor and father figure to Mason. Mark was a successful businessman who worked for an international company. His job required him to travel more than Debbie liked but she had gotten used to it as time went on.

Debbie and I threw together a makeshift dinner out of what we found in our kitchens. The hamburgers and bratwursts were sizzling on the grill a little after six when Heather and Isaac turned up. Heather brought some homemade no-bake chocolate oatmeal cookies and a pasta salad to share. Isaac brought a bottle of Maker's Mark. They were both being incredibly stubborn about sharing their good news. They insisted we eat first.

After dinner, Isaac lined up the shot glasses and poured the Marker's Mark into each one. He passed them out to each of us while Heather grinned from ear to ear anxious to share their news with us.

"I figured it only appropriate that I share our good news with you all because of the spectacle I made of myself the last time I was here. Although I honestly have no memory of it, Heather was kind enough to tell me all about it and I literally have the scar on my ass that proves she was telling the truth." Isaac stood at the head of the patio table. "Therefore, I wanted to tell you all personally that I have been accepted into medical school. I will be starting the fall term in two weeks."

We all congratulated him repeatedly and toasted to him. Isaac beamed. I couldn't have been happier for him. I knew how hard he had worked in the short time I had known him.

"We've got so much to do in this next week. It's been crazy," Heather told us. "I've got so much packing to do."

"Packing?" I looked between them. "Where are you going?"

"Boston," Isaac stated proudly.

"Wow, I guess I just figured you'd be staying closer to home." I hated the thought of my first college friend leaving. "And you're going with him?"

"Yes, we talked about it when he started applying to schools out of state. I've already got several interviews lined up." Heather couldn't have been more excited.

"I'm so happy for you both. I'm just sad that you're leaving. I'm going to miss you so much." I got up and hugged them both.

"I'm going to miss you too. You've been such a wonderful friend to us. But don't worry, we'll keep in touch." Heather squeezed me tightly.

"You'd better," I informed her.

"Besides, now you have a place to stay and an excuse to visit the east coast," Isaac remarked, pouring himself another shot.

"I love the east coast. It's so beautiful," Debbie said.

"The architecture is amazing," I concluded.

"What? Are you telling me you don't like the vinyl villages that have sprung up all around us? They are simply breathtaking," Mark added sarcastically.

It didn't take long for Mark and Isaac to polish off the Maker's Mark. After that, they finished off another bottle of whiskey and then worked on the beer after Debbie and Heather refused to make a liquor store run for them. I was happy that Mason had the sense not to drink nearly as much. He paced himself and wasn't one who enjoyed hard whiskey very often.

Heather sat beside Debbie and me with our feet in the water. She was ecstatic about the move. They were flying out there the next week to find an apartment and tour the school. She confessed that she and Isaac had discussed getting married but that she was the one who wanted to wait. She claimed it was because she wanted to focus on her career before making a lifelong commitment, but something in her voice said different. Although she had said numerous times that Isaac's flirtatious nature never bothered her, I believed it to be the true reason she wasn't ready to take the plunge. I honestly didn't believe she trusted Isaac, although she loved him enough to move halfway across the country with him.

* * *

Mason and I took a quick, yet playful shower upon our return home. I had been teasing him all day that tonight was going to be special for him. He was doing extremely well with his classical conditioning and the positive reinforcements were paying off nearly as well as the negative ones. I had been denying him ejaculation for almost two weeks, but playing with him every opportunity I was given. He loved the pure torture of it, the sweet agony, and even the painful swollenness of his thick cock.

I toweled Mason off in a seductive manner and led him by the hand to our bed. I nodded to it, signaling for him to climb up. He complied. I followed and perched myself up so that I was sitting on my feet along the edge. He lay down in a prone position with his head resting on a mountain of pillows. His hair was still damp and the little ringlets around his face made him appear even more youthful than he already was despite the ever-present scruff on his face. He placed his hands behind his head with the corners of his mouth turned up slightly. His eyes never left mine.

I pulled out a couple of white silk scarfs from my nightstand and tied both his hands to the bed posts in the same fashion as I had done before.

"You're enjoying this," Mason noted, watching me carefully.

"And so are you."

"Very much so." The slight grin on his lips broadened into a full smile.

I carefully pulled out the black silk scarf and tied it loosely over Mason's eyes. He playfully squirmed against his bindings just to check his boundaries. "Lexie?"

"Yes." I paused a moment, holding the bottle of lubricant in my hand.

"You are a sick and twisted lady for doing this to me." He grinned.

"And what does that make you? You're the one allowing me to do it to you?"

"I know." He chuckled lowly.

I smiled to myself and carefully placed a few droplets of lubricant over the head of his penis and watched it run down slowly. I added just a smidge to my own hands and rubbed them together to spread it evenly. Then I lightly traced the tips of my fingernails in a feather light fashion over the inside of his thighs, his pelvic region, scrotum, and genitals before starting a full lingam massage. Mason wiggled around the bed in delight.

The lingam massage or caress had quickly become a favorite of Mason's over the last several weeks. I had stumbled across the tantric technique in one of the books I'd found in an old bookstore after class one day when I was wandering around the city doing some window shopping. It was very erotic, very tantalizing, and an extremely deep intimate caress. And Mason was an addict.

For the lingam massage I alternated my hands, one over the other, beginning at the base of his penis, including his testes, stroking firmly upwards to the head towards his navel. Every few minutes I changed the tempo of my rhythm. Mason was purring softly, completely lost in his own little paradise. I leaned up beside his face and kissed him softly on the cheek, lingering there for a few strokes so he could feel my hot breath on his neck. I traced my fingers teasingly around his perineum, his scrotum, then firmly grasped his cock at the base and slid my hand upwards, massaging the head.

"Lexie, please . . .," he begged.

"Do not cum." I spoke softly and let go of him.

Mason's breathing was labored. A bead of sweat glistened over his brow. His body glowed under a soft layer of perspiration. His cock was swollen and bright purple. It twitched uncontrollably. I gently massaged his anus, spreading lubricant over the area. He moaned softly and rocked his hips towards my hand. I watched his facial expression, loving the exquisite pain and pleasure I could plainly see him experiencing.

With a little pressure I inserted two fingers into him and caressed his prostate gland. Mason spread his legs further apart and groaned loudly. He arched his hips towards me begging me for more. The intensity of the sensation drove him ecstatic. I followed his lead and continued to massage his prostate. With my free hand I took out the surprise I had been teasing Mason about all day long.

About a week ago I found myself shopping online for a toy for Mason. I wanted something enticing with a realistic feel to it. What I found was seven inches long, medium girth, and had a lovely new skin covering that felt very real. I was very careful not to get anything that was the typical hard rubber that most dildos were made of. The last thing I wanted to do was ruin this experience by purchasing the wrong toy to introduce to him.

I carefully applied a large amount of lubricant and coated the toy heavily. Then I teasingly rubbed the toy around Mason's scrotum.

"What is that?" Mason's head shifted from side to side searching helpless under the blindfold.

"The surprise I bought you."

"Are you serious?"

"Do you want it?" I continued teasing him while stroking his throbbing cock.

"Yes," he whispered.

Gently, I inserted the head of the toy into Mason's rectum. He groaned in pure pleasure and arched his hips up further towards me and into the toy. I pushed a little more into him, teasing him, and continued stroking him slowly with long, firm strides. He began rocking his hips forcefully, loving the feel of the toy in him, wanting more. So, I obliged. I slid it out just a bit then offered a little more repeatedly until Mason screamed out in ecstasy and came across his chest.

"Oh, my God!" he gasped. "Oh, my God!"

He lay there breathless, his whole body quivering uncontrollably. I slipped the toy out and set it aside on a towel. I leaned up and kissed him softly before I removed his blindfold. Mason blinked a couple of times to adjust to the soft hues of the room. His eyes searched desperately for my own and embraced them with a pleading for understanding.

"I can't believe you did that." A couple of tears escaped from the corner of his eyes.

"It's okay." I kissed his tears away. "I know it can be a little intense the first time. You're fine," I assured him.

"That was amazing. I've never cum that hard before." I untied his hands and he quickly embraced me. "Thank you so much," he whispered in my ear.

"I'm happy you enjoyed it so much," I said softly.

I kissed him passionately, yet the uncontrollable trembling continued. It was clear to me how freaked out Mason truly was. I hadn't realized it would be such an emotional experience for him. I never expected him to break on me. I held him in my arms and tried to get him to calm down just a bit. He was shaking and holding onto me for dear life.

"I don't know why I can't get the tears to stop." He laughed uncomfortably, brushing them off the sides of his face.

"It's normal. It's just your body reacting to the intensity of it," I carefully explained.

Wow! I didn't mean to break him. Stage one complete.

I lay there with my head on his chest and his arms still holding me tightly. His breathing had calmed, the trembling had almost ceased. But he seemed unwilling to move. It wasn't long before he drifted off into a sound, peaceful sleep.

Chapter 14

THE BOYS RETURNED HOME the Sunday before their first day of school the following Wednesday. Mason and I picked them up at the airport late in the evening. Both were excited and worn out from their travels. They talked nonstop as we waited at the baggage claim. By the time we got them in the car, both had dozed off before we were halfway home.

Mason carried Max into the house while I followed him with Henry. We tucked the boys into bed. Mason went back out to the car to retrieve their luggage while I lingered in the hallway between their two rooms, silently watching them sleeping. I was so overcome with joy and relief to have my sons back home with me and in their own beds. My life felt complete again. I felt rejuvenated from our short time apart and ready to tackle the new school year, theirs and my own.

The next morning after we got the two chatterboxes through breakfast, Mason and I took the boys shopping for their school supplies and some new clothes. It was already hot and humid by mid-morning when we arrived at the outside mall. The sun was beating down upon us as we moved from store to store trying to gather all the necessities they needed. I bought them each a new pair of sneakers and a pair of casual shoes. They got new jeans, cargo shorts, various shirts, socks, and accessories.

Max was starting Intermediate School this year and getting to the age where he was starting to really develop his own style. He was concerned about his hair and insisted on putting product in it now. He wanted a watch, bracelets, and more expensive styles. It was fun to watch him declare his individuality, make decisions about who he wanted to become and figure out how he wanted to express himself to the world.

After picking up a large assortment of paper, pens, art supplies, backpacks, and folders along with ten million other things, Mason and I took the boys out to dinner. I got them settled into the booth and once our entrées were ordered, the boys talked nonstop about football practice starting back up and speculated who their new teachers would be. It was so wonderful to hear the excitement in their voices. I had missed them so much in the weeks they spent with Danny.

*   *   *

Over the next two weeks the boys and I fell back into our previous routine consumed with school and sports. My classes kicked in a week after the boys started back to school. I was taking five classes this semester and Mason was taking six. Our schedules couldn't have been more opposite, but he was still staying with us after the term kicked back in. However, when I had to run the boys to football and karate, he stayed back at the house to study. The pace of our hectic lifestyle was wearing thin on Mason's study habits and challenging my ability to find some sort of balance between school, my sons, and Mason.

Three weeks into my semester, the head of the psychology department, whom I had only met a couple of times before briefly, stopped me in the hallway just after my Abnormal Psychology class.

"Excuse me, Mrs. Rose. Do you have a moment?" He was a middle-aged man who fit the perfect mold of a college professor with his tweed jacket and trimmed mustache and beard.

"Yes, Dr. Johnston. Of course." I followed him to his office.

He held open the door for me and motioned to one of the chairs placed in front of his desk. "Please, have a seat." He walked around his desk and sat down behind it.

I tried to make myself comfortable, but my stomach had suddenly twisted into a knot. I couldn't imagine why this man had singled me out and requested my presence in his office. I couldn't think of anything I had done to draw his attention to me.

"I have spoken with several of your professors regarding your academic performance and I must say I am very pleased with their reports," he began.

"Thank you, sir."

"I am looking for someone who can spend a few hours a week tutoring a couple of our athletic students who seem to be struggling in their Psychology 104 class. As I am sure you are aware, our university requires our athletes to maintain a C average to remain eligible for participation," he continued.

I nodded.

"Of course, you will be compensated for your time." He shuffled some papers and placed them on the corner of his desk. "Are you interested?"

"Yes, sir. When would you need me to start?" I felt a rush of relief flood over me.

"Here is their contact information and their class schedules. Please get in touch with them as soon as possible. They could really use your help." He reached across his desk and handed me a piece of paper. "Please keep track of your hours each week and turn them into me every Friday. The university pays fifteen dollars an hour for their tutors. Is that acceptable to you?"

"That would be fine." I tucked the paper inside my textbook and stood up with my hand outstretched. "And thank you Dr. Johnston for the opportunity. I will do my best to help them."

"I know you will." He shook my hand firmly.

*   *   *

I laid my backpack down on the floor before I collapsed on the couch. I closed my eyes and listened to the sound of silence. I had another hour before the boys would be home from school and another two before Mason returned from his afternoon classes. All I wanted to do was lay there.

The next thing I knew Henry was kneeling beside me waking me up with a kiss on my cheek. "Are you all right, Momma?"

"Hi, sweetheart." I pulled myself up to a seated position. "I must have drifted off. How was school today?"

"Fun. We played kickball in gym." He climbed up on my lap.

Max walked into the family room from the kitchen with a bag of Doritos in one hand and a juice box in the other. "Hey Momma," he said with his mouth full.

"How was school?"

"Boring. But I did find out that Kayla has a crush on me." Max smiled with chips stuck in his teeth.

"Who's Kayla?" I inquired through my grimace.

"She's in my class. She's cute." He sat down on the ottoman and flipped on the television. "But she's always giggling with her friends and staring at me. It's kind of annoying." I couldn't help but laugh.

"Do you have any homework?" I watched him fire up the X-box and start playing Halo again.

"Nope. Finished it at school."

"What about you?" I turned back to Henry on my lap.

"Spelling words."

"Okay, Mister. You know the drill." I gave him a gentle squeeze before he hopped down.

"I know. I know. Kitchen table. Five times each." He grinned and picked up his backpack on his way to the kitchen.

I sighed heavily and got up myself. It was time to start dinner and I still had to look over the schedules of my new students, wondering how in the world I was going to fit them into my already insane schedule.

*   *   *

After I got the boys tucked in for the night and the house had finally returned to calm, I sat down at my desk and laid out all the material I should be studying. Mason was lying on the couch engrossed in some textbook. He had missed Henry's football practice this evening and had seemed more stressed than usual with his coarse load.

I straightened out my schedule and compared it with the two athletes I was supposed to tutor. I scribbled for some time for them on Monday and Wednesday mornings and maybe a small chunk of time on Fridays. It was going to be difficult to find time for me to study for my own classes. I turned towards Mason and decided to interrupt his reading.

"Hey sweetie, guess what happened to me today?"

"What's that?" He looked up from his text.

I went on to recount my earlier conversation with Dr. Johnston. He listened intently to all I had to say before he responded.

"You really think you can find the extra time this semester?" he asked.

"It's gonna be a little rough, but I think I can manage it." I picked up the new schedule I had just created and joined him on the couch to show him.

"I guess you'll be spending more time on campus studying just to keep up." He looked the paper over carefully before he handed it back to me.

"I think I'll have to." I glanced back over it considering all possible options.

"Who are you tutoring?" he asked.

"Um . . . let me look," I returned to my desk and picked up the paper Dr. Johnston has given me. "A football player named Derek Jennings and another player named Nathan Blair." I shrugged. "I have no idea who they are."

"Seriously? You don't?" He gave me the strangest look, but I just shook my head in reply. "Jennings is our starting wide receiver and Blair is our center," Mason explained.

"Whatever," I muttered. "I don't care who they are. All I know is that they're not doing so well, and I'm supposed to help them."

"They are classic party jocks. I'm surprised you've never heard of them. Both have a good chance of making it to the NFL," Mason remarked.

"Well, good for them." I sat back down in my desk chair. "Either way, I've got to call them and set up a time to meet them tomorrow." I picked up my phone and typed in the first number on the list.

"Good luck," he muttered and went back to his reading.

I called Derek first and decided to meet the following morning before my first class. He seemed nice enough but a little slow on the uptake. I talked with Nathan, or rather Nate as he corrected me, next. He was a jovial guy who expressed his extreme dislike for psychology and how ridiculous it was that the university required it for all majors. I set up a time to meet with him after my morning class.

*　*　*

I arrived on campus a half hour before I was to meet Derek. I grabbed some coffee from the little café shop in the student center. I brought along a file folder that I had stashed away at the end of my first semester that contained all my study guides for the course. I set up my laptop and got out my guides for the first two chapters. I sat back on the couch and took a sip of coffee waiting for him to arrive.

It was seven thirty and the student center was slowly coming alive. There were a few classes that started at eight but most of them didn't kick in until nine. Out of the corner of my eye I saw a tall muscular kid headed in my direction. He had brown hair that was badly in need of a trim and his face had strong angular features that only enhanced his looks. He was wearing an Indianapolis Colts t-shirt and a pair of running shorts. He looked like he'd just rolled out of bed.

"Hey, are you Alex?" He stopped next to the couch and looked down at me.

"Yes," I said.

"Cool. I'm Derek." He dropped his backpack on the floor. "I'm gonna get some coffee. Be right back." Before I could even reply, he was trekking across the center toward the café.

This should be fun.

Several minutes later, Derek returned with a steaming cup of their largest mug of coffee. He set it down on the table and sort of flopped down on the couch beside me.

"Dr. Johnston said you were really good at this crap." He dug around in his backpack and pulled out a notebook and text. "I must tell you. I really hate this class. I don't know why they make us take it."

"What's your major?" I asked out of curiosity.

"Elementary education," He informed me, setting his things on the table, and opening his book to the chapter they were covering in class.

"Really? Why elementary education?" I couldn't help but think this kid must tower over elementary children.

"Little kids are cool. They are so much fun to be around. I'll most likely go to the NFL after college if my knees hold out, but then I'd like to teach like second grade." I noticed he had the most charming smile.

"I have a second grader. It's really a great age." I smiled back at him.

"You're a mom?" He paused for a moment and really looked at me. "You don't look old enough to have a kid in the second grade."

"Thanks. I should have said my youngest is in the second grade. I also have a son who just started in the sixth grade," I informed him.

"I thought Dr. Johnston said you were a student here."

"I am. I'm just an older student."

"Huh . . . You're not wearing a ring." I saw him glance briefly at my left hand. "Are you divorced?"

"Yes," I replied politely. "So, what chapter are you covering?" I wanted to change the subject since we were already late getting started.

"We're starting chapter three today. We took our test for the first two chapters last week and I didn't do so hot. So, Dr. Johnston thought it would be a good idea if I got a tutor. This class doesn't really make any sense to me," he confessed, looking a bit embarrassed.

"What did you get on the test?" All the exams for this class were taken at the computer lab and your score was given to you immediately after you hit submit.

"Forty-six," Derek's face turned a little red.

"Well, yeah . . . I guess you do need some help. You do know that the material from those chapters will be on the final exam?"

"Yeah, I know." He sighed deeply and slumped back on the couch. "Do you think you can help me? I can't lose my spot on the team because of this class, and I can't lose my scholarship." He looked genuinely concerned.

"Of course," I said cheerfully despite my own doubts from my lack of experience. I had never been someone's tutor let alone teacher.

"Okay then, Alex, let's get started." His tone lightened with forced enthusiasm as he sat back up beside me.

"All right. Chapter three covers human development. Your interest in working with elementary children will help you a lot when studying this chapter." I smiled. "And I believe will give you a better understanding of child development and make you a better teacher."

"Okay, you've intrigued me." He picked up his textbook ready to learn.

*   *   *

I hurried from the student center shortly before nine trying to get to my English Lit class on time. Unfortunately, the building was across campus, and it had just started to rain. I bobbed and wove my way through the hordes of students rushing in fourteen different directions, also trying to get to class on time. I rushed down the catwalk then cut through the library trying to avoid the elements as much as I could.

Once I reached outside, a steady rain was falling from the skies. I put up my umbrella against the wind and rain. My mind kept returning to my first session with Derek. He was a charming individual and once I broke down the terms of the material into laymen's terms and gave him examples, he could relate to, he picked up the material rather quickly. By the time we departed, I felt he wouldn't have any trouble at all learning the material. It was just the way the text conveyed the information that he had difficulty translating into real life applications. I also thought, after spending such a short amount of time with him, that he would indeed make a fabulous teacher with his easygoing spirit and quick-to-smiling attitude.

*   *   *

Nate was already waiting for me on the third floor of the library when I arrived after class. He was seated on one of the oversized chairs that a lot of students had a habit of taking naps in between classes. He had extremely large shoulders and a solid muscular barrel chest. His blond hair was short and messy. I could tell right away he was an all-American jock and the stereotypical frat boy.

"Nate?" I asked in a low voice.

"Yep, you found me." He chuckled and stood up. "You're Alex, right?"

"Yes." I held my hand out to him, but instead he caught me completely off guard and wrapped me in a big bear hug.

"Thanks so much for agreeing to help me," he said when he finally released me. "You have no idea how much I hate this class. It just makes no sense. I've read the chapters, more than once, reviewed the study guides and I'm telling ya, it just doesn't make sense." He shook his head and flopped back down on the chair.

"Don't worry, the key to understanding psychology is finding the right way to relate to the material with real world applications." I sat down and made myself comfortable.

*   *   *

Mason arrived as I was putting dinner on the table. He didn't look to be in a very good mood. He set his things down in the family room and joined me in the kitchen. He kissed me briefly on the cheek before climbing up on a bar stool at the island.

"How did your day go?" I asked, pouring lemonade into the glasses.

"Fine. Did you know I have an econ class with Nate?" he asked before taking his drink and carrying it over to the table.

"Really? Why didn't you tell me that last night when I mentioned him?" I put the other three glasses on the table. I started to leave the kitchen to get the boys, but Mason grabbed my arm.

"Cause I really don't know him, but he does sit next to me in class." He let go of me and stood there for a moment. "Did you meet with him today?"

"Yeah, why? You knew I was going to tutor him." I couldn't understand why he was upset.

"Did you mention us to him or that you were involved with anyone?" he questioned in a rough tone.

"No. I don't talk about my personal life. I'm his tutor."

"What did you talk with him about?"

"Psychology," I replied, getting a little bit annoyed.

"Well, do you have any idea what I had to listen to this afternoon?" he asked, raising his voice at me.

"I don't have a clue. And where the hell do you get off talking to me in that tone?" I took a step away from him.

Mason's face immediately dropped like a little kid being chastised by a parent. "I'm sorry. I just got so mad." His voice dropped barely above a whisper. "Nate spent most of class telling a bunch of us guys about his hot new tutor. He called you a MILF!"

I couldn't help but laugh aloud which only seemed to annoy Mason even more.

"I don't think you realize how determined he is to sleep with you. He was making bets that he'd nail you before mid-terms," he said clearly ticked off.

"Just because he wants to, doesn't mean he gets to," I explained. "I have no interest in Nate." I wrapped my arms around him and pulled him closer to me. "I am extremely happy with you. You have nothing to worry about." I kissed him softly. "But I think it's really cute when you get jealous."

"I'm not jealous," he declared. "I just thought you should know what he is saying about you."

"Somehow, I am not surprised," I laughed. "He's a college boy and a very immature one at that. Who cares what he said? I don't."

"But I do." His eyes narrowed. "I don't want him talking about you that way. It's rude and disrespectful."

"Oh, good grief, Mason." I dropped my arms and stepped back. "Our dinner's getting cold. I'm going to get the boys."

Chapter 15

MASON HAD BRIEFLY mentioned something about reserving a cabin for Labor Day weekend back in May. At the time I hadn't thought much about it. But as the holiday weekend drew closer, he brought it back up. It sounded phenomenal and I couldn't have been more excited until he mentioned a little too casually that we would be sharing a rather large cabin with several of his friends from school, namely Nick, Jared, and Josiah, their girlfriends, and a few other couples. This, I was not too pleased to learn about.

I dropped the boys and Billy off at my parents' house after dinner on Friday evening. I kissed them both goodbye and wished them good luck on their games the next day. I hated missing them, but I had to admit, a long weekend at a cabin in the mountains in Tennessee with Mason sounded like the perfect getaway. I climbed in my car and headed back towards my house.

I drove down Main Street looking at the old buildings that had been there since long before I was born. It was a beautiful late summer evening. The humidity had died away with the last days of August and left us with a warmth that covered our nights like a comfortable old blanket. The sun was setting behind the library filling the skies with soft hues of pink, purple and orange. It was a breathtaking sight.

I couldn't get my excitement level back up to where it had been before Mason had told me about our weekend roommates. The prospect of spending the holiday with a group of late teens and early twenty-something year old sounded more like an unpaid babysitting job that I would rather skip than the romantic retreat he had promised me. But I had agreed to go and now there was no way of backing out of it.

Time to grin and bear it.

*   *   *

We headed south down the highway in Mason's beautiful Camaro at the butt crack of dawn. The early morning chill still hung heavy in the air and the ground was saturated with dew. I pulled my jacket a little closer around me trying to keep warm. Being the social morning person I am, I rested my head against the passenger window and dozed back off again. Mason was listening to *Thirty Seconds of Mars* and singing quietly along. We had a good five-hour drive before we arrived at Dale Hollow Lake in Byrdstown, Tennessee.

When I opened my eyes again, I was blinded by the bright sunlight pouring in through the windshield. I reached into my bag and pulled out my sunglasses, thankful that I'd left my glasses at home and decided to wear my contacts instead. I put them on and stretched my legs a little. My whole body felt stiff and cramped from sleeping in such an uncomfortable position for so long.

"Where are we?" I shifted towards Mason.

"About an hour from Dale Hollow. How'd ya sleep?" He grinned slightly in my direction before turning his eyes back on the road.

"I didn't mean to sleep so long. Want me to drive?" I offered.

"Naw . . . We're almost there. I can't wait to get out on the lake. Everyone is probably already there. I believe they all went down yesterday." His voice was dripping with anticipation.

"I'm sorry we couldn't. The boys had school," I apologized again.

"No biggie." Mason shrugged. "We're going to have a great weekend. Have you ever jet skied?"

"Not in the last several years."

"Well, you're going to this weekend." He reached over and squeezed my hand.

"Sounds fun." I gave him the best smile I could muster up.

I turned back towards the scenery and watched the flat lands roll into foothills. I could see the mountains still some ways in front of us. Drifts of white cotton clouds strolled across the mountain peaks kissing them lightly. The sky had turned into a clear robin's egg blue and the air had warmed up a great deal. I peeled my jacket off and tossed it in the backseat.

* * *

A small cabin in the woods? Hardly.

The size of this place stunned me. It was fashioned after a cabin, but one built for a wealthy individual. Mason grabbed our bags from the trunk and carried them up the walkway. I followed him hearing the muffled sound of loud music playing in the near distance through the trees and occasionally the sounds of playful laughter and squeals.

The inside was not nearly as luxurious as the exterior of the cabin had conveyed. It was nice in a plain wholesome country charm sort of way. Nothing I would have written home about but perfect for the purpose it was going to serve this weekend. The foyer led into a huge two-story great room with the back wall almost completely glass. The view of Dale Hollow Lake and the mountains was breathtaking. There was a huge stone fireplace against the far wall, an oversized flat-screen TV, and several comfortable sofas and chairs tastefully arranged.

Jared was the first to spot us and literally pounced on Mason before he even got the chance to set our bags down.

"Hey! Took ya long enough," Jared declared, giving Mason a big hug. "I feel like we never see you anymore."

"You see me all the time," Mason laughed.

"Hello, Alex. You look beautiful." He surprised me by hugging me also.

"Well, thank you, Jared." I gave Mason an odd glance. "So, do you."

"Come on in and meet everyone, Alex." He took me by the hand and dragged me to the center of the room. Luckily, most of our roommates were already out on the lake.

"Hey Jared," Mason called. "Which room is ours?"

"The master's up the stairs down the far end of the hall." He nodded towards the stairwell.

"Are you sure?" I was sure someone would have claimed it by now, especially since we were the last ones to arrive.

"Yep. Nick insisted." Then he leaned a little closer. "And boy, you should have seen the look on Courtney's face! She had a complete meltdown."

"Courtney?"

"Nick's new girlfriend. They started dating at the end of last semester. She's cute, but she's also a total bitch. I think she keeps his balls in a jar on her nightstand." Jared shook his head. "Oh, and she hates my girlfriend. Well, Emma's not really my girlfriend. I mean, she sort of is . . . we just started dating the first week of this term."

"Okay. Okay. I understand." I placed a hand on his arm to stop his rambling.

"Yeah, right. Anyway, they don't get along very well, which sucks. We drove down with Josiah and his girlfriend, Tricia." Jared started walking towards the back deck.

Mason rejoined us and the three of us walked outside. Josiah, who I recognized immediately because of his ginger hair and freckles, was standing over the grill flipping hot dogs and hamburgers. Two girls were lying on the patio lounges in their bikinis soaking up the noon sun. One of them was a stunningly cute girl with long blonde hair and a damn near perfect figure. The other had more of the girl next-door kind of look, a little above average with mousey brown hair. I noticed her legs were a little stockier than the blonde's.

"I was wondering where you disappeared to." The brown-haired girl stood up and walked over to us. "Hi, I'm Emma. You must be Alex," she said in a warm voice.

"Yes, hello."

"And this is Tricia." Jared gestured towards the blonde.

"Hi." Tricia smiled and lifted her sunglasses. "Nice to meet you, Alex. I've heard so much about you."

"Don't believe any of it," I replied, elbowing Mason playfully.

"Don't worry, I don't." She smiled.

"Hey, you guys hungry? We've got plenty of food." Josiah approached, nibbling on a hot dog he'd skewered.

"Starved," Mason answered.

"Good. Why don't you guys change into your suits and then we'll eat lunch," Emma suggested before turning her focus on Jared. "Are we still taking the boat out this afternoon?"

"Yeah, if Nick ever brings it back."

"Where is Nick?" Mason's eyes scanned out across the lake.

"He and Courtney took Blake, Stewie, Mike, and Lori out on the boat. Hopefully, they'll be back soon. They said they'd be back by lunch," Josiah explained.

"I figured they'd be back by now," Jared remarked.

"I guess we'll go change." Mason took hold of my hand.

"We'll be here," Josiah said with a smile and returned to his grilling duties.

*   *   *

Mason opened the door to the master suite, or at least that's what it was supposed to be. Apparently, the owners were using the term loosely. It didn't resemble any master suite I'd ever been in. It was rather plain with nothing on the white walls but a gaudy western print over the king-size bed. There was also a dull looking dresser and armoire, but it had a spectacular view of the lake and its own personal deck. Plus, the bathroom had a Jacuzzi tub and a separate stand-up shower.

"My dear," Mason mocked an extreme gesture and bowed. "Your bed chambers."

"Oh my, thank you sir." I curtsied and kissed him on the cheek.

He chuckled and scooped me up in his arms, kicked the door closed and carried me over to the bed with a devilish grin. He laid me down gently and leaned over me.

"Correct me if I'm wrong, but I believe that it's our civic duty to christen the room to make it truly ours for the next three days." He kissed me softly.

"I believe you're right." I wrapped my arms around his neck and pulled him to me.

He kissed me fiercely, his mouth devouring mine and reached beneath my shirt unclasping the fastener on the front of my bra. It slid down under my arms while Mason brought his lips down to my breast. He ran his tongue gently over my nipple and cupped it with his hand. He took it into his mouth and teased my erect nipple before he squeezed it tenderly.

I tugged at Mason's shirt and pulled it over his head. I paused for a moment and ran my hands admiringly over his torso. I loved the sculptured structure of his body. I rolled him over and straddled him. He helped me take off my shirt and slip my arms out of my bra. I grinned down at him and held the gaze of his sea blue eyes. His sandy blonde curls were tousled perfectly making him appear angelic. In that moment I realized just how attached I'd become to him and how he had managed somehow to bring such an intense intimacy and love back into my life.

I leaned down and pressed my lips to his with ferocity. I wanted to devour him completely. I raised my hips just enough to slide my hands down to undo his shorts. With a mischievous grin, I slid down his body and took his shorts and boxer briefs with me. I tossed them aside and removed the rest of my clothing.

"You are so damn sexy," I remarked in a low sultry voice as I climbed back over him.

I caressed his thick throbbing cock with my mouth and listened to the low moan that escaped from Mason. Then I ran my tongue teasingly down his shaft. I absolutely loved sucking on his cock and how turned on it made him. He squirmed beneath me and rocked his hips to the rhythm of my mouth. I loved teasing him, torturing him, watching the exquisite pain on his face as I made him wait to be inside me.

Finally, I relented. Not because he wanted me to, but because I wanted to. I crawled up his body and kissed him hungrily, lowering my hips down on his dripping cock. I loved the feeling of him entering me slowly. I could feel myself caressing him as he filled me completely.

A soft moan escaped from deep inside me as I sat fully down upon him. Mason took hold of my thighs and moved my hips in perfect timing with his. My hands reached for his pecs as I picked up our pace. Mason pulled himself up and kissed me with such force it took my breath away. He shoved his tongue deeply into my mouth then kissed me roughly over my neck and shoulder. He buried his face in the small curve between my neck and shoulder and I could feel his hot breath on my skin, his teeth nibbled with just enough bite that I let out a small scream. Not from the pain, but from the jolt it sent through my body all the way down to my toes. His hands grasped my ass, increasing the depths of each thrust. His pelvic bone rubbed deliciously against my clitoris causing the perfect amount of friction to launch me into pure ecstasy. Mason arched his hips into me and grinded mine down upon him trying to get as deep as he could in me as he came.

Both of us collapsed back onto the bed completely spent. I lay on top of him listening to his heart pounding in his chest. I looked up into his eyes and smiled softly.

"I love you," I whispered.

"I love you, too."

*   *   *

Mason's friends were all relaxing on the deck finishing their lunches by the time we came back downstairs.

"It takes an hour to change?" Josiah asked with a knowing look.

Thankfully, Mason just smiled, but didn't offer an explanation. Neither did I.

"The food's inside on the island. Help yourselves," Emma informed us.

"Thanks," I said, and we headed to the kitchen.

They had an assortment of chips, baked beans, potato salad, and fruit to go along with the hot dogs and hamburgers. I fixed my plate with some cantaloupe, watermelon, potato salad, and a hamburger while Mason loaded his up with a variety of everything.

"Hungry?" I rolled my eyes at him.

"I told you I was starving. And that was before we went upstairs. Now I'm famished." He stuck a deviled egg in his mouth and kissed me on the cheek.

"Aw, Mason," I wiped off the overly wet kiss, making him laugh.

"You're the one dating me."

"True." I opened the refrigerator and took out a Coke for myself. "What do you want to drink?"

"Just grab me a beer, please."

I picked out a Rolling Rock and handed it to him.

The boat crew had returned from their morning on the water by the time Mason and I walked out on the back deck. The only one I recognized in the group was Nick. The other three girls were also wearing their bikinis and sporting their golden tans left over from summer. All of them seemed to have started drinking already.

To be 21 again . . .

Mason and I found an empty lounge chair. He climbed on back and put his plate behind me. I sat down in front of him and held mine on my lap.

"Nice to see you guys finally made it. We got down here yesterday around noon," Nick told us as he grabbed another beer out of the cooler.

"That was my fault. I had to wait until the boys got out of school and drop them off at my parents," I explained.

"The boys? You have kids?" a girl with amber colored hair asked.

"Yes, two sons."

"Aw, really? How old are they?" Emma inquired.

"Max just turned eleven and Henry is seven."

"You have an eleven-year-old? Damn, how old are you?" The girl with the amber hair asked rudely.

"Let me guess, you're Courtney." Both Emma and Tricia giggled while Josiah and Jared tried not to make eye contact.

"Yes. Why?" Courtney demanded.

"Just a lucky guess." I looked over at Emma and Tricia and winked.

"So, are we taking the boat out or what?" Mason intervened.

"Sure. You guys ready?" Jared picked up a heavy cooler which I'm sure was full of beer.

"I'm ready." Mason stood up and threw his plate in the trash can.

I followed suit and was happy it was Emma, Jared, Tricia, and Josiah joining us on the lake.

"Hey guys," Nick shouted. "We're gonna run over to the Marina and rent some jet skis. We'll find you out there."

"Okay," Josiah yelled back from the docks.

They had rented a speed boat for the weekend that only fit six to do some skiing. Jared climbed into the driver's seat, which honestly made me a little nervous at first. I hoped his usual flippant attitude didn't translate to his driving. But as we headed out into open waters, I began to realize he knew what he was doing and began to relax.

"Hey, I'm sorry about Courtney." Emma turned in her seat toward me. "She's not exactly the nicest person in the world."

"Are you kidding? She's a bitch. I don't know what Nick sees in her. She treats him like shit," Tricia added.

"I'm just glad she didn't want to join us," I remarked.

"No. She wouldn't have as long as I'm going," Emma snickered. "She hates me. I've known her since grade school. We graduated together. After graduation I was sure I'd never have to deal with her again. Imagine my surprise when I started dating Jared and found out that not only does she go to the same university as me, but that our boyfriends are best friends."

"I'm sorry. That must suck," I empathized.

"Yeah. Well, what can you do?" Emma lifted her arms despairingly and giggled. "I'm not going to let her ruin my weekend. I'm just thankful we have different majors, so I don't have any classes with her. At least, so far I haven't."

"What's your major?" I asked.

"Elementary education. What's yours?"

"Psychology and nursing," I told them.

"Double major?" Tricia inquired, and I nodded. "Maybe we'll have some classes together. I'm a nursing major too."

"Maybe, but you're probably further along than I am. I'm just starting my second year." I shrugged.

"Probably not then. I graduate in May," Tricia stated.

"So, what made you decide to go back to school?" Emma questioned.

"I figured it was time. My youngest had started school full time so . . ." I answered.

"I think it's great." Tricia smiled.

"Can I ask you a question?"

I nodded.

Emma hesitated a little. "Are you divorced?"

"Yes. Almost six years ago."

"It must be hard going to school full time and being a single mom," Tricia noted.

"Sometimes, I guess. It gets a little crazy with their sports and school activities and trying to keep up with the house and finding time to study." It sounded exhausting just saying it aloud. "But Mason makes it easier." I looked over at him carrying on a conversation with Jared and Josiah.

"Jared said you guys are living together," Emma probed.

"I guess. I mean we never really discussed it. He just sort of never went back to his dorm and then one day I realized I was doing his laundry too." I shrugged in a casual way.

"What do your boys think?" Tricia asked.

"They really like him. It took Max a little longer than Henry to come around but once Max learned that Mason played sports in high school and was willing to practice with him and give him a few pointers, his attitude changed. Now they get along well." It was strange discussing something so personal with these girls I'd just met.

"What about your ex? He can't be too thrilled about Mason spending so much time with his sons," Emma pointed out.

"He moved to Arizona several years ago. So, his opinion has very little weight. He did meet Mason this summer when he came out to get the boys."

"That must have been awkward." Tricia grimaced.

"A little. He made a few remarks about our age difference, but most people do. But I think he was more upset about being replaced by someone so much younger than himself," I concluded.

"How old is he?" Emma inquired.

"Thirty-five." The two of them exchanged a knowing look. "And for the record, I'm thirty-three," I said politely.

"We weren't gonna ask," Emma gushed.

"Yeah. It's none of our business," Tricia added.

"It's okay. I don't mind." I laughed at their discomfort.

"You really don't look your age," Emma threw in for good measure.

"Yeah. I mean, we thought you were like twenty-six or seven. That's why when you said you have an eleven your old, we were all surprised," Tricia explained.

"I understand. Don't worry about it. My friends give me a hard time about our age difference also," I informed them.

"Okay, who wants to go tubing?" Josiah stood up and hooked up the large inner tube before tossing it overboard.

"Want to go?" Mason asked me.

"Sure," I replied cheerfully. It had been years since I'd gone tubing.

* * *

Later that evening, Emma, Tricia, and I cleaned up the mess made by dinner before we joined everyone else on the back deck. Someone had started a fire in the bonfire pit and the fire was blazing. Several people were roasting marshmallows and making s'mores. Everyone was drinking heavily, and the music was blaring. I sat down in front of Mason on the lounge and leaned back against him sipping my glass of wine.

"Would you like a beer?" Nick held out a beer for me.

"No thanks. I don't drink beer." I smiled, and he handed the beer to Mason instead.

"Thanks." Mason finished off the one he was drinking and popped the cap off the new one.

"You don't drink beer?" Courtney walked over to us. "But you drink wine."

"I don't care for the taste of beer," I informed her.

"I guess older, more sophisticated people drink wine on their holiday weekends." She smirked.

"What the hell is your problem? My age or the fact that I'm here?" I said with a sharp edge.

"My problem?" Courtney laughed and tossed her hair over her shoulder trying to act superior to everyone else. "My problem is that you can't get a man your own age, so you seduce someone who's over a decade younger than you. It's pathetic."

Mason jumped out of the lounge. "Where the hell . . ."

"Mason, don't." I stood up and put my hand on his arm and faced her. "Courtney, I don't care what you think of my relationship with Mason. Frankly, it's none of your fucking business. If you have a problem with it, then it's your problem. Not ours."

"Don't you see how ridiculous you look? You're thirty-five years old hanging out with a bunch of college kids. It's sad really that you can't spend time with people your own age. You know, the other pathetic soccer moms." She smirked.

Nick came up beside her and grabbed her arm. "Who the hell do you think you are talking to my best friend and his girlfriend like that?" he demanded.

She shook her arm away from him. "I'm just saying what everyone else is thinking."

"The only one thinking that is you," Nick fired back.

"I think we should head home." I turned to Mason, who was fuming.

"Good idea." Courtney flashed a hateful smile.

"No, you're not leaving." Nick shook his head and looked directly at Courtney. "But you should."

"What? You're taking their side? That's such bullshit," Courtney shouted hatefully. "And how do you propose I get home. We're in Tennessee for Christ's sake."

"Not my problem. You can walk for all I care!" Nick sneered.

"No, Nick. She doesn't have a car. Don't worry about it. We'll leave." I reached out and gently placed my hand on Nick's arm. "It's no big deal."

"No. It is a big deal. I promise you; no one here has given your relationship a second thought. I know how good you two are together. I've seen it. Please don't go," he said affectionately.

The atmosphere on the deck shifted dramatically. No one was talking, drinking, or roasting anything. I suddenly realized all eyes were upon us waiting to see what would happen.

Talk about uncomfortable.

Mason finished off his beer and walked over to the trash and tossed the bottle in. "I'll get our bags," he said softly to me and headed back into the house.

"No. Mason, wait . . ." Nick called after him, but Mason didn't stop. "I can't believe you." He glared at Courtney.

"Why don't you be honest? How many times have you called her a cougar and said that she sank her claws in Mason?" she shot back at him.

"Yes, I said that . . . more than once. But you're twisting the meaning of what I said. It wasn't a negative comment. Good God, Courtney. Alex is gorgeous!" Nick looked over at me with a smile.

"Oh, so you're saying if she'd picked you, you'd be with her instead of me?" Courtney inquired with glaring eyes.

"Definitely!" Nick laughed.

"If you want to be honest, Courtney. Why don't you be honest with Nick for once? Tell him why you really pursued him?" Blake stepped forward.

"What?" Nick turned to Blake.

Courtney's face turned an even brighter shade of red and her eyes narrowed in on Blake. "Shut up!"

"She only started dating you to get to Mason. She told me so herself." Blake gave Courtney a fake smile.

"She's lying, Nick." She took a step towards him and he took a step back. "You know I love you. Blake's just trying to turn you against me."

Nick appeared to be speechless. He looked around at everyone staring at him and shook his head slowly in disbelief. "I can't believe you."

"Nick, it may have started out that way, but I fell in love with you. Not Mason," Courtney pleaded.

"Just leave me alone." Nick walked quickly across the deck and down to the water's edge. I felt so bad for him. I thought about going after him but somehow it didn't seem to be my place. Everyone was silent for several long moments. Courtney finally got her bearings and turned towards me.

"This is all your fault. If you'd find yourself some sad little divorcee and stop trying to relive your youth, we'd all be better off."

"If it makes you feel better to blame me for your short comings please do. However, if I were you, I would try to assess why you need to blame others for your situation and learn how to take responsibility for your own actions," I said in my best mom voice.

Courtney stood rooted in that spot and stared at me fuming. Everyone else just started laughing. I looked over at Emma and Tricia and said, "I'm gonna check on Nick."

I still didn't think it was my place, but since no one else had bothered, I didn't want to leave with him feeling like no one cared.

Before Courtney had a chance to respond, I walked across the deck to the side stairs that ran down to the lake's shoreline. Nick was sitting in the sand tossing stones in the lake absentmindedly. My heart went out to the poor guy.

"Nick?" He turned his head and gave me a weak smile. "Mind if I join you?"

"Sure." He turned back towards the lake and threw in another rock.

"Are you alright?" I took a seat beside him in the sand.

"I don't understand what I'm doing wrong. I always pick the wrong girls. I mean, your friend Lisa never returned my calls and I'm not saying I expected her to. I knew I was just a one-night stand. No big deal. I never expected it to turn into something like you and Mason, but still . . ."

"Lisa isn't looking for anything serious. I'm sorry. She went through a nasty divorce recently and believe me, it's hard to put your trust into someone after you've been through one of those," I explained.

"But you did," he pointed out.

"Nick, my divorce was almost six years ago and to be honest, Mason is the first guy I've gotten involved with since. And it is hard even now. You can ask him. I pushed him away a lot in the beginning."

"But you guys are so good together," he observed.

"I think so. But no relationship is perfect. It's a lot of time and patience. And there's still no guarantee."

"Do you think it will last?" He looked at me with hopeful eyes.

"I don't know, to be honest. But I hope so." That was the best I could tell him.

"Me too. You guys seem so perfect for each other."

"Yes, we seem to complement each other well," I agreed. "And you'll find someone too. I promise. You're a very sweet and good-looking guy. Any girl would be happy to be with you."

"Really? Who?" he laughed but it was hollow.

"Don't worry so much about it. I've found that if you stop looking for love, that's when it finds you." I nudged him in a playful manner. "And it will!"

"Mason's pretty lucky."

"Thanks. I'm not so sure he'd agree with you all the time about that." I chuckled.

"Yeah, I heard about your ex. And your mother." He grinned.

"I'm sure you did. That was a little rough, I admit. That's why I didn't get too bent out of shape over Courtney's remarks. I figured it was my turn to take some of the heat from his friends about our age difference." I shook my head slowly. "I honestly expected it."

"Does it bother you? The age difference, I mean," he inquired.

"Not when we're alone. It doesn't matter. But when we're out, sometimes. I mean, people sometimes look at us funny or make comments they think we can't hear. My boys love him, but my folks, well, my mother has been very open about her disapproval of our relationship. Even my friends tease me about my 'college boy toy.'"

"That sucks," he remarked, slightly bumping his shoulder against mine in an affectionate way.

"I just tell them all they're jealous and they agree." I put my arm around his shoulder. "You see, every relationship has obstacles."

"Awww," Nick sighed heavily. "Why does everything have to be so difficult?"

"To make it all worthwhile and more valuable when you find it. So, when you do find that special someone, you won't throw it away lightly. You'll work through your differences together rather than be so quick to call your lawyer," I attempted to explain.

"You sound as if you speak from experience."

"Let's just say I was always certain that I would only get married once and that there was nothing I wouldn't do to make my marriage work." I rolled my eyes at my own words.

"And yet you got divorced anyway."

"Yes, I did."

"Can I ask why?" Nick looked over at me briefly.

"My husband had an affair with his boss to get a promotion. He got the promotion, a transfer to the Arizona offices, and a divorce for his troubles. I found I could not forgive him his transgression," I answered honestly.

"Do you still love him?"

"I still love the man he used to be. Not the man he has grown into. I will always care for him—even love him in some strange way because he's the father of my sons. That creates a bond between two people that is nearly impossible to break. We share a responsibility and an unconditional love for the two sons we created out of the love we once shared for each other."

"I can understand that one. Does Mason?"

"Honestly, we've never discussed much about my ex-husband. Mason knows why we got divorced, he knows I talk to him occasionally when it has to do with our sons, but he's never inquired much more than that and I've never offered any insights. I guess some things are too painful to discuss."

"Is there any chance of you two getting back together?" Nick looked concerned.

"Nope. None."

"Then Mason knows everything he needs to. I'm sure with time he will figure the rest out, but if he is secure in your feelings for him then he has nothing to worry about." Nick placed his hand over mine and squeezed it gently. "I wish you two nothing but happiness."

"Thanks, Nick." I smiled sweetly at him. "Are you ready to go back?"

"No, but I guess we should. I'm sure Mason has already packed all your things and is waiting with the car idling in the driveway." Nick stood up and held out his hand to me.

*   *   *

Nick was not far off. Mason had our things sitting by the front door and was talking with Jared, Josiah, and their girlfriends when we walked in. The others were still out on the deck and said nothing when we passed by them. I felt Nick stiffen up when he saw Courtney still sitting smugly on the lounge. I put my hand in his and gave it a gentle squeeze. He held his head up proudly and passed her by without uttering a word.

"Are you ready?" Mason asked as soon as he saw us walk through the patio doors.

"Are you sure you want to go?" I walked over and wrapped him in my arms.

"I think it would be best if we did."

"I don't. Why would you let some bitch run you off? So, she only dated me to get to you. Big deal. I say you two stay for the weekend and let her be miserable seeing how happy you two are together. Plus, the place is already paid for." Nick leaned against the island and opened another beer. "Might as well enjoy it."

"So, Courtney isn't leaving either?" I asked the five who had been at the cabin the entire time.

"Not that we're aware of," Emma answered. "I don't think she has a way to get home."

"Well, she'd better make some arrangements. She can't seriously think she's riding back to campus with me on Monday," Nick said hatefully.

"We are in Tennessee, Nick. You just can't leave her here," I pointed out despite my dislike of the girl.

"Yes, I can. After what she did, I don't want her staying in this house. I paid for my portion of this weekend, and she was here as my guest. She's not staying here one more night." Nick raised his voice just a little.

"And how am I supposed to get home?" Courtney's voice came from the patio doorway.

We all turned in her direction. How long she had been standing there listening to us, none of us knew.

"Frankly, my dear. I don't give a damn," Nick quoted Rhett's last line from *Gone With The Wind*.

"Very cute," Courtney snorted. "I have no way of getting home, let alone another place to spend the night."

"That is not my problem, but you're not staying here." Nick took another swig of his beer and set it down loudly on the island. "You're always bragging to me about all these guys who want to go out with you, call one of them to pick up your sorry ass."

"It's almost midnight," Courtney declared. "I am not calling anyone this late." She put her hand on her hip and looked ready to kill someone, namely myself or Nick.

"Fine," Nick relented just a smidge. "You can sleep on the couch tonight, but I expect you to call someone in the morning."

"Wow," Courtney huffed. "Thank you so much for such a simple act of kindness and not making me sleep on the deck!"

"You're most unwelcome, you, heartless bitch!" Nick fired back.

"You're such an asshole!" Courtney screamed and slammed the patio door behind her as she returned to the deck.

"So, I guess you're staying then," Josiah chuckled, looking at Mason and me.

"What do you want to do?" Mason looked over at me.

"Why should we let her ruin our weekend? We came down here to enjoy your friends. I don't see how that's changed," I said.

"I guess it hasn't." A broad smile slid across Mason's shapely lips.

"Oh . . . good! I'm so glad you two are staying!" Emma squealed and we all laughed at her.

Chapter 16

WE SPENT THE NEXT day out on the boat with Josiah, Jared, Emma, and Tricia. The others had rented jet skis and we alternated throughout the day. Courtney had stayed behind alone at the cabin. A part of me worried that she would do some damage to the place just to get even with Nick, Mason, and me and to ensure they wouldn't get their security deposit back. She seemed like the type of person who would take pleasure in doing something so devious. Fortunately, she didn't touch anything.

The weather couldn't have been more ideal. The sun was shining brightly in the clear blue skies, its rays dancing off the crystal waters. The air was hot, and the humidity was high. Thankfully, being out on the water kept the spa feeling in the air at bay from us. The trees surrounding the lake were a dark green and accented the scenery like a photograph. The lake was full of people enjoying the holiday weekend. Houseboats were out in abundance, as were the pontoons, ski boats, and jet skis. The alcohol was flowing freely and even I had a decent buzz going by the time we stopped for lunch.

Emma, Lori, and I pulled together a makeshift dinner out of the leftovers we found in the kitchen. I'd noticed Courtney's bag was missing by the front door upon our return. I wasn't sure when she had left while we were out on the boat or how she had managed to get home. I nudged Emma and nodded towards the front door.

"Good riddance," she remarked with a small grin.

After everyone had gorged themselves on dinner—it was amazing how hungry spending a day on the lake made all of us—Jared started the bonfire back up on the deck. We all settled in with the music playing loud enough for us to hear, but not so loud that we couldn't talk. Everyone was spent and fried. Even with sunscreen, my tan had renewed itself to a full dark golden. Emma, Tricia, Lori, and I decided to make orange dreams. As muggy as it was on the deck, they tasted incredibly refreshing. Blake decided to drink beer with the rest of the guys especially after Mike and Josiah went out and picked up a keg while the rest of us put dinner together.

The sunset over the water cast the most brilliant colors I'd ever seen. Colors like that just didn't exist in the suburbs outside the city. Vibrant hues of pink, purple, yellow, orange, and red blazed over the top of the tree line across the lake. The edge of the humidity softened with the evening hours. Mason and I snuggled close together on the lounge near the fire. He sat behind me with an arm draped casually around me. He seemed so relaxed and comfortable. We all did. Everyone felt relieved that the tension had passed when Courtney fled. How she managed to get home, no one ever asked or said.

The drinks flowed freely and the more everyone drank, the rowdier they became. And along with intoxication, always came speculation, teasing, and good old fashion rousing. The boys jeered each other about past relationships, one-night stands, taking one for the team, and numerous other disgusting things that I could have died peacefully not ever hearing.

"Okay, enough of lifestyles of the sick and the twisted." Tricia looked at them with disbelief. "Let's play a game."

"What kind of game?" Mason asked.

"Truth or dare." Tricia laughed and most of the guys rolled their eyes.

"We're not in junior high anymore, Tricia. Or would you rather us play spin the bottle?" Mike pumped the keg and refilled his cup.

"Now that could be fun." Jared picked up an empty beer bottle left on the deck railing and gave his a jingle.

"Oh, come on. It'll be fun," Blake squealed, ignoring Jared's comment.

"Fine . . ." Mike caved and rejoined the circle around the fire. "Who goes first?"

"I do. I thought of it," Tricia announced. "Okay, Stewie. Truth or dare?"

"Well, I've done too many things to be truthful, so I've only got one choice: dare," Stewie boasted.

"Fine. I dare you to strip down to your birthday suit and take a lap around the cabin."

"Is that all? Hell, I can do that." He jumped to his feet and without a second thought, stripped down right where he stood and skipped down the deck steps.

We scurried over to the railing and watched him let it all hang out without a care in the world. He was skipping, dancing, and singing his fool tail off as he faded off around the corner of the cabin. Two minutes later he rounded from the opposite direction still singing at the top of his lungs, drunk as a monkey. We were almost all in tears by the time he returned.

Stewie slipped back into his shorts and t-shirt and sat back down looking extremely proud of himself "My turn. Let me see . . ." He slowly eyed each of us. "Jared. Truth or dare?"

"Truth." Jared looked over at Emma. "Don't judge me," he said with a wink.

"What's the meanest prank you've ever pulled on someone?" Stewie asked.

"Meanest? Um, let me think?" Jared quickly took a drink of his beer while he thought for a moment. "Okay. I've got it. Once when I was nine I had the biggest crush on my older sister's best friend. They were about fourteen at the time. Well, I kept bugging them all night just because I wanted her to notice me. So, when I overheard her tell my sister I was the ugliest little kid she had ever seen, I was crushed and almost started crying. Then I got mad and thought I'd get even with her and that she wouldn't be so pretty when I got done with her." A devilish grin slid across his lips. "Well, Diane, that was my sister's friend's name, she had the most beautiful long almost black hair. It was so silky and smooth . . ."

"Oh my God, you cut her hair." Emma smacked his arm.

"No, I didn't cut her hair. That would have been too easily traced back to me. Now hush and let me finish." Jared took a drink and continued. "She always brought over her own shampoo and conditioner when she spent the night. She was just that anal about her hair. Anyway, when everyone was in the family room watching a movie, I snuck in and took her shampoo and conditioner bottles. I poured in some hydrogen peroxide, shook them up well and put them back. A couple of hours later when she took a shower, she came out with the most hideous orange hair you'd ever seen. Naturally, she was screaming to high heaven. I thought for sure I'd be skinned alive for it, but luck was on my side. Turns out she'd had a fight earlier with her own brother who was twelve and he got blamed for it. Of course, he insisted he didn't do it and I played complete ignorance. So, in the end, he got grounded for a month and no one ever figured out it was me." He grinned like a Cheshire cat.

"That's awful," I declared.

"You are terrible!" Tricia said between her laughter.

The guys thought he was brilliant, not only for thinking of such a thing at the age of nine but also having escaped punishment for it as well.

"All right. Now I get to pick." Jared narrowed his eyes. "Alex. Truth or dare."

"Truth." I wasn't about to risk running naked around the cabin.

"What's the worst thing you ever did to someone?" Jared inquired.

"I'd be careful asking her that. She's been through a divorce. That puts her in an entirely different league than the rest of us," Nick said, amusing everyone at my expense.

"You best remember that too, Nick," I teased him back and got an even better reaction than he did. "The worst thing I ever did. Well, I guess it would have been my senior year of high school. I found out my boyfriend had cheated on me and I was pissed. So, my best friend and I snuck over to his house about two in the morning. He lived on a farm and since the dogs knew me, they never barked at us. Plus, there were lots of cats, you know, farm cats out in the barn. Well, he had a prized Z28 that he loved more than life. So, we fed about six of these cats a bunch of X-lax and put them in his car. Let's just say the interior was ruined." I couldn't help but smile at the memory.

"Did he ever find out it was you?" Tricia asked.

"I'm sure he knew, but he could never prove it."

"I can't believe you'd do that to his car." Mason looked at me completely stunned.

"That's one way to get even with a cheating bastard," Blake laughed.

"Okay, so now we know not to cheat on Alex. Mason, I'd hide my car keys if you two ever have a fight," Josiah remarked with wide eyes.

"Couldn't you think of a less painful way of getting even with him?" Mike asked.

"Oh, I did. But that came much later when we got divorced."

"That was Danny's car?" Mason looked shocked.

"Yep." I sipped my drink with a coy smile.

"Why did you ever marry him if he cheated on you?" he asked.

"Because I was young and stupid and believed him when he said he'd never do it again." I shrugged and eagerly changed the subject. "Josiah, truth or dare?"

"Truth."

"What's the worst thing you ever did?" I figured I'd keep with the common trend.

"Well, back when I was in high school there was this guy, Jake, who was a real douche. And I don't mean he was an ass; I mean he was a real prick. Anyway, he had a party at his house following our homecoming game. He got really wasted and kept hitting on my little sister, Julia, who was just a sophomore. He didn't seem to understand 'go to hell.' Well, sometime during the party, he got her pinned in a corner. He was trying to kiss her and had forced his hand up her shirt. My buddy noticed her struggling with him and intervened. Julia was shaken and understandably so. She wanted me to take her home. So, on our way out, we passed through the garage. My friend got the bright idea of pissing in his water softener. I mean, it's not like I could have kicked Jake's ass. He was one of the linemen on the football team and this guy was huge." Josiah outstretched his arms. "He would have mopped up the floor with my scrawny little ass and I knew it." He chuckled. "So, when my buddy suggested it, it seemed like a great idea. Julia stood look out while we both relieved ourselves." Josiah was still clearly proud of what he'd done.

"You have any idea how gross that is?" Lori asked. "That's their drinking water. They washed their clothes and showered in your piss!" She wrinkled her nose.

"I know," Josiah declared with pride.

"That's sick!" Emma looked truly appalled.

"If you think that's horrible," Tricia began, "there was a guy I went to school with who was pretty much like the one your sister encountered. He was always hosting parties. His parents traveled a lot and he pretty much had the run of the place. So, when he attacked me, the only thing that saved me was my right knee. I kicked him in the nuts. He went down like a sack of potatoes. Well, after that, he bragged how he'd turned me down that night. So, the next time he hosted a party, my best friend,

Andrea, and I went and bought a special treat just for him. A little travel sewing kit and a bottle of deer urine. My dad and brothers like to hunt," she explained. "Anyway, we waited until he was doing beer bongs in the kitchen and then we snuck off to his bedroom. We locked the door and tore the sheets off his bed. Did I mention he had one of those old waterbeds from the eighties? Those ones with the rubber-like mattresses." She laughed. "So, Andrea opened the sewing kit and took out a couple needles. She started poking tiny little, microscopic holes all over his mattress while I pulled the plug up, you know how those things are." She demonstrated using wide drunken gestures by pretending to pull up the nozzle and unscrew the cap. "And poured in the entire bottle of deer urine into the mattress. Then we quickly remade his bed like it was before."

"You people are sick," I roared with laughter. This was a woman after my own heart.

"Says the lady who gave cats chronic diarrhea and locked 'em in a classic car!" Mike stated.

"All right, all right. This truth stuff is getting far too serious. So, I dare everyone to go skinny dipping," Josiah said as he held up his beer for a toast. "What say you all?"

"Hell yeah!" Lori was the first to jump up.

Seconds later, everyone else joined in and began undressing. I looked at Mason to see what he was thinking. He just grinned real big and said, "Come on, baby," and took my hand.

"What the hell." I shrugged.

Eleven naked bodies trampled down the deck stairs and headed straight for the lake. I held Mason's hand as we splashed into the cold water. It felt like someone had filled the lake with ice cubes since our last meeting earlier in the evening. By the sound of the screams coming from the rest of our party, they must have shared my sentiment.

*　*　*

The following day was spent much like the one before. The weather was perfect, hot, and sunny with just a hint of a breeze. I sunned with Emma on the boat deck, soaking up the final days of summer listening to the *Fun.* CD. I felt so calm and relaxed. The mist from the waves created by the speedboat was so refreshing. I could feel all the tension in my body melting away. The stress from being a single parent, all the school functions, the sports, the conferences, the bills, the housework, and my own responsibilities associated with college all drifted from my muscles, leaving me with a calmed spirit that soared across the waters.

I listened to the music floating above the water, the roar of the jet skis and the boat motor humming evenly and playing as a backdrop to the laughter of Mason and his friends. I eyed Mason out of the corner of my eye. He was out on one of the jet skis, and he and Jared were jumping the waves left behind by our boat and many others that were racing around on the lake. They were having the time of their lives.

* * *

I got out of a hot shower with my hair still wrapped in a towel. I slipped into my deep lavender silk robe and sat down on the end of our bed. I shook my hair out of the towel and began brushing it out. Mason walked in from our private patio and sat down beside me.

"I've got a surprise for you," he whispered, kissing my neck.

He pulled my robe down just a little off my shoulder and kissed it gingerly.

"Really? You certainly bolted from the shower quick enough," I pouted. "You know how much I love showering with you." I playfully pulled away from him.

"Follow me," he flashed a mischievous look and led me out onto the private master deck.

"Mason, what are you up to?" I let him pull me along.

Much to my surprise, he had spread out several candles, covering the fold-out cushioned lounge with pillows and a blanket. He had even put a bad bottle of cheap wine in one of the coolers to chill. The stars and moon glistened off the small ripples in the lake. It was so incredibly beautiful and romantic. I loved him for wanting to do something special on the last night of our retreat from life.

"I wanted to make sure you remember our last night here." He pulled me into a loving embrace.

"It's perfect. Thank you." I stood on my tiptoes and kissed him lightly. "You are so wonderful to me. I love you."

"I love you."

Mason reached down and scooped me up in his arms, carried me over to the lounge and placed me down gently. I looked up at him standing over me and couldn't believe how fortunate I was to be here in this moment with him. His hair was till damp from our shower and curled in loose waves in a purely masculine angelic way. His bright blue eyes gleamed in the soft hues from the candlelight and the little stubble on his face made him look incredibly sexy.

I reached up and placed my hands on his chest. It was still warm from baking all day in the sun. I played with the little patch of hair on his chest in a suggestive way. I crouched up on my knees and pulled him down to me, so I could help him out of his shorts. My favorite thing to do.

*   *   *

Mason and I woke up around ten thirty the next morning. We took a quick shower, packed up our bags, and joined the rest of our weekend roommates shortly before eleven. Everyone was congregating around the kitchen having breakfast. Mason left our things by the front door with all the other bags before joining us.

I had such a good time with Mason and his friends. I was almost sad to go back home. Of course, I missed my boys, but I had forgotten what it was like to be young with little or no responsibility except for schoolwork. A part of me truly envied them. They had their whole lives ahead of them and so much to look forward to. True, so did I, but a part of my book had already been written.

I poured myself a cup of coffee and Mason helped himself to a glass of orange juice. I sat down on one of the bar stools and grabbed a bagel. I started smearing some cream cheese on it and looked around at everyone. They were unusually quiet this morning. Most of them looked like the long weekend of excessive drinking had taken a toll on them. Thankfully, we had gotten a one o'clock check-out time.

"Could you two have been any louder last night?" Nick asked Mason.

"What? We slept on the deck," Mason replied.

"You might as well been in the same room with me. I could hear everything," Nick said.

"Us too," Jared stated, and Emma nodded.

"Yep." Blake and Stewie along with the rest all agreed.

"Sorry," I blushed. "I thought since we were outside you guys wouldn't hear us."

"Nope. And I would imagine everyone else on the lake did as well," Tricia added.

"I mean, good Lord. It was bad right after you arrived, but you two never stop," Mike piped up.

"What? Didn't anyone else have sex this weekend?" Mason stammered.

"Ya didn't exactly make it easy with the porn movie being made down the hall," Jared concluded.

"That didn't deter you any," Lori threw in. "We were on the other side of your wall." She tossed a bagel at him.

"Thanks," Jared said and took a big bite out of it.

"Guess, I'm the only one who didn't get any this weekend?" Nick pretended to pout. "Well, not since Friday anyway."

"Considering you were in there alone, I'd be a little concerned if we'd started hearing those noises from your room," Tricia declared.

It was hard saying good-bye to everyone. I had come to adore all of them and their unique personality quirks. So, I decided to invite them all over to my house for a Halloween party the weekend after we all finished mid-terms. I figured we would all need to blow off some steam by then. But I also made them all promise to wear costumes. The girls thought it would be a riot to get all dressed up, but the guys all groaned. However, in the end, they all promised.

Chapter 17

I MET UP with Derek and Nate twice a week for one or two hours a piece to help them with their psychology class. Adding them to my already hectic routine was extremely stressful at first but once I got into a rhythm, they fell into place like everything else in my crazy world.

Both did much better on their next exam covering human development and the following chapter on how stress affects your health, but the fifth chapter over psychological disorders were a little more challenging for each of them. There was a lot of information in this chapter and some of the disorders were like each other, which made it hard for them to pull out key terms that differentiated one disorder from the other.

Despite what Mason had said about Nate's classroom antics, he was a gentleman around me. He never made a rude comment or said anything that alluded to him having any sort of sexual interest in me. Derek, on the other hand, asked me out to dinner after our fourth session. I told him he was on an adrenalin rush from getting a B on his chapter four exam. He denied it, so I kindly thanked him but told him I was involved with someone. Since that awkward moment, he'd returned to his charming self.

Mason, on the other hand, was struggling a lot with my tutoring two well-known fit college athletes. He tried to hide it as best he could. I knew it had a lot to do with his age, so I tried my best to ignore it. On the plus side, he was being more attentive than usual. He stopped skipping the boys' football practice during the week and instead insisted on coming with us. And twice in the last two weeks he had made me breakfast in bed when he didn't have an early class in the morning.

Nate and I were finishing reviewing his terms and concepts late on a Thursday morning when he paused and put his note cards aside.

"Can I ask you a question, Alex?" he began.

"Sure," I replied naively, thinking it was related to the chapter we were covering.

"Would you join me for dinner tomorrow evening?" he asked confidently.

"Oh." He'd caught me completely off guard. "No. I'm sorry. I can't."

"Why? It won't interfere with you tutoring me. I promise."

"That's not it. I'm already involved with someone, and he makes me very happy. In fact, he's in your econ class," I admitted.

"Who?"

"Mason Brooks."

"Seriously?" He raised his eyebrows at me.

"Yes. In fact, we live together," I said proudly.

"No shit. Huh . . . I never would have guessed he'd have the balls to go after someone as hot as you." He looked perplexed. "How long have you guys been together?"

"About six months."

"And you're already living together? That's fast."

"Well, he lived in the dorms, and I have a house so . . . he just stays with me." I couldn't help but smile.

"Oh, I see." And he let the subject drop.

I didn't give our conversation much thought afterwards. I was too busy with my own classes and upcoming exams. By the time I finally made it home, I had all but forgotten it until Mason arrived and came up behind me while I was cooking dinner. He wrapped his arms around me and leaned down kissing me softly on the small of my neck.

"Thank you," he whispered.

"For what?" I spun around so I could give him a proper kiss.

"I think I just became Nate's hero today."

"Huh?"

"He came into class this afternoon, walked over and shook my hand and said he was proud of me and that I was a lucky man. When I asked him what he was talking about, he admitted that he'd asked you out and you told him you were happily involved with me and that we live together." A smile of pride spread across his shapely lips.

"Oh, okay. Yeah, that was this morning."

"I know. He said I was lucky because you're very sweet and he also said you were so freakin' sexy." He laughed. "I told him I couldn't agree more. But then he took it a step further and told all the guys sitting around us that I was the one who was dating his hot tutor. I think they were all a bit envious."

"Yeah, I'm sure they were."

*   *   *

The house was finally quiet. It was almost midnight. Mason was in the family room studying for some exam he had tomorrow with the television rambling on in the background. I stepped out onto the back deck and sat down on the swing. The night air was cool and crisp. The glorious smells of early autumn flooded the air. Some of the leaves had started turning this week, adding a little character to the scenery. It was going to be stunning in the next couple of weeks with all the brilliant reds, oranges, and golds shining through.

I gently rocked back and forth listening to the sounds of nature chirping off in the near distance. The moon was almost full and there was an abundance of stars scattered across the sky on this cloudless night. There wasn't much of a breeze, and I was comfortable in my long silk soft blue nightgown. I had a light shawl draped over my shoulders that was just about perfect to keep the night air off my bare skin.

"What are you doing out here?" Mason's voice jolted me out of my thoughts.

"Relaxing." Our normal tones sounded loud against the natural silence.

"Everything all right?" He came over and sat down beside me, drawing me into his arms. "It's a little chilly out here."

"It's not too bad," I said. "Are you done studying for the night?"

"Yeah, I was on my way to bed, and you weren't there." He leaned his head down against mine.

"I didn't want to interrupt you."

"You look beautiful tonight." Mason lightly traced his finger over the top of my thigh.

"Stop that." I giggled and brushed his hand away.

"No," he whispered and leaned down kissing me forcefully.

I moved my body against his and wrapped my arms around him, eagerly kissing him back. I shifted myself up and sat down on his lap facing him. I caressed the side of his face with one hand and the other entangled in the back of his hair. I loved the way he tasted, like salt and sweet sweat with subtle hint of the mocha coffee he was drinking while studying. His arms enveloped me, his hands running up and down my back, caressing my ass. He rocked his hips into me and I could feel him hardening in his gym shorts.

"Take them off," I whispered into his ear.

Mason wiggled himself around and removed his shorts and boxer briefs down around his ankles. I slid my nightgown up around my waist and slowly lowered myself down upon his hard cock. It filled me deliciously. He scooted down just a bit for me to wrap my legs around his waist crushing his lips against mine, his tongue searching, teasing my own.

With his hands on my hips, he guided each thrust into me. I arched my back and bit my lip, trying not to let out the scream I felt with each tantalizing lunge. I loved the way his cock moved within me, gloriously ripping me apart and filling me completely. I could feel it throbbing within me with each thrust. My clitoris rubbed beautifully against his pelvic bone, sending a sensation through my body to the tips of my toes.

I was off in my own little world, filled with ecstasy and desire, loving every thrust of his pelvis into me. Our momentum picked up, his hands tightened on my hips as he pushed harder and faster, loving every enchanting second. I arched my back, lifting my face towards the stars as Mason sucked on my breast. I let out a loud moan not caring who heard me. Then there was a loud crack and instant pain.

Mason and I went crashing down to the deck as the old wooden swing broke beneath us. It knocked the wind out of each of us and took us both a second to realize what had happened.

"Ouch!" Mason screamed loudly in my ear.

"Oh, my God! Are you alright?"

"I think I broke my ass! And my dick!" he exclaimed.

"Don't move," I shifted my legs around to get my footing and stood up straightening my nightgown.

Mason looked up at me with big, rounded eyes. I wasn't sure if he was going to laugh or cry. "Damn, that hurt." He pulled himself up using the side of the swing and rubbing his ass with his other hand.

"You okay?" I looked him up and down as he struggled to get his shorts back up.

"Yeah." He stood back and analyzed the damage. "But you get to explain this one to the kids," he laughed.

"Great. Thanks!" I gave him a playful smack.

We crawled into bed exhausted and spent and slightly frustrated with having our finale spoiled. I rolled over and put my head down on his chest. The strong rhythm of his heart sounded like a lullaby. I closed my eyes and draped my arm across him. He wrapped his arm around me and I felt so safe and secure in his arms.

Despite how this relationship came about, I had grown to love this young man. He treated me better and with more respect than my ex-husband ever had. Whenever Mason was late coming home for dinner or went out with his friends, I never worried about him cheating on me. The thought never even entered my mind and I loved that about him. I could trust him, I believed in him and he had proven over time, I could trust him with the two most important things in my life, my boys and my heart.

Chapter 18

LISA AND I SAT on the hard aluminum bleachers watching our sons run up and down the football field. At this level the boys were still learning the sport and mastering the essence of the game. They used flags and were not allowed to tackle although most of the boys did anyway, supposedly to capture the flag from the opposing team's player.

It was a gorgeous morning. I could still see the dew upon the grass twinkling in the sunlight. I had on a light-hooded sweatshirt and a pair of shorts. The temperature was supposed to reach the low seventies by mid-afternoon, but currently there was a strong enough breeze that my legs were covered in goose bumps.

Lisa was rambling on about her date last evening with some attorney named Erick. He had taken her to a nice restaurant downtown and afterwards they simply walked around the city getting to know one another. He was also divorced and had a daughter with his first wife that was eight years old. She said he stopped at one of those quaint little parlors for ice cream during their walk. I hadn't seen her this excited about a man since before she'd gotten divorced.

I looked over my shoulder to see where Mason and Max had gone. They were a distance from us, throwing the football back and forth getting Max warmed up for his game right after lunch. I grinned to myself before turning my attention back to Lisa. Over my left shoulder I heard a couple of cliquey moms make a snide comment about me dating a child. I did my best to ignore them and concentrate instead on what Lisa was saying.

Then I distinctly heard Becca, the mom of one of the boys on Henry's team, call me a slut loud enough to ensure I would hear it.

"Excuse me?" I turned around to face her. "What did you call me?"

"I called you a slut." Her cold eyes glared at me.

"I don't appreciate that. You don't even know me."

"Look, lady . . ." Lisa began, but I put my hand on her arm to silence her.

"You're involved with someone who is barely legal. I think it's disgraceful."

"So, because you don't approve of who I date, that makes me a slut?"

"Yes . . . running after a boy who is barely out of high school," she huffed. "You're just one of those cougars!"

Lisa snickered next to me, and I fought to keep a straight face.

"So, you're calling me a slut because I'm dating someone younger than me? That's very narrow minded of you," I said politely.

"That was rude!" she spat.

"No. That was an honest assessment."

"Do you even care what message you're sending your children?" she stammered.

"And what exactly is that message? Not to judge someone by their age or by societal standards?" I asked.

"You must realize how ridiculous you look with him," she scoffed.

"Becca, just because you're miserable, do you really have to deny everyone else happiness?"

"I am not miserable!" she raised her voice drawing the attention of others around us.

"I feel sorry for you, Becca. You take pleasure in talking about others behind their back, judging people who don't live by your idea of right and wrong and treating people around you like it's their fault your life didn't turn out the way you envisioned. Perhaps if you spent more time focusing on yourself and making a better life for you and your children and a little less time spreading your unhappiness, then you might find something to make you happy again," I said in the sweetest voice I could manage before turning my back to her.

"That was magnificent. I only wish I'd gotten to be the one to say it to her," Lisa leaned in and whispered.

"I've been dying to say that since baseball season," I whispered back.

*   *   *

I spent the rest of the afternoon sitting on the back deck covered in study guides, notes, and textbooks. Midterms were coming up and I always felt unprepared for them regardless of how much I studied. It was an endless sea of stress and panic. Not nearly at the same level as finals, but close. Luckily, not all my classes had midterms this semester and I was thankful for that.

Mason was studying in my bedroom for his midterms, so my boys occupied themselves on the X-box. It still amazed me the transformation my sons had gone through with my return to school. My first semester back, I spent half my time telling them to keep the noise down, so I could study. Now, they don't bother me for trivial things if I was buried under schoolwork.

My cell phone rang right when I was in the middle of a research study on schizophrenia. I almost didn't answer it until I looked at the caller ID. It was Danny.

"Yes?" I said, trying not to sound too annoyed.

"Am I interrupting something?" He sounded a little too cheerful.

"I'm studying, Danny. What do you want?" Now I didn't care if I sounded annoyed. I was.

"I was calling about Thanksgiving." He hesitated a moment.

I closed my eyes and leaned back in the swing knowing full well what was coming next. Another disappointment for my sons.

"What now?"

"I don't think I can take the boys that weekend. I'm really swamped at work and I'm trying to put together this project . . .," he stammered.

"Seriously?" I took a deep breath and checked my temper. Blowing up at him would serve no purpose whatsoever. "Fine. Whatever. I'll let them know."

"Hopefully, I'll have things wrapped up soon, so I can spend some time with them over Christmas break."

"Sure, Danny. But forgive me if I don't hold my breath." I hit the off button and tossed my phone aside in disgust.

Danny pulled the same stunt last year. Now I was the one who had to go in there and try to sugarcoat their dad's behavior and then deal with the fall-out for the next six months. Hopefully, Max would take it better this year although I seriously doubted it. He was so sick and tired of being dismissed by his dad and I really couldn't blame him. I was beyond sick of his excuses myself.

* * *

Henry cried and crawled up into my lap. Max's face just turned a deep red, but he remained silent. He sat there for several minutes silently fuming. He laid the controller down on the couch and walked out the front door. Through the front window I saw him leaning up against the tree for a few minutes and then eventually he slid down hugging his knees.

Max tried so hard to be tough, to be a man. My heart broke for my son, and I wished there was something I could do to fix this for him. But I had been fighting this battle for years. Danny was never going to change. And there was nothing I could do to hide that reality from my boys. I was always careful not to badmouth their father. I never had to tarnish him in their eyes. He was doing a fine job of that all by himself.

I let Henry cry it out, consoling him the best I could and telling him how much his Daddy wished he could spend the holiday with him, all the while keeping one eye on the broken heart in my front yard. When Henry had calmed down, I let him return to his video game and went outside to check on Max. I sat down beside him on the dead leaves that had gathered at the bottom of the tree.

"I'm sorry, Max." I thought about putting my arm around him and decided against it. Lately, he'd push me away when I did and said he was too grown up to be hugged by his mom. As much as that hurt, I didn't push.

"Why are you sorry? You didn't do anything," he muttered and continued to dig at the little hole he'd dug with a stick.

"You know what I mean."

"I don't know why I believed him anyway. He never keeps his word." He angrily tore at the ground.

"Because he's your dad and you love him," I offered.

"Yeah, but he doesn't love me!" He looked over at me for the first time and I saw the heartbreak in his red puffy eyes that were glistening with tears. "I hate him!"

"No, you don't."

"Yes, I do," he declared. "Don't you think I know who he's spending Thanksgiving with?"

"Who?" I had no clue.

"Amanda," he spat the name out like it was poison. "He'll be with her and her three brats. I guarantee it."

"Who's Amanda?" This was news to me.

"Some girl he's dating. She and her brats met us in Florida. They went to Disney World with us," he informed me.

"I didn't know that. I thought it was just the three of you," I apologized.

Danny's declaration of love and wanting to give our relationship another try on his visit last summer flashed through my brain. *Boy, he really hasn't changed!*

"He told us not to tell you, but I don't care. I'm not going to lie to you if he's going to lie to me."

"You don't have to keep secrets from me, Max. But I understand why you felt you had to."

"We stayed inside the park in some hotel. Dad and Amanda had their own room and Henry and I had to share one with her kids."

"You stayed in a hotel room by yourself?"

"Yes, but there was a door between their room and the one we were in," Max explained.

"Oh, I see." At least Danny wasn't a complete moron.

"But her kids . . . I hate her kids. Her oldest son kept picking on Henry and making him cry and Dad wouldn't do anything about it. And she has a daughter, Ariel, that's four years old. Dad carried her around all the time and gave her anything she wanted. He ignored me and Henry most of the time."

"I'm so sorry, Max. I had no idea," I said in a low voice. Now I was glad my boys wouldn't be going to spend Thanksgiving with Danny. From the way it sounded, they would have been miserable.

Then Max surprised me. He climbed into my lap and rested his head on my shoulder. I wrapped my arms around him as he let go of his anger and finally cried it out.

Chapter 19

I DROPPED THE BOYS at my parents' house before three o'clock the Saturday afternoon before Halloween. My folks were starting to get used to Mason despite their repeated objections to our relationship. But still, my mother maintained a cold politeness towards him. At least my dad seemed to be trying never to say anything negative about us in my presence.

"Don't worry. We'll drop the boys off tomorrow after supper." My mom edged me out towards the door. My parents were planning to take my sons to the haunted house at the Children's Museum as soon as they could get me out of their hair.

"Okay." I kissed them goodbye one more time and warned my father once again about scaring Henry and the possibility of nightmares. He never did well with scary things although his brother absolutely loved them. "Have a good time," I called as I climbed into the car.

The four of them waved to me as they headed towards my mom's SUV. All I could think about was having to stay up with Henry for the next couple of weeks while he overcame the nightmares, he was certain to get thanks to my folks, mainly my father's inability to listen to me concerning all that had to do with my sons.

Mason was setting up the decorations around the kitchen, dining, and family room by the time I returned. We had picked up a few things when we went shopping for food, drinks, and alcohol. Halloween and Christmas were my favorite holidays, and I had an abundance of decorations for each. I even had a themed porcelain village for each to adorn my mantel. Although, I loved my Christmas village, the Halloween one was my favorite with its Potion Shop, Witch's Brewery, pumpkin patch, graveyard, and the little people dressed in scary and comical costumes.

I arranged all the appetizers and desserts on the island along with the disposable plates, napkins, and plastic silverware. I put the ice chest next to the plastic cups and arranged the soda and alcohol so that it could be easily assessable. I set out the Jell-O shots that I had made earlier. I used vodka instead of water, boiled it and added it to various Halloween candy molds. We had cherry, blue raspberry, and strawberry banana flavored shots and they tasted so delicious.

I was a tad leery of hosting this party to begin with even though it was originally my idea on the last day of our Labor Day weekend getaway. I had tried to add a little balance to the party by inviting Debbie, Mark, and Lisa and Erik. I was hoping against all odds that their presence would hold the antics to a mild roar. Although I knew my friends, at times, had the tendency to be much rowdier than Mason's ever thought of acting.

I slipped back into our bedroom to put on my costume. As I undressed Mason walked in to change also. He was as excited as a small child anticipating a birthday party. He was jabbering on a mile a minute as he climbed into an orange prisoner jumpsuit. There was a black prisoner number over his left breast and County Prisoner was printed in large black letters across his shoulder blades. To match him, I had gotten a sexy little cop's uniform. It had short little shorts, a cropped officer's shirt that showed an obscene amount of cleavage, and a patrolman's hat. I put on my knee-high black boots with four-inch heels and borrowed Henry's plastic holster, cap gun, and handcuffs. I even had his little officer's badge.

I stood in the mirror pinning the badge on my left breast pocket when Mason stepped up behind me and smiled from ear to ear.

"You look edible."

"Is that how you speak to an officer?" I gave his reflection a coy look.

"Well, it's not like I can call you by your name? You don't have a name tag," he observed. "Hold on a second."

"What are you doing?" I called after him as he left the room.

Mason didn't reply. I looked at my reflection for a moment longer then decided to go in search of him. I found him at the island fiddling with the masking tape.

"What are you doing?" I repeated coming up beside him.

"Making you a name tag. I had an old one from Steak n' Shake in my glove box from when I worked there for a summer in high school. I'm covering it with masking tape and . . ." He pulled a black sharpie out of the drawer and wrote something across the top of the tape.

"There. How's that?" Mason held up the name tag.

"Officer Jackie Mehoff," I read aloud and laughed. "This is fabulous!"

"I thought it appropriate," he stated proudly and pinned it below my badge.

Lisa and Erick were the first to arrive. Lisa was dressed as Little Red Riding Hood and Erick came as the Big Bad Wolf. I loved his pointed fuzzy ear extensions and gave his tail a playful yank when he walked by. Erick helped Mason build a bonfire in the pit on the back deck while the two of them had a couple beers and discussed football. Lisa and I fired up the blender and made the best mudslides I'd ever tasted. After our second ones, we decided that the alcohol content we added to the mix cancelled out the calories in the ice cream, chocolate syrup, and whipped cream. We sampled a couple of the Jell-O shots in each flavor. I couldn't believe how smooth they tasted and how easily they went down.

We joined the men out on the deck just as the sun began to disappear into the western sky. I sat down on the swing beside Mason and snuggled up into him. Erick took a playful bite at Lisa's neck when she sat down on his lap. Shortly after we'd sat down, the doorbell started ringing and people showed up in droves.

We had a wide assortment of characters wandering about my kitchen, family room, and backyard. It didn't take long for the appetizers and the desserts to disappear and the alcohol to run low, even though almost all our guests had brought some as well. Apparently, we were all cutting loose after taking our midterms.

Emma, Tricia, Jared, and I all went on a liquor store run. Tricia was driving since she was the only one who wasn't drinking. The liquor store was in the same strip mall as a grocery store, and suddenly I got an idea for the best Halloween prank. I'm not sure what possessed me, maybe it was the alcohol, maybe it was that small part of me that never really grew up, but I thought it would be fun to pay Becca a little visit.

I pitched the idea to the others, and they all thought it was brilliant. We took off at an awkward drunken jog over to the grocery store. We must have appeared a comical bunch, coasting on a grocery store cart: the sexy police officer, Alice in Wonderland, the Mad Hatter, and the nun. We were loud, obnoxious, and having a great time. People just didn't look at us, they stared. And we were all fine with it. We picked up twelve packs of toilet paper, a four pack of bar soap, four dozen eggs, and a box of fifty count plastic forks.

Becca lived on the outskirts of town with her two kids in a small older ranch house that sat a good distance off the road with plenty of mature trees. We parked about a quarter of a mile from her place in a little alcove where our car would be hard to see. It was almost midnight and Becca's car was parked in her driveway but all the lights inside were out.

We crept down the road trying to contain our giggling. It wasn't easy. I felt like I was sixteen years old again. We stood at the corner of her front yard and divvied up our stash. We each took a dozen eggs, a couple rolls of toilet paper and a bar of soap.

"What's with the forks?"

"You'll see." I opened the box and gave each of them a handful. "These are for last. And make sure you don't hit any windows. One, we don't want to break any. And two, we don't want to wake anyone up."

We redecorated her lawn, garage, driveway, and the front of her house. There was toilet paper hanging off every tree, eggs, and soap on every surface. We soaped up her car widows and every window on the outside of her house. There was a strange sense of justice in it no matter how juvenile it was.

I met up with the others under a big oak tree on the side of the garage. "Okay, here is what you do with the forks." I squatted down to the grass. "Prong side down." I jammed the fork in the ground. "And break." I snapped off the handle leaving the prongs sticking up out of the yard about an inch. "It makes their clean-up that much more fun." I smiled widely.

"You are evil," Jared grinned. "Brilliant, but evil."

"No, but my son is. Max told me about doing this to a bully at school," I laughed.

When we had completed our task, we made our way back to our car. I almost wanted to be there tomorrow morning when Miss Judgmental saw our decorating job. She was going to blow a gasket.

Mason, Josiah, Erik, Lisa, Nick, and Mark were playing poker on the deck by the time we made it back to our house. Debbie was in the kitchen fixing more Jell-O shots as we had already run out. Blake, Lori, Mike, and Stewie were lounging on the deck with some other people I didn't recognize around the fire pit discussing something or other with lively gestures.

I fixed myself another drink and followed Emma out on the deck. Debbie joined us shortly thereafter. I sat down on the swing and warmed myself by the bonfire. Debbie sat beside me and raised her glass to mine.

"When did you get the new porch swing?" Debbie asked, running her fingers over the soft cushions.

"Mason got it for me for our six-month anniversary," I said casually, taking a long drink.

"I loved your old wooden one. It was beautiful," she remarked.

"I did too, but I think it finally rotted through and wasn't safe anymore."

The party was a huge success in many ways. I was thrilled that nothing got broken or destroyed. Most every one of Mason's friends spent the night and my house looked like *Jonestown* the morning after. Everyone was at least respectful enough to stay out of my sons' rooms, so my family room was crammed full of college students sleeping it off. There were blankets and pillows everywhere, and I couldn't even walk into the kitchen to make coffee the next morning.

Chapter 20

THE FOLLOWING WEEK on Halloween I went to Henry's class to volunteer to help with the Halloween party. Becca's son, Steven, was also in Henry's class this year and she happened to be there as well. Luckily a couple other moms had also signed up to help so I wasn't stuck with dealing with her alone. The other two moms, Stacey, and Tara were both around my age, perhaps a few years older, but not much. Stacey was also a divorced mom with three children. She was attractive and had a very successful career. Tara was one of the few happily married people I knew. She was always involved with school activities and served at vice president of the PTA.

I arrived at the school around noon, signed in, and made my way to my son's classroom. The kids were at lunch and then headed outside to recess so we had almost an hour to set up things for their party. I walked down the hall with Stacey talking about how we both thought it was ridiculous that the kids could no longer dress up for Halloween like we did as kids. Some parents several years back made a big stink about Halloween being a satanic holiday, blah, blah, blah, and the school board banned the kids from dressing up after that. They also renamed the Halloween party to Fall Harvest just to appease those few self-righteous individuals who liked to suck the fun out of childhood.

Becca and Tara were already in the empty classroom when we arrived. They were trying to hang a pumpkin piñata and having a difficult time. Stacey and I busied ourselves in the back of the room putting the treat bags together with poppers, various candies, and other goodies. We could hear the other two arguing over how to secure the piñata when finally, Tara told Becca she could do it alone. Stacey and I looked at each other and tried to keep a straight face.

We finished the preparations quickly since there wasn't much we were allowed to do. So, the four of us just stood in the back of the classroom talking quietly and waiting for the kids to get back from recess. Becca leaned over and said to Tara, "I'm sorry, I didn't mean to be so grumpy. I'm just having a bad week. Some kids decided to toilet paper my house, soap my windows, egg it and I don't know what they did to my lawn but there's little plastic things sticking out everywhere and we can't even walk across the yard."

"That's horrible. I'd be really upset too," Tara said sympathetically.

"I questioned my oldest daughter, Carla, about it. I mean, it has to be one of her friends or someone who's mad at her or something. She swears she has no idea who could have done it. But I made her clean it all up anyway." Suddenly I felt so bad for Carla. It hadn't occurred to me that she would be held accountable for what we did.

"Did you call the police?" Stacey asked.

"Of course, I did. If someone thinks they can mess with my house and not pay for the damage they did, they've got another thing coming," Becca huffed.

"I thought you just said they redecorated your house with toilet paper, soap, and eggs. That's not considered property damage." I looked over at her.

"Yeah, worthless police, they gave me the same speech. 'It's just a Halloween prank,' they said. They're not the ones who had to clean it up," Becca fumed.

"Neither were you," I remarked, and Stacey snickered.

"It was Carla's fault it happened, so she had to clean it up. It was her mess," Becca stated hatefully.

"Who knows, maybe it was somebody trying to teach you a lesson, not your daughter. You know, since you're always so sweet to people," I said just as I heard the kids coming down the hall.

Becca narrowed her eyes and glared at me, and I was positive she knew it was me and there was nothing she could do about it. She couldn't even respond because thirty little second graders came pouring through the door all hyped up from recess.

* * *

Mason was a quick study, and his sexual education was progressing beautifully. I was proud of how much he had learned since our first encounter. He was not even close to the same fumbling awkward little boy I had brought home from the bar that night. Now he had grown into quite the amazing lover, open-minded and submissive to anything my heart desired. He loved the growing exploration of his sexual awareness and never questioned any of the techniques I tried.

I tweaked my technique depending on Mason's body language rather than his verbal opinions. I loved trying new things with him and so far ejaculation denial seemed to be the most powerful tool for submissive behavior. I had pushed him up to three weeks at a time and he had in turn become the most pleasurable man a woman ever had. He went out of his way to endear himself to me. He had also gotten to the point that he absolutely loved his toy and craved it often. The intense sensations it aroused in him ways something that could not be matched in any other way.

And it was fun. Mason and I loved exploring this whole new sexual realm together. The level of intimacy it created between us was something neither of us had ever experienced before with past lovers. There was a level of trust, honesty, and devotion that only strengthened as time went on. As I moved forward in our adventures together it made me think on all the possibilities yet to be explored.

Chapter 21

MASON ZIPPED UP his duffle bag and walked back over to the bathroom door. I was standing over the sink brushing my teeth and getting ready for bed.

"Why don't you just come with me?" he pleaded for the hundredth time.

I spit out the toothpaste and rinsed my toothbrush off before putting it back in the holder. "Mason, we've been through this. No." I grabbed my mouthwash.

"Your parents will be happy to watch the boys? Or we can take them with us?"

"Seriously?" I rinsed and turned the water off. I brushed past him and climbed into bed. "One, I'm not leaving my boys over Thanksgiving. Two, your parents know you're dating *someone*. They know my name, but not my age. And three, do you really want them to find out in front of your entire family when the four of us show up? I don't think so." I turned off the lamp on my nightstand and snuggled down under the covers.

"Then I'll stay here." He climbed into bed beside me. "I don't want to leave you for four days."

"It's four days. It's not like it's four weeks or months. Besides, it will do you some good to see your family," I said, reasoning with him.

"But you three are my family." He leaned over and turned off the light on his nightstand.

"You know what I mean."

I rolled over and put my head on his shoulder. Mason wrapped his arm around me tightly and kissed the top of my head. "I'm going to miss you," he whispered.

"I'll miss you too."

I climbed up on him and ran my fingers over the sculpted muscles in his chest and broad shoulders. I loved the feel of his warm skin beneath my fingertips. My eyes held his and I could feel my heart rate beginning to increase. I playfully squeezed one of his nipples, making him smile up at me. I traced a finger slowly down the side of his face, across his jawline and over his lips . . . his full, shapely red lips. The corners of them turned up in a slight smile before he kissed my finger.

I leaned down and let my lips linger on his chest. I sucked on one of his nipples while pinching the other lightly. I could feel his hard cock beneath me twitching with anticipation. I moved my lips up to his shoulder and kissed it softly. I could taste the delicious salty taste of his skin and smell the faint fragrance of his cologne. My lips lingered on the small of his neck as I ran my tongue over it. My face hovered over his, our eyes locked together. I leaned a little closer and kissed his eyelids, then the tip of his nose. Finally, my lips found his. I brushed mine against his featherlike at first, then with a great deal more force. My tongue hungrily searched for his. My hands cradled his face. He entangled his fingers in the back of my hair and held me tightly against him. After a summer of instruction, Mason and I had mastered the art of sensual sexual pleasure. His hands ran over my back, feeling the warmth of my skin against his. He tightened his hold on me and rolled me over. I lay on my back looking up into his eyes. He kneeled in front of me and rested my feet against his chest. He entered me slowly, thrusting deeply as my body fully enclosed his hard cock. He leaned back slightly to feel the full pleasure of his thrust. He clasped my ankles and kissed my toes, running is tongue softly over them. I arched my back, pressing my pelvic bone against his and moaned loudly. My eyes held a smoldering contact with his as we melted into each other.

I wrapped my legs around his waist and pulled myself up into a seated position on his thighs. I kissed him with the fiery passion that was burning inside me. I loved the taste of him, the feel of him inside me. I could not get enough of him. I pushed him over onto his back. I straddled him, riding him in perfect rhythm. Our bodies moved together as one in unadulterated harmony. Mason moaned softly, enjoying each thrust of my hips back and forth as I allowed his hands to guide my body in synchronization with his.

He lifted his knees up to support my back and placed my feet on his shoulders. I could feel the spark of erotic energy move through our bodies. I moved gently, but firmly, back and forth feeling him deep inside me. I could feel our muscles contracting together, my clitoris rubbed deliciously across the small patch of hair at the base of his beautiful cock causing the perfect amount of friction. Mason's grip on my hips squeezed with more pressure, his rhythm back and forth increased. His hips arched trying to get as deep as he possibly could inside me. My hands grabbed his buttocks pulling into me. I let out a loud moan and leaned back against his knees, my dark hair cascading out over his shins.

I could feel the euphoric heat sizzling through my pelvic region and spread throughout my chest, across my arms reaching my fingertips while simultaneously enveloping my thighs and flowing down to my toes. The sensation engulfed my head leaving me in a state of adrenaline high that capped the mountain tops. My entire body quivered as I exploded in a glorious orgasm all over his hard-thick cock. Mason squeezed my hips and arched his back with all his strength as he screamed in pure delight. I could feel his hot cum shooting deep inside me. His beautiful face contorted in a mixture of uninhibited ecstasy and pure agony.

I collapsed forward, my body completely spent. I smiled into his eyes and kissed him with all the love I felt for him burning inside me.

Chapter 22

MASON LEFT for Thanksgiving in Chicago with his family on Wednesday afternoon. He left directly after class and headed north. I finished my last class before break and was looking forward to the long weekend. My folks picked the boys up from school and kept them for the night, so they could help my mom bake some pies for tomorrow. Now, with Mason gone, and no kids, I didn't know what to do with myself.

I stuffed my laptop in my backpack and walked out of the science building. It was a rainy autumn afternoon, and the temperature was dropping. The trees had already shed their leaves and the bare branches quivered in the wind. I opened my umbrella and fought against the wind trying to make my way across the large campus to where my car was parked in the lot by the student center. I was quickly losing the battle as my umbrella got turned inside out the third time by the wind.

Across the street from the main quad on campus was a bar and grill. I had never been there, but I knew it had been Isaac's favorite place to hang out between classes. I took off at a near run but was still completely soaked by the time I made it in the door. I figured I'd stay here for a while at least until the rain let up.

I sat down on a barstool and ordered myself a long island iced tea. I picked up the menu and thought I might as well have some dinner while I wait.

"Alex?" a voice said from behind me.

I turned around and saw my social psychology professor, Dr. Jefferson, waving from a corner booth. I waved hello back. She motioned me to join her. So, I picked up my drink and bag and walked over to her. She was surrounded by a pile of papers and was drinking a dirty martini.

"Please, join me." She waved at the seat across the table. "Sorry, about the mess." She gathered up her papers and stuffed them back into her bag. "I figured I'd get some grading done and have dinner while I was waiting on the rain to let up."

"Thanks, Dr. Jefferson," I slid into the booth. "I had the same idea; except I'm not grading papers."

"Please, call me Michelle. How is your semester going?"

"Busy." I took a slip of my drink.

"Dr. Johnston told me you've been tutoring a couple of the football players."

"Yes. It's been interesting. They are doing much better." I picked up the menu and began browsing again for something that looked good.

"He told me you've done an incredible job with them. He's been tracking their progress." She smiled and stirred her drink. "Have you thought about what path you're going to take after you finish school?"

"Some," I shrugged. "Right now, I am a double major for nursing and psychology. I was considering going after my nurse practitioner license specializing in mental health. But now I'm not so sure. I've been in the medical field for the better part of twelve years. I got my LPN right after high school and now I'm not so sure I want my RN."

"Have you considered teaching? I think you'd be good at it."

"Teaching? I don't know. It would depend on the grade."

"College level. I need a teaching assistant for next semester, and I'd love to have you work for me." She smiled.

"Really? I'd love that."

"Wonderful. We'll get together before the spring semester starts so you can fill out the paperwork. It's just a formality. The university loves paperwork." She sipped her drink as the waitress came over to take our orders.

Michelle and I ate our dinners and chatted about everything. I discovered that she was only two months old than me, was married, and had twin sons that were three years old. She loved teaching but was considering branching out more. She only taught two classes a semester and spent half her time at the VA Hospital counseling returning soldiers. That was her true passion. It turned out her brother had served in the Marines and was killed in a convoy bombing in Iraq several years ago. This was her way to stay connected to him.

I told her about my sons, Danny, and even Mason. She seemed to find it amusing and wonderful that I was involved with someone so much younger than myself. I confided in her that the relationship was not without its obstacles. Outside of college and sex, we had absolutely nothing in common and sometimes that put a real strain on our relationship. We had different tastes in music, hobbies, books, friends, and even how we spent our spare time.

She confided in me that her relationship with her husband was far from perfect also and that I shouldn't focus so much on the differences between Mason and me, but rather enjoy our similarities. By our third drink and halfway through our entrées, the subject turned to what classes I had taken. When I mentioned Dr. Wilson's Sex and Society class she let out a roar of laughter.

"I love that man. Don't you? I sat in on one of his classes after I'd heard several students discussing the material. It was outrageous and so open-minded. I blushed just sitting there listening to him. And he acts like it's no big deal. As if he was teaching biology or physics, not deviant desires of the flesh."

"I had to do a speech on female dominance for his class and let me tell you, I learned a great deal from it. More than I would probably ever admit. But so much that afterwards, it made me think about the aspects of classical and operant conditioning and combining them with the sensual art of tantric sex and female dominance. As in combining the techniques together in a complete sensual dominance of a man and controlling all aspects of his sexual desire. Things like teaching him how to use his cremaster muscle to control his ejaculation, adding pressure to the prostate gland to heighten his intensity, and rewarding him with an organism if he has pleased me," I admitted and ordered a fourth long island for myself.

"You're kidding me." She finished off her drink as if she was lost in thought. She motioned to the waitress to bring her another. "Have you actually tried this hypothesis?"

"Yes," I said as the waitress set down our drinks. "And it works." I raised my eyebrows and smiled.

"You should do your capstone research on that," she laughed. "I'm on the committee for grading those and at least that would be something outside the box and very intriguing. Have you considered turning your beanie boy into the topic of your research paper?"

"Oh, I'm sure he would love that," I laughed aloud.

"It's not like you should tell him. You're in your second year, correct?" I nodded. "Then by the time you get to your final year you should have plenty of complied data to write a paper. The age difference could make it even more appealing. You could title your project, The Freudian Slip." She couldn't restrain her laughter. "You should really forget about nursing and enroll for your masters at the Kinsey Institute in Bloomington."

"How about, The Pleasure Principle?" I suggested.

"Oh, my God. That's perfect. I love it."

"You really think I should keep a record of everything and turn it into my capstone research paper?"

"Of course, you should. Obviously, I would change the names and look up some more research on the topic. See if anyone else had conducted research like yours. I would imagine Dr. Wilson would be an invaluable resource in that area," she concluded.

"I don't think I could share such intimate details with the Capstone committee." I admitted.

"How much control do you have over this guy?" Michelle asked, raising one eyebrow.

So, I took a gulp of my long island iced tea and started at the beginning of Mason's training. I decided to take advantage of getting the perspective from someone who knew a little more about classical and operant conditioning than myself and told her the entire truth.

I began with the lemon drops, where it all started last April. I told her about the disastrous first attempt, his clumsiness, his lack of knowledge, and inability to control himself. I told her about the research I'd done, and finally, the way Mason's toys had affected him and how the ejaculation denial process had given me extremely promising results in creating a completely endearing young man.

As we finished off our dinners and drinks, I told her about the silk scarfs, the toys, the edging, and rewarding Mason for good behavior, control, and progress. She listened attentively and sipped her third dirty martini. I could tell she was completely captivated by my story or research. Whichever you wanted to call it.

"My goodness. That is amazing. Dr. Wilson would absolutely love it. You may have tapped into something that hasn't been studied yet. I mean, this gives a whole new spin on Freud's Oedipus complex during the phallic stage of development," she remarked.

"Honestly, I just thought it would be fun for me and it's not like he wasn't benefiting from it as well." I shrugged with a coy smile.

Michelle started laughing. "I'm sure he has been traumatized by the entire experiment."

"Well, not overly so, I hope." I thought of the night Mason broke down in tears and trembled in my arms.

"What do you mean?"

I went on to confess what had happened that night I introduced Mason to his new toy.

"I'm sure the intensity was new to him and shocked his system. I'm sure it did not lasting damage." Michelle assured me.

"I hope not. He kind of scared me that night, seeing him so vulnerable, but it brought us much closer." I confessed.

"I would imagine so. You probably created a level of intensity that no other woman would ever be able to duplicate for him." She raised her eyebrow at me.

"I guess I hadn't thought about that."

"What I'm saying is you've obviously built up a certain level of trust with Mason that allows him to let you control him. He's putting his physical and emotional wellbeing in your hands. I just can't escape the Freudian aspects of this whole cougar thing," she said more to herself than to me.

"That had crossed my mind, but as you can imagine, I quickly dismissed it. Especially considering I have two sons myself."

"Yeah, I can understand that. When you put it that way it's kind of creepy." She sighed and checked her watch. "Oh, my goodness. I need to get home. I still have to make a couple pumpkin pies for tomorrow."

I glanced down at my watch, and it was almost seven. We talked for nearly three hours. I couldn't believe it. She paid for both our dinners and drinks, and we gathered up our things.

"Thank you, Michelle. You didn't have to do that."

"No. Thank you. It was my pleasure. You saved me from eating alone. Plus, I've now got a teaching assistant for next semester."

We walked over to the door. Thankfully, it had finally stopped raining. "You have a great Thanksgiving, Alex. And don't worry about what others say. If you're both happy, that's all that matters."

"I will. Thanks. Happy Thanksgiving!"

Chapter 23

FOR ONCE I got to sleep without setting my alarm clock. I was thankful, but it felt odd waking up alone to a quiet house. I had become so use to having Mason beside me, and the boys making a racket trying to tell each other to hush. The silence was almost painful.

I crawled out of bed and turned on the shower. I let it warm up while I brushed my teeth. I still had a couple of hours before I was expected at my parents' house. I was absolutely dreading it. My older brother was going to be there along with his perfect wife and perfect children. I had no desire to see them. The two or three times a year when I was forced to be in their presence were more than enough for me. My brother, Colin, was a successful corporate attorney who lived in Chicago. Personally, I thought he was about as sleazy as they came, but then again, a lot of attorneys were. He was married to Charlotte, the single most pretentious woman this side of the Mississippi River. They had their two darling children who go to an elite private school that costs more in one year than my mortgage. Their eldest, Hunter, was fifteen and on the lacrosse team. He was class president and a straight A student. The perfect son. Their daughter, Misti, was 13, a diver and not just a diver on the school team. This kid competed on a national level and trained six days a week with a personal diving coach. And of course, she was also an A student. In comparison, my sons might as well be inbred, heathens born with tails.

On the brighter side, my sister Samantha was also going to be there. Most likely with her flavor of the month. She was the typical middle child who always felt deprived of parental attention. My mother had coddled and doted on Colin since the day he was born and my father . . . well, I was always Daddy's little girl. So where did that leave Sam? Apparently, doing anything and everything to draw attention to herself. She was the attention whore, the wild child, and admitted on more than one occasion, as someone who was only as faithful as her opportunities.

Her presence, if anything, would draw the topic away from my relationship with Mason and add some comic relief to the day. My sons adored her and thought she was hilarious because Sam lacked that brain mouth filter that we all tend to develop sometime in late adolescence. She was now thirty-six years old, never married, and had no children. Strangely enough, she was very successful in her career as some medical analyst something or other. It was her personal life that was always a train wreck of sorts. She traveled globally all the time and was rarely around. We were lucky to see her once every couple of years.

I let the hot water rain down over me. I felt as if all the energy had been sucked right out of me. I was so exhausted, and I hadn't even realized it until I got a chance to pause for half a second. I still had to make a pumpkin roll and sweet potato casserole to take to my parents' house. I stayed in the shower until the water ran cold.

I slipped into a teal tank top and a pair of teal, lime green, and royal blue polka dotted ladies boxer briefs. I brushed out my hair and pinned it up with chopsticks to keep it out of my face. I walked into the kitchen and noticed Mason's old iPod sitting on the island. I picked it up and began scrolling down his playlist. I knew he didn't use this anymore and had in fact given it to Max a few weeks ago because Max enjoyed many of the same tunes. I paused on the *Fun.* album. I remembered hearing it repeatedly over Labor Day weekend out on the lake. It was one of Emma's favorite groups. I placed in on the speaker dock on the corner of the counter and turned it up.

The music soared through the air and vibrated through the floor. I danced over to the refrigerator and took out the ingredients I needed. Somehow the music made me feel so much better. Almost as if it breathed some life back into my body. I even surprised myself with how many of the lyrics I remembered.

* * *

I arrived at my parents' house by one. My brother and his family were already there. Charlotte was in the kitchen talking with my mother, but not helping. Charlotte does not cook. She also does not clean. I'm not even sure if she knows how. She has a full-time housekeeper that takes care of all of that for her. The only thing she does do is raise money for various charities and sit on the PTA board. As far as I could tell, she was pretty much a useless snob.

My dad and Colin were in Dad's study discussing investments my brother thought my dad should be making. My sons were watching football and playing on their DS's. Hunter was reading on the sun porch while Misti was typing on her laptop.

I set the pumpkin roll and sweet potato casserole down on the island on my way to the family room to kiss my boys. Both of them looked miserable as they always did whenever my brother's family was in town and they were forced to spend time with them.

"Can we go now?" Max whispered. "This is so boring."

"I know. But we have to at least have dinner first." I kissed him on the cheek.

"Can we get it to go?" He smiled mischievously.

"I wish." My sons understood there was no love lost between my brother and me.

"Promise we'll leave as soon as dinner is done," he pleaded.

"Promise."

I kissed Henry hello, took a deep breath, and made my way back into the kitchen. Charlotte was seated at the island wearing a designer dress suit and regaling Misti's latest triumph on the national diving team. My mother had her hair pinned up the way she did on every holiday. She was wearing a dress and heels and a nice apron covering it in case she spilled something on it. There was a bead of sweat on her brow as she was trying to accomplish ten things at once.

"Hello, Mother," I kissed her on the cheek. "What can I do to help?"

"Can you please set the table and fix the drinks?" She pulled the twenty-pound turkey out of the oven.

"Sure." I went over to the hutch in the dining room and got out my mom's good china that she only used on holidays.

"Hi, Alex," Charlotte said with fake sincerity. "How have you been? How is college?"

"Fine. Just fine." I set the plates down on the table and started passing them around.

"I think it's wonderful for someone your age to go back to school. It takes a lot of guts to go back and take classes with a bunch of kids. But your mother told us you like them. In fact, she said you're dating a twenty-one-year-old kid. Why would you do something so absurd and humiliating?"

"What I do is none of your business, Charlotte." I went over to the drawer where the silverware was kept. "Thanks, Mother." I whispered as I passed her by.

"I didn't think Mason was a secret," my mom replied.

"He isn't," I flashed an annoyed look her way.

As I put the last of the silverware in place, my brother came up and kissed me on the cheek. "I hear you're shopping in the junior section these days and not for your sons," he casually remarked.

"Mind your own business." I shoved past him.

"Oh, come on," Colin remarked. "Alex, it was a joke. Albeit not a humorous one. Sort of sad really."

"Colin . . ." I began but quickly stopped myself. I had played this game with him a dozen times and knew it wasn't worth it. Colin was an SOB, always had been, always will be. And nothing I ever did was ever going to be good enough in his eyes. Not me, nor my children.

My dad was sitting down in the family room between my sons watching the game. It amazed me how Colin and I came from the same background yet could not be more different than night and day. I was more laid back and tackled life head on like our father, while Colin was very uptight, judgmental, and arrogant like our mother.

Just then, the front door opened, and Samantha blew in like a hurricane, tugging with her a nice-looking man who looked painfully uncomfortable. She was wearing brown slacks and an ivy sheer blouse. Her dark brown hair was styled perfectly and flowed gracefully over her shoulders. She immediately took off her gorgeous cream-colored dress coat and laid it across the back of the chair by the front door and dropped her pocketbook in the seat.

"Alex!" She wrapped me in a bear hug. "How are you? You look great. Where's my boys?" She immediately grabbed both my sons and wrapped her arms around them. "Oh, I'm so rude. I'm sorry." She turned back to the man she'd left standing in the foyer. "This is my fiancé, Oliver." She dragged the poor man front and center. "Oliver, this is my baby sister, Alex and her two sons, Max and Henry. And this is my father, Jack Carlton."

The two men shook hands and exchanged pleasantries while I pulled my sister off to the side. "Fiancé? When did this happen?"

"He asked me when we were in London last month." She showed me the huge rock on her finger.

"How long have you been dating this guy?"

"About a year." She glanced over and saw him looking scared and nervous. "I'll tell you all about it later." She left me standing there and rejoined Oliver.

I quickly went back into the kitchen and set another place at the table. I briefly heard Charlotte rambling on about a near disaster she recently experienced when someone bumped into her spilling her gourmet coffee all over this "gorgeous pair of suede boots, ruining them forever." To hear her describe the tragedy, I would have thought several people were standing around staring at her in horror as tears poured down their cheeks. I rolled my eyes behind her back getting a grin from my mother.

"Did I hear Sam come in?" mom asked.

"Yes, and she brought a friend."

"Oh good, Oliver came with her. I've been dying to meet him." My mom wiped her hands on her apron and smoothed out her dress before waltzing into the family room.

"Who's Oliver?" Charlotte inquired.

"Samantha's fiancé."

"I didn't know she was engaged. No one said anything to me about it." Like it wasn't important because she wasn't consulted.

"Huh? Imagine that." I muttered on my way out of the room, leaving her alone in the kitchen.

I joined Max off to the side of the family room watching the various greetings and introductions. Charlotte wandered in shortly after I did and took a hold of my brother and waited for the right moment to turn the conversation on her and her sparkling children. Max looked up at me and rolled his eyes. I smiled back at him in agreement. True, my kid might not be a diver on the national team, but I could guarantee Ms. Prissy Pants over there didn't share this kind of bond with her child.

When we were all finally squeezed into my parents' large dining room table, Mom said grace before we dug in. The food smelled delicious, and everything looked picture perfect. My dad stood up and carved the bird. It wasn't long before everyone started talking at once and no one was listening to anyone else. Colin started grilling Oliver about his financial portfolio until Samantha finally reached her limit.

"Okay, big brother. This is supposed to be a holiday dinner, not a job interview," Samantha said lightly, hoping he would take the hint.

"I'm just curious. I wasn't trying to offend." Colin smiled in a fake manner.

"So how is school going, Alex?" Samantha tried to change the subject.

"It's great. I love it. I'm tutoring this semester. I'm working with two guys on the football team helping them with psychology as a social science. I really enjoy it." I smiled at her from across the table.

"Tutoring?" Charlotte turned towards me. "Isn't that a little humiliating? I mean, it's a student's job."

"Charlotte!" Samantha glared at her.

"What?" Charlotte tried to look innocent.

"Enough." Sam held her glare.

"Well, it is. I'm just stating the obvious." Charlotte looked back over at me. "You can't tell me you aren't humiliated tutoring jocks and doing a job that a nineteen-year-old can do."

"I don't know why she would be; she apparently likes college students so much she's forgotten that she's an adult responsible for two impressionable young sons. I honestly cannot believe Danny has not intervened," Colin said with an authoritative voice.

"For your information, asshole, I take very good care of my sons. And I am very proud of being a tutor, and I work very hard in school. I've made the Dean's List every semester. I am the one who does all their school activities, their sports, helps them with their homework, cooks, cleans, and tucks them in bed every night. How dare you question anything I do. You can kiss my ass, you, pompous jerk." I stood up and threw my napkin down on the table. "You can all kiss my ass."

Everyone froze. All eyes were locked on me. I moved my chair out of the way and walked over to the head of the table. "I'm sorry, Dad," I leaned over and kissed him on the cheek. "I just can't." I reached for my sons' hands and pulled them to their feet. "Get your things," I told them, and they immediately took off down the hall to my parents' guest bedroom. Henry looked confused, but Max was smiling.

My boys came back in with their backpacks. I rushed them off to the car barely grabbing my purse on our way out. "Thanks, Momma." Max looked relieved. "I really don't like Hunter and Misti. They always gloat about how much better they are than us and they brag about how much money they have."

"Hunter and Misti don't have any money. Neither does that money sucking leech wife of his. Colin is the one with a job," I remarked and immediately regretted it. "I'm sorry guys, I shouldn't have said that."

Henry giggled from the backseat. "It's okay, Momma. I don't like turkey."

"Me neither," Max added.

"You know what? I don't either." I pulled into the nearest grocery store. "I say we start our own Thanksgiving tradition." I smiled at my sons.

The boys cheered.

"So, what sounds good to you guys?" Max pushed the cart and Henry skipped along beside us happily.

"I don't care," Max muttered.

"I want Twinkies," Henry sang out.

"I hate Twinkies," Max stated.

"Okay, we've got to agree on something." I stopped in front of the bakery. Not a good place to stop with children.

"Let's have tacos," Max suggested. "Like soft tacos with chicken or that spicy steak."

"Yeah, yeah! Let's have tacos!" Henry agreed.

"Okay. Tacos it is. What about desserts?"

"No pumpkin pie," Henry stated. "I want an apple one."

"With ice cream on top," Max added.

We gathered up everything we needed to make our feast. I even tossed in a box of Twinkies for Henry and gave him a wink. We also threw in several things that weren't required but, considering how this day had started, were necessary. This was positively the most bizarre Thanksgiving dinner I had ever prepared.

The boys and I danced around the kitchen while the spicy chicken and steak sizzled on the stove. I had promised the boys we could put up the Christmas tree and decorations after we finished our feast. We normally waited until tomorrow, but it was something I thought we could all use.

As the three of us were dancing around the kitchen, singing at the top of our lungs to *City of Angels* by Thirty Seconds to Mars, I spun Max around and ran smack into my dad.

"Is this *The Voice* or *Dancing with the Stars*?" he laughed at me.

"Dad? What are you doing here?" I walked over and turned the music down.

"I wanted to make sure you were all right. And I thought I would see if you would consider coming back with me?" He walked over to the stove. "That smells fabulous. What are you making?"

"Spicy chicken and steak tacos," Henry told him.

"For Thanksgiving?" Dad's eyes shifted from the boys to me.

"We decided it was time to start our own Thanksgiving traditions." I smiled over at my sons who nodded in agreement.

"Mind if I join you?"

"Won't you get in trouble?"

"Ah, I'm sure they'll eat without me." He sat down at my kitchen table and lifted Henry up on his lap. "After all, the turkey was dried out." He tickled Henry a bit.

"Nana's gonna be mad at you," Henry told him.

"She's always mad at me. Why should today be any different?" My dad tousled Henry's hair.

We ate cafeteria style. The boys seemed much more relaxed than they did at my parents' house. Even my dad seemed to be in a better mood. My dad confessed that he got into a huge blowout with my three tormentors shortly after I left. He even told them that he was tired of my brother meddling in his finances, advising him on his retirement and told all of them that he was tired of their 'holier than thou' routine.

I tried my best not to laugh, just for the sake of my sons, not my dad. I'd heard most of this before. It happened about every other holiday in our family. No matter, things would return to normal, at least normal for our family, by Christmas. Therefore, it was hard to take these constant little family spats too seriously.

*　*　*

I sat down on my couch at the end of what turned out to be probably the best Thanksgiving of my life. Nat King Cole was singing Christmas carols softly from my CD player. The luminous glow from the Christmas tree lights gave a warm hue to my family room. My dad stayed the remainder of the day and helped us drag the Christmas tree box out of the shed along with several boxes of decorations. It took us almost four hours to get it all put together. Once the lights were on the tree my dad and sons decorated the tree together while I put the village on the mantel. Afterwards, the four of us gorged on popcorn and M&M's and watched our favorite Christmas movie, *Christmas Vacation*.

My mom had called my dad several times, but he ignored each call. She also tried my phone twice to no avail. Danny never even called to wish his sons a happy Thanksgiving. I took a sip of my red wine and relaxed. The boys were sleeping soundly, and I was sure my dad was getting an earful for spending the day with us. Colin and his family were staying with my parents through the weekend. I couldn't imagine them coming by my house, but I feared my dad was in for a very long weekend.

Chapter 24

THE TIME BETWEEN Thanksgiving break and final exams is a long and excruciating marathon for every college student. It involves an endless stream of papers, notes, study guides, and textbooks. For the majority of students, it was a time of pure panic and wishing they'd paid closer attention in class or took better notes. It was a period of long nights spent hunched over textbooks and cramming in an entire semester's worth of knowledge into their brain. An overachieving student determined to graduate with high honors functions for these two and a half weeks on pure anxiety, caffeine, unbelievable stress, exhaustion, and extreme mood swings. Unfortunately, both Mason and I fell into the latter category.

The boys were wonderful. They helped around the house more than they usually did. Max attempted to fix dinner for everyone: grilled cheese and tomato soup. Henry tried to load the dishwasher. I thanked him and paid him a dollar for it then rearranged the dishes in it after he went to sleep. I truly appreciated their effort. It was so sweet of them to try to help out. They were both unusually well behaved. However, I wasn't sure if it was them being considerate of my finals or the fact that Christmas was creeping up on us. Either way, I wasn't going to argue.

Lisa was invaluable. She took Henry to his basketball practice the week of finals and my dad took Max. My mother still wasn't speaking to me for walking out on Thanksgiving, but I didn't have much time to give it any thought.

I worked diligently with Nate and Derek for their psychology final. They both really dug in their heels and put in the hours. It was a struggle, especially having to go back and learn those first two chapters they'd bombed the exam over. But they did it. Nate tracked me down at the library after his final and was ecstatic about his eighty-six percent. He hugged me tightly literally jumping up and down. I couldn't help but laugh at his enthusiasm and told him repeatedly how proud I was of him.

Derek surprised me the most. He really went above and beyond, determined to succeed. He even showed me a couple poster boards he created diagraming various topics and material. He'd made himself flash cards for the terminology from all ten chapters along with chapter outlines. I was impressed by the amount of time and effort he put into learning the material. He walked away with one of the highest scores out of all the classes for the semester. I was so incredibly proud of him.

And between worrying about my finals and when I was going to find the time to go Christmas shopping, I hadn't given my talk with Michelle much thought since Mason returned. We were both so busy and worn out from studying, we had no energy left for playtime.

*   *   *

Mason and I left campus together after our last final of the semester. We had six days until Christmas, and we were spent, both mentally and physically. I had more coffee running through my veins than blood. We headed straight to the downtown mall to begin our Christmas shopping for the boys. Mason had insisted on accompanying me even though he wasn't going to be there to see them open them up. He was going back to Chicago in two days to spend the entire break with his family. He wasn't planning to return until a week after New Year's.

He mentioned it briefly when he got back from his Thanksgiving trip. We had barely discussed it. I was hoping that since he went home for Thanksgiving that he would stay with us for Christmas. I knew the boys were disappointed that he was leaving even though neither of them had mentioned it.

Mason and I raided the toy store first. I got Henry a new RC monster truck, an Star Wars Legos set, and a ton of other things Mason kept sticking in the cart. He was the easy child to shop for. I picked up a couple X-Box games Max had mentioned and a game for Henry. Then I got them both some new clothes and a Colts hooded sweatshirt from the sports shop. I also got Max a new pair of casual shoes Mason picked out. I wanted to pick up something for Mason, but I couldn't find a way to get rid of him for a while. I was running out of time, not to mention I had absolutely no clue what to get him.

* * *

The boys played video games with Mason while I cooked dinner. I fixed a roast and all the trimmings along with some homemade yeast rolls. The fragrance that lingered over the kitchen was heavenly. All I could hear was yelling and jibbing at each other from the family room. Sometimes it was almost impossible to tell exactly which ones were the children.

After dinner was cleaned up and the boys finished their schoolwork, we all settled around the family room with blankets and pillows. Mason had started a fire to take the chill out of the air and I surprised the boys by putting in an old favorite of theirs, *A Christmas Story*. The boys had most of the dialogue memorized and would recite it back and forth to each other.

I turned off all the lights except for the Christmas tree. Between them and the fireplace the room felt warm and toasty. I snuggled in with Mason on the couch with Henry sprawled out beside me with his head in my lap. Max flopped down across the loveseat with Billy munching on kettle corn. I swear that boy was a bottomless pit. He did nothing but constantly eat.

Later, Mason carried a sleeping Max to his bed. He had gotten so big in the last year, so I was no longer able to carry him. Max didn't even flinch when Mason picked him up or put him in his bed. A tornado could tear the roof off our house and Max would never even budge. I couldn't believe the child was such a sound sleeper.

I lifted a sleeping Henry off the couch. He wrapped his little arms and legs around me and put his head down on my shoulder. I carried him to his room and put him down gently on his bed. He barely stirred and whispered, "I love you, Momma." I brushed soft brown hair away from his eyes and kissed him on the forehead.

"I love you too, little buddy. Sweet dreams," I whispered before I snuck out of his room, closing his door partway.

I checked the doors one last time just to make sure everything was locked up tightly for the night. On my way to my room I paused in the hallway in front of my sons' room. From this angle I could see them both sleeping soundly. Henry curled up in the fetal position with his little hand tucked up under his face. And Max, lying out on his back with his legs kicked out and arms above his head. He looked as if he'd been knocked out cold.

My angels. I could have easily stood there all night and watched them sleep. They looked so peaceful and beautiful.

Mason was already in the shower when I made it to my room. The bathroom door was closed, and I could hear him singing something. I couldn't quite make out the words. I snuck in only to be hit in the face by a wall of steam. I could barely see across the bathroom. I quickly slipped out of my clothes and climbed into the shower with him.

"I'm going to miss you so much." He took me in his arms and looked down at me. "Especially this."

"Me too," I reached up and brushed my lips over his. "I wish you didn't have to go."

"It's only for a couple weeks. I'll be back before the semester kicks back in," he reassured me. "I wish I was going to be here to see the boys open their gifts."

"I know. I do too. They are really going to miss you."

I shampooed my hair and then poured some body wash on my loofah. I lathered it up well and began washing Mason's body very softly, tracing it longingly over every muscular ripple, every luscious curve. With my other hand I lightly ran my fingertips through the suds. I loved the stature of his frame, the strength of his muscles, the way they bulged, glistened in the light with the shower raining down upon them.

I slipped my hand between his legs and stroked his already hard dick. I lathered it up and teased him until a low moan escaped his chest. I gently nudged him back beneath the water and played with him until the bubbles were washed away. His eyes embraced mine as I kneeled down before him and took him into my mouth. He was throbbing with desire as I slipped it down my throat. Mason braced himself against the side of the shower and tilted his head back under the water letting it wash over the both of us. I loved tormenting him, tempting him, making him crazy with desire. I wanted to make sure that I haunted his thoughts and his dreams the entire time he was away.

The last of the hot water drifted down the drain. Mason reached behind him and turned the faucet off. He slipped a towel over my shoulders and drew me to my feet kissing me deeply. We barely toweled each other off before we stumbled into bed fully embraced. I untangled myself from his arms and opened the top drawer of my night table. I emptied a few droplets of massage oil into my hand and rubbed my hands together, fully coating them.

Mason rested back against the pillows and relaxed, watching me intently. I kneeled beside his body at his waist and prepared to give him a lingam massage, a favorite technique of his. Rather than pleasuring him quickly, I wanted to draw this night out fully. I began teasing him longingly, caressing the thickness of his erection, letting my fingers explore his entire genital area.

Our eyes locked onto each other as we synchronized our breathing. I used long hand over hand strokes moving from his testes to the base and upwards at a firm snail pace. Every few minutes I would change up my pace and the firmness of my grasp from strong to featherlike just to watch the expression of pure torturous desire on his face. He squirmed beside me and tried to take a hold of his cock, but I pushed his hand away.

"No," I said in a sultry voice.

"Please . . .," he pleaded.

"You know better." I paused to let him gain some control over his excitement.

"I'm sorry." He drew in a deep breath and tried to refocus himself.

His muscles relaxed, and his breathing returned to matching my pace. My fingers gingerly explored the glans, the underside of his shaft, the base where it connected to his body, slightly tugged on his balls, and ran lightly over his perineum. Mason struggled to remain focused and keep his breathing with mine. I interlocked my fingers and moved them up and down at a steady speed. I purposely ran my thumbs over the extremely sensitive frenulum area on the underside of the head of his cock. Mason squirmed in pure agony.

I reached into the nightstand and brought out his favorite toy. He smiled at me with a devilish grin and squirmed a little more. I coated his toy with lubricant and rubbed it lightly across his scrotum, teasing him and enjoying the torture it brought about in him. Mason lifted his knees and spread his legs a bit further apart to give me easier access to him. I loved how much this excited him.

I entered him slowly, knowing how badly he wanted it. A low moan escaped from deep inside him as I pushed just a little further in. He arched his back and rocked his hips towards me, his body begging for more. I eagerly complied. I increased my rhythm watching his breathing becoming more labored as the intensity of the toy rubbing against his prostate almost brought him to the peak of his desire.

Leaving his toy securely in place, I relented and pulled him on top of me in a compact embrace. He pressed his lips on my mouth, his tongue hungrily devouring mine. I gazed into his eyes as an unspoken message telling him to slow down. Mason immediately complied. He brought his hand up beside my face and stroked it lovingly, never breaking our eye contact.

I kept my legs together in this causing a delicious snugness between us. His cock rubbed against my clitoris in parallel movements. He would pull himself almost all the way out and then reentered me fully. I had to fight against my own orgasm. It wasn't long before I felt myself losing control. Mason kissed me again, but with less urgency as he knew how tormented I truly was by his actions.

I lifted my hips off the bed and parted my legs, wrapping them completely around him. Mason raised his body to match my own. On his knees, he placed one hand on my hip and caressed my thigh with the other. I thrust upward into him with all the strength I had in me. He felt so amazing, so hard. We quickened our speed until we both collapsed in pure ecstasy.

We fell against the pillows and let our breathing return to normal. I was lightheaded and numb from the waist down from the intensity of our orgasm. I think I could have slept for a month.

"I'm really going to miss you," Mason said breathlessly.

"And I'm really going to miss your cock!" I reached over and grabbed it making him jump. "Touchy." I kissed him playfully on the cheek.

Chapter 25

I DROVE UP to campus on Monday afternoon before classes resumed on Wednesday for a meeting with Michelle. The temperature had dropped dramatically after Christmas. Our mild start to winter had disappeared overnight. Big grey clouds hung heavy over the city and large fluffy flakes drifted down covering the world below it in a cold wet blanket.

I parked in the lot across from the science building and hurried over the wet snow as quickly as I could as the wind picked up in intensity. I knew this meeting was just a formality of paperwork, but I hoped it wouldn't last too long. I was afraid the roads were only going to make my drive home that much more miserable. Not to mention Mason was driving down from Chicago today and according to the weatherman, the weather was even worse where he was at.

Michelle was sitting at her desk surrounded by piles of papers and books. She had pictures of her twins in various sized frames on the window shelf and snapshots of them pinned on her corkboard. There was one plant in the corner that looked like it had seen better days and a large plastic Mike Wazowski wearing his *Monster's Inc.* hardhat leaning against a file cabinet. I tapped lightly on the open door.

"Dr. Jefferson?"

"Alex?" She looked up and put her pen down. "Hi, I'm glad you could make it. Have a seat." She motioned towards the chair in front of her desk. "How are the roads?"

"Getting slick," I said, sitting down.

"I was afraid of that. I think I'll be leaving here early." She moved some papers around and pulled out a stack from the bottom of a pile. "I've just got a few papers for you to fill out." She handed them over to me.

I filled out the employment application and signed all the necessary forms in a few minutes. I double checked it all and handed the packet back over to her. "I think that's it."

She browsed through them quickly before dropping them in her top drawer. She gave me a brief description of my new position, informing me for the first time that I would be teaching her classes one day a week and she would conduct the other. I would also be responsible for administering all exams, helping students with their papers, and grading assignments. I was both excited and terrified at the prospect of this new position.

*   *   *

I was surprised when I turned the corner down my street to see Mason's car sitting in the driveway. I barely got my car in the garage before I hopped out and ran inside. He was in the kitchen making a snack when I came through the garage door.

"Hello, darling." I quickly wrapped my arms around him and immediately kissed him. "I'm glad you made it back in one piece. I was worried. The roads are getting bad."

"I couldn't wait to see you." He held me tighter and pressed his lips against mine.

"I missed you so much."

"I missed you too. How was your break?"

"Fine. How's the family?" I inquired.

"Good. Loud." He grinned and let me go. "My parents' place was like a circus."

"But that's a good thing."

"Not when you're trying to sleep. My little brothers and sisters like to get up early and they don't believe in letting anyone sleep in. I'm glad your boys aren't like that." He took a bite of his sandwich.

"Anything exciting happen?" I climbed up on a bar stool and relaxed for a moment.

"Not so much. Lots of family and all that," he remarked casually.

"Did you have a good time?"

"My dad grilled me on what I was learning in school and 'how important it is that I be prepared for the real working world'," he said, mocking his dad.

"He's just being a concerned dad," I grinned.

"Whatever. It's not like I'm goofing off. To hear him lecture you'd think I was preparing for med school or something." He took another bite and washed it down with a Coke. "It's not like I can argue with him. He's paid for my education." He shrugged with his mouth full.

As a parent I understood exactly what Mason's dad was saying and agreed with him completely. I patted him on the shoulder and Mason picked up his bag and went to unpack his things. He was home.

*   *   *

The semester began without fail. I sat in on Michelle's Thursday morning back-to-back classes. I sat over at her desk while she introduced herself and me to the classes and listened intently to how she spoke and managed her students. It was a totally different experience viewing things from this seat as opposed to when I was sitting in one of the others. I was terrified of taking over on Tuesday morning and doing this on my own.

After class, Michelle and I walked together over to the Bar and Grill for lunch. She handed me a packet that contained the class syllabus, study guides, worksheets, and various teaching techniques as helpful guides.

"Don't worry. I'll be here if you have any questions," Michelle assured me.

"Thanks." I put everything in my backpack. "They look a little intimating," I admitted.

"You'll do fine. It's just like working with Nate and Derek, just on a larger scale. Would you like a drink?" she asked as the waitress approached.

"Just regular iced tea. I've got an honors speech at one fifteen and I don't want to show up for the first class with a buzz," I grinned.

"Yeah, probably not a good idea." She ordered two iced teas for us.

We scanned over the menu for a moment deciding what looked good. The waitress returned with our drinks, and we placed our orders.

"So . . . how are things with you and Mason? Did you meet his family over the holidays?"

"No, he went back home to Chicago, and I stayed here. I don't believe his family knows much about me."

"Have you thought about why he's keeping you a secret?" She raised a quizzical brow.

"I don't know." I fiddled with my straw. "I'm sure he's concerned they'll react the same as mine, probably even worse." I chuckled. "I know if he was one of my boys, I wouldn't be too happy about it."

"But as a mom, all you ultimately want is for your sons to be happy." She pointed out. "Even if they decide to be with someone you don't approve of." Michelle stated.

"True. I just hope it never comes down to that."

"As a mom, no one is ever going to be good enough for our sons." She laughed. "At best, just hope you can tolerate their choice."

"Good to know." I snickered.

"Have you made substantial progress with Mason?" she asked as the waitress placed lunch on the table.

"Not as much as I'd like. Since he went home for Thanksgiving and Christmas breaks. He just returned Monday. And of course, there was that sort of lull period between Thanksgiving and Christmas break when we were both focused on finals so not much new training was involved. But he is gaining ground on control of his erection, his stamina has improved greatly and finally, he's mastered the ability to only ejaculate with permission. We're still working on mastering the art of having an orgasm without ejaculating."

"You do realize that you've ruined this guy, right?" she asked, drowning her fry in ketchup.

"How do you mean?"

"He's so attuned to you that no other woman will ever be able to please him with an intensity that would even be comparable," Michelle explained.

"Huh?" I wasn't sure what to think of that.

"I'm just saying, you've told me you don't foresee this as a relationship with longevity, correct?"

"He's twenty-one," I said as if that said it all.

"So, what happens when he moves on to his next relationship?"

"Dustin Hoffman seemed to turn out fine despite his affair with Mrs. Robinson," I remarked lightheartedly.

"Touché." She held up her drink and we clinked glasses.

Chapter 26

I NEVER WOULD HAVE thought about it before, but I dearly loved being a teaching assistant for Michelle. Our students were a great group of young adults to work with, some more than others, but for the most part I couldn't have asked for a better group. It didn't take me long to fall into a new routine. I was getting used to my life switching drastically every four months now and it wasn't as difficult as it once had been.

Mason had been bugging me to let him sit in on one of the classes I got to teach. At first, I was too nervous to let him, but by the end of February I caved in only under the condition that he sit with the other students and keep his mouth shut. A silent observer.

We parked in the lot across from the science building. It was almost a balmy fifteen degrees out with a good six inches of snow on the ground. The roads were still a little sluggish despite all the salt the city had tried to lay down when they cleaned the roads. We trudged across the parking lot shivering against each other. I slipped on the sidewalk in front of the building as soon as we crossed the street. I came down hard on my right knee and almost took Mason down with me.

"Damn it!"

"Are you all right?" He helped me back to my feet.

"Yeah," I muttered although I had my doubts.

Mason helped me into the building and held the door open for me. I leaned on him just a bit as we made our way to the classroom. I arrived about ten minutes later than I usually did, and most of the class had already beaten me there. I let go of Mason's arm before we reached the doorway. He walked in after me and took a seat in the back of the room over by the windows.

I hobbled up to the front and set my backpack on the top of the teacher's desk. I unzipped my coat and removed it along with my scarf and laid it down on the chair.

"Are you all right, Miss Rose?" Megan, one of my students, asked.

"Yes, I just smacked my knee on the ice outside the building." I walked around to the front of my desk and pulled myself up on it. Normally I would never sit at the desk to teach the class but today, all I could think of was getting weight off my knee.

"Ouch," Ian remarked.

I let the students chat with each other for several minutes after the start of class while I tried to get my stuff out of my backpack and somewhat organized beside me. "Okay guys, settle down."

"Miss Rose . . ." Megan nodded towards the dry erase board behind me.

I spun around still seated on the desk and looked at what she was referring to. Someone, I had a pretty good idea of whom, had scrawled across the board in big sloppy letters: I love you Alex, you are a hot MILF.

"Megan, please erase that." She immediately complied. "Who wrote that?" Several of the boys couldn't hide their smiles very well, but they were all trying to look as innocent as possible. "Christian?"

"How did you know it was me?" His smile gave him away.

"Honestly?" He giggled. "How old are you?"

"Legal." Christian grinned from ear to ear. I gave him my annoyed mom look and he sat up straight in his chair and answered. "Eighteen."

"Do you think that was an appropriate comment?" He shook his head. "What were you expecting to accomplish by writing such a thing on the board?"

"I don't know," he replied sheepishly.

"See me after class."

"Yes, Miss Rose."

"Okay, today we are going to begin our discussion on relationships. What makes people attracted to one another? Do opposites really attract or are people who have common interests more likely to have a successful relationship?"

A little over an hour later I dismissed the class. Today's topic had spurred a lively discussion and we barely got through the necessary material. As the students filed out of the room, Christian made his way up to my desk. He looked terribly young and uncomfortable as he stood before me.

"I'm sorry, Miss Rose. It was only meant as a joke," he explained.

"Not a very humorous one, I'm afraid and quite disrespectful, wouldn't you agree?"

"Yes, ma'am."

"Food for thought, Christian. Treat every female you meet as you would like someone to treat your mother."

"Yes, ma'am. I'm sorry." He looked down at the floor.

"Fine. You may go now." He hurried out as quickly as he could without looking back.

Mason finally walked to the front of the classroom as I was putting my things back into my bag. He clapped his hands with a big smile across his shapely lips. "You were amazing. I had no idea you were such a great professor."

"Thanks," I blushed.

"I almost said something to you when I sat down and saw what was written on the board."

"It's not a big deal. I just wanted to embarrass Christian for it." I shrugged.

"I almost said something to him. That was most disrespectful to you."

"I can handle myself, thank you very much. Now I've got another class to teach, if you're going to stay, take your seat. If not, you'd better get going." I kissed him briefly on the cheek.

"I'm staying, but I'm going to grab some coffee. Would you care for some?"

"Yes, please."

Once Mason disappeared, I slipped my boot off to have a look at my knee. It was already a little swollen and hard to get my jeans over, but I managed. There was a rainbow of colors covering it in all shades of red, purple, blue, and black. It looked grotesque, but I could bend it without any problem, so I was sure I didn't do any real damage to it. Most likely, it was just going to be sore for the next week.

Chapter 27

MASON SEEMED unusually cheery as he waltzed into the kitchen from campus. It was about an hour past the normal time he arrived home. I was in the middle of dinner and Henry was at the table writing his spelling words. Max had retreated to his room to finish his science homework.

"Hey, what smells so good?" Mason inquired with a quick kiss on the cheek.

"I made a chicken pot pie. It should be done in about a half hour. You hungry?"

"Starved. I was just talking with Jared and Josiah." He dropped his backpack on the island and sat down beside Henry and looked at his paper. "Whatcha working on?"

"Spelling words," Henry replied.

"Why bother." He nudged Henry in a playful way. "Isn't that what spell check is for?"

"Mason!" I gave him a discouraging look and my little boy giggled.

"You're in trouble," I heard Henry mumble under his breath.

"It's your fault," Mason whispered back.

"Is not."

"Is so."

"Is not." Henry pushed him as hard as he could. "And no tag backs."

"All right you two. Knock it off," I scolded them both with a grin.

Mason grabbed some animal crackers out of the pantry and leaned against the counter munching on them. He gave Billy one for every two he ate. I had told him and the boys numerous times not to feed her our food but none of them ever listened and Billy had learned a long time ago they couldn't say no to her.

"Have you given any thought to spring break this year?" Mason asked out of nowhere.

"No. Why?" I started setting the table around Henry and his schoolwork.

"I talked with Jared and Josiah after class this afternoon and everyone has decided to go to Cancun and they invited us to go with them," he said excitedly.

"And I suppose you want to go?" It was obviously a stupid question.

"Of course! It will be great! And we need a break," he reasoned, reaching for some more crackers.

"Our spring break is two weeks before the boy's. I can't go," I said, although I hated to tell him that.

"Just leave them with your parents. They'll watch them." Henry immediately looked up with a worried expression on his face.

"We'll discuss this later." I gave Mason a dirty look.

*   *   *

Two days later after the boys were asleep and I crawled into bed beside Mason, he rolled over and wrapped his arms around me. "So, have you given it any more thought?"

"Given what anymore thought?" I had all but forgotten Cancun.

"Spring break." He kissed me sweetly.

"I told you, I can't go, Mason. I've got responsibilities here. I'm not sending my boys to my parents, so I can play on the beach for a week in Mexico."

"Why not? They watched them Labor Day weekend," he reminded me.

"That was two nights. You're talking about a week," I said.

"Nine days, but what's the difference? Your parents won't care."

"Mason!" I sat up completely stunned. "I care. These are my sons you're talking about. I'm not going. Why can't you understand? This is not a game. I'm not playing house. I am responsible for them." I tried not to raise my voice.

"I get that! I do, but you've got to live life a little. You can't put life on hold because you've got kids." He sat up also.

"My life is not on hold," I said angrily. "I am living my life and my kids are the biggest part of it. They will always come first. Don't ever ask me to pick between you and my sons because you will never win that one."

"I would never ask you to choose between me and your boys. Never! Don't you know me better than that?" he huffed. "I just think it would be fun to get away together."

"I'm not saying it wouldn't be fun. I'm saying I can't take off for nine days. Besides, I can't afford it," I tried to explain.

"No problem. I've got it covered." His face softened and he leaned over and kissed me.

"I can't let you do that."

"Yes, you can," he whispered.

"No, seriously. I can't. If you want to go, that's fine with me. I'm not going to deprive you of a week of drunken foolishness with your friends because I can't go with you."

"I don't want you to be upset with me if I go." He sounded sincere.

"I promise, I won't be. Just no fooling around." I kissed him.

"Like I'd ever look at another woman!" He rolled over and kissed me hungrily.

Chapter 28

BASKETBALL SEASON WOUND to a close and I got a small reprieve for the next few weeks before baseball season kicked in. I was really looking forward to it. Our spring break was less than a week away and Mason was bouncing off the walls with excitement. I couldn't blame him though; I would be as well if I was in his shoes. A part of me was even a tiny bit jealous of him and the rest of his friends. Still, I wasn't about to begrudge Mason his youth by throwing a fit about him going or insisting that he stay with me. I couldn't do that to him. He'd worked so hard this year and he really deserved a break.

The weather was still soggy, and spring had not yet gotten a firm hold. The sun never fully made an appearance but would occasionally flirt with the clouds. We were getting more rain than in a typical season but hopefully that would mean summer wouldn't be so dreadfully hot. I sat at my desk in the family room trying to concentrate on the paper I was supposed to be writing for my Stress and Health Psychology class.

I thought the material was interesting enough, but I had learned something very important in my four semesters in college. Nine times out of ten grad student professors were the worst possible professors an undergraduate student had to deal with. It was my experience, as well as others I had spoken with, that graduate student professors seemed to feel like they had to prove something. Either to themselves or the faculty, I wasn't sure which, but they were notorious for being self-righteous hard asses. And the bitch I had this semester was the crown jewel of them.

Professor Reynolds was maybe twenty-three or twenty-four years old. She was a homely woman with a long-pointed face, mousey hair, and a sour personality. There wasn't anything pleasant about her. She was rude to her students, talked down to them, and acted superior to them at every opportunity. She had informed us all on the first day of class that she was getting her master's degree in counseling. I honestly couldn't imagine why. From everything I had witnessed she was a horridly unpleasant young lady that had nothing nice to offer anyone.

I stared at the blank screen on my laptop. I couldn't get my mind to focus. My eyes lifted to the outside world and the rain came down softly. The soft patter of drops danced off the roof. I could hear it pouring down the gutters breaking the silence that fell over my house. Mason was still on campus and the boys wouldn't be home for several more hours. It was a rare opportunity when I had the house all to myself. And the last thing I wanted to do was work on this paper.

I closed my laptop and got up from my desk. I went to all the bedrooms and bathrooms gathering laundry and towels. I figured I'd do something to keep myself occupied. After I got it all sorted and started, I vacuumed the entire house and then dusted it. I finished in record time simply because I didn't want to write some stupid paper.

*   *   *

Mason spent the last night before he left for Cancun on campus at the dorm. I couldn't even remember the last time he slept there. We did our typical goodbye the night before and I reassured him numerous times that I would not be upset with him should he choose to participate in such spring break frivolities. But I did remind him several times as well to keep it in his pants. He promised he would.

The first night Mason was gone I wasn't sure how the boys were going to react. True, Mason wasn't exactly an authority figure around the house, but he was a fixture and the boys both liked him a great deal. Strangely enough, they barely mentioned him. We went about our regular routine, homework, dinner, clean-up, and showers without skipping a beat. Strangely, it was as if we fell back in time to before Mason came into our lives.

Once the boys were asleep, I walked back into the family room and curled up with a blanket on the couch. I flipped through the channels and settled on a documentary on the American Revolution. I've always had a love of history and often watched documentaries late at night. I grabbed my phone and called Lisa.

"Hello," she answered.

"Hi, whatcha up to?" I turned the television down just a bit.

"Just got the kids down. What are you doing?"

"Nothing, watching a documentary on the American Revolution."

"Wow sounds exciting. Any big plans for the weekend?" she asked. "Isn't your little beanie boy on spring break yet?"

"Yeah, he left early this morning. He spent last night on campus because I think their plane left at like four in the morning. And I wasn't getting up that early to drive him and his friends to the airport."

"Who all went?"

"Just the four guys you met. Apparently, it wasn't fair that Mason was going solo, so I guess they all decided to."

"And you're not worried?" I could hear the skepticism in her voice.

"You think I should be?" I honestly wasn't. For some weird reason I trusted Mason, nothing he'd ever done had caused me to think I couldn't.

"Let's see, you just sent your gorgeous, well built, twenty-one-year-old boyfriend down to Cancun with three other drunken, irresponsible, twenty-one-year-old college boys. Nah . . . I'm sure he's going to be a perfect angel. How stupid are you?" Lisa laughed at me.

"No, I know he's not going to be an angel. I'm not stupid. I know exactly what he's going to be doing down there," I insisted.

"And yet you let him go anyways? You're a better woman than I am. Erick is forty years old and I wouldn't let him go running around Cancun with a bunch of his friends on spring break," she stated in her mom voice.

"You don't trust him?" I questioned.

"You trust Mason? Or any man for that matter? After what Danny did I figured you of all people wouldn't be so naïve." Suddenly I felt very foolish.

"I am not naïve. Besides, I don't own Mason. We're not married," I explained.

"I'm not saying you own Mason, but you are in a relationship with him."

"Really?" I wasn't so sure.

"Well, sort of. I mean he's practically living with you."

"Practically? Last night was the first time in almost a year it seems that he stayed at his dorm. I've been doing his laundry and feeding him for a year. So, I guess you could say we're in a relationship," I laughed. "Honestly, I don't know what the hell we are."

"All I'm saying is you're brave to set him loose like that. I wouldn't have," she said flatly.

"I don't own him, Lisa. Let it go. It's fine." I couldn't believe her. She was in worse shape than me, and she was pushing me to return to the dating world.

"If you say so . . ." I could hear the disbelief in her voice.

"Anyway, what are you doing tomorrow night?" I was eager to change the subject.

"Erik is taking me out for dinner with a couple of his co-workers. Yeah rah!" She sounded so thrilled.

"I thought you had the kids?"

"I switched weekends for this stupid thing. I've got to get all dolled up and be impressed by these damn suits and their plastic wives," she complained.

"You sound so excited." It was my turn to laugh.

"Yeah, bite me. You should see this freaking dress I've got to wear to this thing." She went on about her dress, shoes, and everything else required to make her look like some Barbie doll. Even as I listened to her bitch, I knew how much she loved to get all dressed up.

"Make sure you take pictures," I teased.

"You'd better hope Mason doesn't," she fired back with a chuckle.

"You're such a bitch. What about next Friday? Pizza and a movie?"

"Sounds good."

"Call me later and let me know how it goes," I told her.

"Yeah, whatever. Bye."

"Sweet dreams," I chimed in and heard her grunt at me before she disconnected the call.

I set my phone down on the coffee table and flipped the television off. The house felt strange and too quiet. I went around and made sure I'd closed the garage door and that all the doors were locked. Billy tagged along with me wagging her tail. She seemed to be thrilled that Mason was gone. She beat me to my room and jumped up on my bed. She'd taken her spot back in Mason's absence.

I turned on the television and hit play on the DVD player. Part two of *The Fellowship of the Ring* kicked back on from the night before. I absolutely loved these movies and never got tired of watching them no matter how many times I saw them. I flipped off the light on my nightstand and curled up with Billy. She had already started snoring lightly with her head on Mason's pillow.

My conversation with Lisa kept running through my head. I wanted so desperately to believe that Mason was somewhat behaving himself down there, but I couldn't swear to it. He said he loved me, but then again, I'd heard that from Danny too. Of course, Mason wasn't anything like Danny. Still . . . What was this thing between Mason and me? I had no idea really. We never spoke about the future, never once. And I hated to think that was because he knew we had none together. Perhaps this was all just a fun little affair for him as well.

I closed my eyes and tried not to replay the last year repeatedly in my head. All those little moments we shared. The private jokes, the looks when you know exactly what the other person is thinking and you're trying your best not to laugh. The small things that two people shared, the playful laughs in the shower, the games, the times I'd watch him with my boys when they didn't know I was watching. I wouldn't give those moments back for anything, but did it have to mean everything?

Chapter 29

THE BOYS AND I drove over to Lisa's the following Friday evening for a movie and pizza night. It was windy and raining outside and the temperature was hovering in the mid-forties. All I could think about was Mason and his cronies siting in a beach chair in Mexico with a little drink with an umbrella in it. It almost made me sick to my stomach. The more it rained over the last several days and the more the temperatures dropped the worse my mood had gotten.

I was at least glad to get the chance to spend some time with Lisa. I'd gotten so used to seeing her a couple times a week because of the kids' sports. Now having a couple weeks break from it was fabulous, but I'd missed hanging out with her and talking. In a short span of time, we had become such good friends.

I turned down her street with the wipers on my car on high speed, wondering how I was going to get the boys from the car and into her house without the three of us getting soaked to the skin. Fortunately, Lisa was paying attention and left her garage door open. I took advantage and pulled straight in.

I carried in a two liter of Coke for Lisa and me and a gallon of Hi-C fruit punch for the kids along with a couple boxes of microwave popcorn and several bags of M&M's. My sons hurried inside to get out of the cold and immediately disappeared with her children. Max wasn't too happy about being there for the evening ever since I told him his buddy Aaron couldn't tag along. I loved Aaron almost like another son, I truly did, but I didn't want to impose on Lisa. Five children were quite enough for the two of us. Plus, I knew Max and Aaron would ignore Brie completely the entire evening if they were together. This way, I was hoping that perhaps Max would be a little kinder to Brie if it was just him.

Lisa ordered several pizzas, and we got the children wrangled together in the family room. We gave them a list of movie options that were suitable for all five of them. It certainly wasn't easy considering they ranged from four to almost twelve. I figured Max would be our biggest obstacle in this decision, but for some reason, he was in an unusually good mood, so I wasn't going to question it. I was simply grateful.

We told them to choose between *The Incredibles*, the *Toy Story* trilogy, the *Monsters Inc.* duo, or the *Despicable Me* duo. The decision was almost unanimous. We were watching the *Despicable Me* duo. Logan and Henry took off into Logan's room to play until the pizza arrived. Max sat down on the couch and pulled out his DS while Brie disappeared into her room with McKenzie tagging along behind her. Lisa and I stood in the kitchen silently shaking our heads. This was exactly what we knew was going to happen.

Lisa and I hung out in the kitchen while we waited on the pizza to arrive. We fixed the popcorn and added the M&M's and got the drinks ready for everyone. Lisa told me all about her evening out with Erick's co-workers and their dreadful wives. I couldn't contain my laugher as she recounted the tales of the 'old crows' as she called them. Despite all her complaints, I knew she was crazy about Erick and had behaved as a perfect lady.

The pizza finally arrived, and the kids came pouring out of the woodwork. We sat them all down at the breakfast bar with paper plates and their drinks. Lisa's breakfast bar separated her family room from her kitchen and was positioned perfectly for the kids to watch the movie while they ate their pizza. Once they got engrossed, Lisa and I slipped back to the table, so we could eat in peace and talk.

"Have you heard anything from beanie boy since he left?" she inquired.

"No. But I didn't expect to. Would you be calling your boyfriend if you were in Cancun?" I sat down and took a bite of the pepperoni pizza.

"Probably not," she admitted.

"See? It's no big deal." I shrugged it off.

"When's he getting back?"

"Sometime on Sunday. I'm not sure when, but he's got class on Monday." I wasn't in the mood to talk about Mason.

"What's wrong? You're not acting like yourself," she observed.

"I don't know. I've been doing a lot of thinking since he's gone," I muttered.

"Thinking? About what?"

"Us. Where he fits in in our lives or even if he does. I love him. I honestly do. But I'm not in love with him." I looked over at her to see her reaction.

"Is he in love with you?"

"I don't know, honestly." I took another bite and thought about it for a moment. "It's not like it's something we've discussed. We never talk about the future more than a week out. So, I have no idea where he stands, where I stand. I just don't know."

"You've always said that this relationship was never going to survive college," she reminded me.

"I know. He graduates next May, and I'm sure he will return to Chicago afterwards. I'm trying to be realistic. I know what this is." I glanced over at her and she gave me a sad sort of look.

"But you've gotten attached to him." It was a statement, not a question.

"True, I've also been careful," I admitted.

"With your heart . . ."

"Yes, with that too."

By the time we started the second movie the children were all bouncing off the walls and quoting the first one. Lisa and I got out a bunch of pillows, blankets, and sleeping bags and scattered them about her family room for each of the kids.

They were all still hyped-up when the second movie ended so Lisa stuck in *The Incredibles*. She and I curled up on the sofa with a bottle of wine giggling in low tones like a couple of young high school girls over crushes on the jocks on the football team. I relaxed back against the oversized pillows and stretched my legs out across Lisa's lap. I don't even remember the end of the movie. I don't know whether it was the wine or the company, but I felt so relaxed and comfortable. The next thing I realized was the rustling of the children and the morning sun beaming in through Lisa's family room window.

Chapter 30

MASON RETURNED on Sunday evening. He rolled in shortly before eleven o'clock in the evening. He was golden from his trip and his hair was several shades lighter. He had never looked more handsome. I was thankful the boys were sound asleep by the time he arrived. I hadn't realized how much I truly missed him until I saw him standing there smiling at me when I opened the front door.

I immediately rushed into his arms and held him tightly. I looked longingly into his beautiful sea blue eyes before I pressed my lips down upon his. Mason dropped his bag to the floor and backed me up over the threshold. He kicked the door closed with his foot and only broke our kiss long enough to lock the door behind him. We stumbled back a few paces before Mason finally gave up and lifted me up into his arms. He carried me back into my bedroom and placed me hurriedly on my bed before climbing up beside me.

We pulled and tugged at each other's clothes trying to remove them as quickly as possible. He rolled over partway on top of me, devouring me with his mouth. His hand massaged my breast gently. He played with my nipple, squeezed it and then finally brought his mouth down to it. He suckled on it to his heart's delight. I leaned my head back and closed my eyes. I'd missed this so much.

Mason slid down kissing my stomach, running his fingers lightly up my thigh until they found their desired destination between my legs. He slipped his fingers between my lips moistening them before he slid two of them slowly inside me. I arched my back and moaned deeply. He made his way down my body slowly, teasing me while enjoying himself.

He glided his tongue inside me, gloriously, tempting me. His tongue traced lightly over my clitoris, then a little more roughly with more desire while his fingers teased me constantly. I squirmed beneath him, but Mason wrapped his arm around my thigh and held onto me making my escape impossible. I was sweaty and breathless and loving every agonizing second of it. I had trained him extremely well. He knew exactly how to kiss me, where to place his tongue and his fingers, and just how to make me insane with desire for him.

I held out as long as I could. My nails dug into his back as I arched mine just before I reached the peak of ecstasy. But then Mason surprised me. He stopped. In one quick motion he moved swiftly up my body and thrust deeply into me. I screamed out in pleasure and exploded over his thick throbbing cock. Mason held onto me, kissing me to keep my screams to a lower tone. He moaned loudly against my cheek before he collapsed down upon me.

We lay there for several moments, breathing heavily, exhausted. My body was spent. I waited until I regained use of my legs before I slipped into my robe and returned to the living room to turn off the television and shut off the lights. When I returned Mason was snoring softly on the pillow beside mine. His hair was messed up perfectly in a tangle of curls giving him an even more youthful appearance. I stared at him for a while before I crawled back into bed beside him.

*   *   *

The boys were thrilled to see Mason when they returned from school. He had gotten them both T-shirts and flip-flops that they both thought were the greatest things ever. I sat at my desk and watched them both crawling all over him for attention before they dragged him outside with their baseball equipment.

The rain had finally stopped, and the sun found its way back to us. It hadn't warmed up much and the ground was still saturated. I could hear their sneakers sloshing across the grass as I stood on the back deck watching the boys warm up. I was wearing jeans, and a hooded sweatshirt and I was still cold. I wrapped my arms around myself; the wind still had a bit of a bite to it. I only lasted a few minutes before I decided it was time to start dinner and headed back inside.

Chapter 31

I WAS SITTING at my desk grading papers and enjoying the beautiful evening. Max was over at Aaron's house down the street and Henry was watching *The Avengers* with Mason in my room. The house was peaceful, and we had fallen back into a similar routine that we'd shared before spring break. I glanced out the front window and noticed the slow drizzle that had been covering our street with a thick haze had finally lifted. The sun was struggling to break through the clouds and there was a vibrant rainbow hovering over Debbie's house.

I was so caught up in the beauty before me I hadn't seen the black BMW with the tinted windows come to a halt in front of my house until I heard the car door slam. A good-looking man with a strong jaw, wide shoulders, and strangely familiar wavy, dirty blonde hair marched up my driveway. I knew in an instant who this man was. It was Mason's father.

I rose from my seat before the bell even rang. I took a deep breath and painted a smile across my lips. I barely had time to give thought to my response before I was face to face with a very angry father. I was suddenly very glad that Mason had begun parking in my garage.

"Yes? Can I help you?" I greeted him with caution, keeping the screen door closed between us.

"I hope so. My name is Hayden Brooks. I am looking for my son, Mason. I believe he must be dating your daughter, ma'am. I went to his dorm room to speak with him, and his roommate said he spends time with his girlfriend here and he gave me your address."

Daughter? I look old enough to have a daughter in college? You asshole!

"I see." I would have to remember to thank Jared the next time I saw him. "Well, I am sorry you came out here. I haven't seen them this evening. My daughter told me earlier they were going to study at the library after they had dinner. I would imagine she won't be home before nine."

"Wonderful." Hayden ran his fingers through his hair in frustration in the same manner as his son. It took everything I had not to smile to myself. "I can't believe that boy." He paced back and forth a couple of paces while I stood there uncomfortably.

"I can send her a text and have him call you if this is urgent," I offered.

"No. It's not urgent, at least not in an imminent means." He stopped pacing and confronted me. "Did your daughter happen to accompany my son to Cancun over spring break?"

"No. I did not allow her to go." I felt a wave of relief wash over me. I opened the screen door and stepped out on my porch.

"I knew I should have made Mason attend Northwestern where I could keep a better eye on him. He was kind enough to put a couple thousand on my credit card that I gave him for emergency use only." His chest heaved to control his anger. "As soon as I opened the statement I jumped in my car and drove straight down here." A low, hollow chuckle escaped him. "I was hoping by the time I reached him I would be calm enough not to beat his ass and drag him back home like the spoiled inconsiderate brat that he is."

"I'm sorry." I didn't know what else to say.

"It's my own fault. I gave that boy everything. Even that new Camaro was my graduation gift. I wanted to give him everything I never had. Now he's only got one more year left before he finishes school and he's still as irresponsible as he was when he was twelve." He hushed quickly when he saw the astonished look on my face. "Oh, I'm sorry. Please don't misunderstand me. I know my son can be a fool, but apparently, he is a fool who is in love with your daughter."

"Really? I was not aware you knew so much about her." *What in the world had Mason told them? Most likely anything but the truth.*

"I know her name is Alex. I have heard she is quite beautiful with lovely skin, dark eyes, and long dark hair. I would imagine she looks a lot like her mother." He smiled for the first time and I got a small glimpse of how stunningly handsome Mason would surely be in another twenty years.

"Well, thank you. We've been told we look similar." I could feel myself blushing.

"Perhaps I will get the opportunity to meet her while I'm here. Tell me, can you recommend a hotel nearby? I'm afraid I am too tired to drive back this evening."

"Yes, of course." I gave him directions to the Marriott Hotel near the interstate. As I was finishing, I saw Max and Aaron walking down the road, and I knew I had to get Hayden out of here before they arrived.

"Thank you very much, Mrs. Rose."

"It was nice to meet you, Mr. Brooks. I will let them know you are looking for Mason and have him call you." I shook his hand and put my other one on my door handle.

"I appreciate that." He took a few steps off my porch and then turned back around. "Excuse me," he trotted back to me. "Here's my card. Can you please call me if they show up here anytime soon? Is there a number I can reach you at?"

I rattled off my number quickly and watched him type it in his phone. I politely excused myself explaining I had dinner on the stove and hurried back into the house closing the door behind him. I leaned against the door and exhaled loudly. Then I turned around and peeked through the curtain as Hayden climbed in his beautiful expensive car and drove off just as Max and Aaron started walking up the lawn.

"What in the . . ." I rounded the corner and almost ran directly into Mason. He had apparently been eavesdropping on my entire conversation with his father.

"I can explain," he began, but I shook my head and silenced him.

"Your daddy's pissed." I walked into my bedroom with Mason on my heels. I closed the door behind us. "I think you may be grounded. Words I never thought I would ever utter to anyone I was dating, but . . . oh, my God, Mason. What in the hell were you thinking of putting that stupid trip on your dad's card. Are you a complete idiot? He should beat your ass for that! I would if you were my son. And from the look on his face, he's going to."

"I know. I was going to call him. I just got busy once classes resumed and forgot to," he offered.

"Oh, come on, Mason. My sons could come up with a better excuse than that. You're not a child. You didn't forget. You didn't want to face him because you knew how upset he was going to be." I was so disgusted with him.

"I will deal with my dad. He just likes to be a bully. I can't believe he drove all the way down here just to have an argument with me over money."

"And he has every right to. It's his money," I tried to explain, but he just couldn't see it. It was clear that he'd never had to work for it.

"He's got more than he can ever spend. It's not a big deal." Mason rolled his eyes like an impatient child.

"It is a big deal. Damn, Mason, grow up." I pushed past him and walked out the door.

Max and Aaron were sitting in the family room playing on the X-Box when I entered the room. "Hi, Momma," Aaron greeted me. He always called me momma.

"Hi, sweetheart," I said without thought.

"Are you all right?" Max inquired.

"Yeah, honey. I'm fine." I left the room and walked through the kitchen and out onto the deck.

I took a seat on the swing and swayed back and forth. I wasn't sure who I was more upset with. Me, for lying to Mason's father or Mason, for acting like the irresponsible kid I knew in my soul he still was. I covered my face with my hands. It wasn't my place to jump all over Mason for what he did, but in some weird way I felt responsible for him as well. Just as my own sons' behavior reflected on me when they were outside my presence, I sort of felt Mason's did too. And for the first time, I was really appalled by his actions. If one of my boys had done that to me, there wouldn't be anyone who could save them from my wrath.

"Momma?" Max was standing in the doorway holding my phone.

"Yeah, baby?" He walked over and handed it to me.

"It was ringing."

"Thanks." I glanced at the screen and didn't recognize the number or the area code.

"Are you okay?" He sounded concerned.

"I'm fine, sweetheart. I'm just really tired." I stood up and gave him a hug. "Can you do me a favor? Can you keep an eye on Henry for me for a little while? Mason's here, but just help him for me okay? I'm gonna run over to Lisa's for about an hour."

"Sure. Can Aaron and I have a snack?" We walked back into the kitchen.

"Don't make a mess." I grabbed my purse and keys. "I'll be back."

And without a word to Mason, I pulled out of the driveway and headed down the street. I turned up the radio to drown out the voices arguing in my head. I just needed some fresh air, some time alone to consider everything. I loved Mason, but I wasn't in love with him. I knew that. But I didn't believe he did. I knew he was in love with me, and I knew we were both going to get hurt when this ended.

My phone went off again. I glanced down at it resting on the console between the seats. It was Mason. I didn't answer. Instead, I turned down the main street and sat back trying to relax.

Several minutes later my phone buzzed at me again. Without even looking positive it had to be Mason again, I answered.

"Yes?" I huffed.

"I'm sorry, is this a bad time?" An unfamiliar male voice replied.

"No. I'm sorry. Who is this?"

"Hayden Brooks. Is this Mrs. Rose?"

"Yes, sorry. I didn't recognize your voice."

"I am afraid you have an advantage over me. I don't even know your first name," he said in a charming voice.

"It's Leah," I quickly offered my middle name.

"Hello Leah," he greeted.

"Hi, Hayden." I passed the turn onto Lisa's street.

"I have two questions for you. First, have you managed to locate my son?" he inquired.

"Not yet I'm afraid."

"All right, then. Secondly, would you care to join me for dinner?" He completely caught me off guard.

"Dinner?" I stumbled.

"Yes, dinner. It seems you are the only one I know in town, and I was secretly hoping you would know which restaurants are good in this area."

I didn't know what to say. A part of me was intrigued. This was a great opportunity to learn some more about Mason and his family. But it also felt like a betrayal. I knew Mason would be extremely upset with me if I went, regardless of how harmless.

"Leah? Are you there? Did I lose you?"

"No. I'm still here. I was just trying to think of a decent place to eat around here," I quickly lied.

"I saw a place called Leo's Pizza. Is it any good? Do you even like pizza?" At least it was casual enough.

"Leo's got the best pizza in town."

"Wonderful, I will be by in a half hour to pick you up." Panic.

"No!" I said a little too loudly. "Sorry, what I mean is I was on my way to pick up a few things at the store when you called. I'm already in town."

"Oh, I see. Well then, how long will it take you to get there?"

"About three minutes," I laughed. "I'll get us a table."

"Wonderful. I will be there shortly."

Leo's was only two lights up the road and sitting in a little strip mall on the left. I pulled in the parking lot and turned my car off, but I didn't open the door. I wasn't sure what I was doing or why I was even here. I shouldn't be having dinner with this man. He was the father of my boyfriend.

What the hell am I doing?

Hayden joined me in the corner booth ten minutes later. I watched him walk in and scan the room. His face lit up just a bit and he gave a brief wave before walking to me. He walked straight, shoulders squared, and head held high. He had the proud confident walk of a successful man. He also had the same chiseled features as Mason, but Hayden's eyes were a bright green instead of sea blue.

"Hello Leah, I hope I didn't keep you waiting too terribly long." He slid into the padded seat across from me. "Thank you for joining me. I've gotten to where I really hate hotel food." He smiled, and I immediately noticed that Mason had also inherited his father's dimples and the small cleft in his chin.

"Do you travel a lot?"

"Yes, about once a month. But not nearly as much as I did when I first started my firm almost twenty years ago. I suppose that's why Mason and I don't get along so well. I hardly spent any time with him when he was growing up. I was always working." He opened the menu in front of him and began to scan it over.

"You had to have been home occasionally considering how many children you have."

He gave me a quizzical look. "What do you mean? I only have two. Mason and his older sister, Kennedy."

"Oh. I thought Mason had said he had a bunch of younger siblings as well." Now I was confused.

"He does, but they aren't mine. His mother and I divorced before his second birthday. She remarried about eighteen months later and had more children with her second husband," he explained.

"Mason never told me his parents were divorced. I just assumed . . ." I didn't have the right words to finish the sentence without making it sound like his son never mentioned him to me. "He did tell me you own a marketing firm."

"I'm sure that's all he ever told you. We aren't exactly close."

"Sons can be difficult at times. I have two of them," I said with sympathy.

The waitress came over and took our order. We both got an iced tea with lemon and Hayden ordered a large pizza, mushroom, ham, and onion on my half, meat lovers on his. As soon as we got our drinks, I tried to figure out why I was even here and how I could possibly keep up the charade.

"Leah, I don't mean to sound rude, but you don't look old enough to have a daughter in college," he commented, stirring some Sweet'n Low into his tea.

"Well, you don't look old enough to have a son in college either. Not to mention a daughter older than him," I replied.

"I was seventeen when Kennedy was born. She was a surprise to say the least and we had Mason almost two years later. I was young and determined to build my own business and take care of my family. Unfortunately, the more successful my business grew, the less time I had for my family, and my wife wanted more." He shrugged it off. "I noticed you're not wearing a wedding ring either. I'm guessing you are divorced as well."

"Yes, six years now."

"I'm sorry to hear that. You must have been a very young bride as well," he commented with a smile.

I sat there for a moment absentmindedly stirring my tea and trying to figure out how to get myself out of this ridiculous mess. The only possibility I could see was coming completely clean with Hayden. With hesitation, I put the spoon down on the table and straightened the napkin in my lap. I wasn't sure how this was going to go.

"Yes, I was a young bride. I was nineteen when I got married. But I'm ashamed to tell you Hayden, I have not been completely honest with you. Personally, I don't handle deception well and I'm not a good liar. So, I think it's time I told you to whole truth." My stomach was tied in a knot.

"I don't understand, Leah."

"You will." I took a sip of my tea trying to decide where to begin. "When you arrived at my house this afternoon, I could tell how upset you were and I didn't want a big scene in front of my neighbors. So, when you assumed my daughter was involved with your son, I went along with it. Mainly because you offered the out and slightly because I was insulted that you assumed I was old enough to have a daughter in college."

"I never intended to insult you. I realized after I said it that you did not look old enough to have a daughter in college, but I thought that maybe she was your stepdaughter or perhaps even your younger sister. Alex is not your daughter?"

"No. I'm Alex." I sighed waiting for it to fully sink in.

"But you told me your name was Leah." Confusion clouded over his brow.

"My middle name is Leah. My first name is Alexandra. Your son calls me Alex or Lexie. And I'll be thirty-three years old next week. I am divorced, and I have two sons. Max is almost twelve and Henry is eight."

Hayden was quiet for what felt like an eternity. "Well, I guess that explains why he wouldn't bring you home for Christmas." He sat back and waited while our server put the pizza down between us.

"Is there anything else you need?" she asked politely.

"No, thank you. This is wonderful." I smiled awkwardly, wanting her to just go away.

"But Mason had told us he met his girlfriend in sociology class?"

"That's true. We did meet in sociology class."

"I don't understand. Were you, his professor?" He leaned forward a little.

"No. Just another student. I decided to go back to college when my youngest started school full time. I work as a teaching assistant and am finishing my second year right now," I informed him, feeling completely foolish.

"How long have you been sleeping with my son?" he inquired.

"Since his twenty-first birthday," I admitted.

"I see. Well . . ." He shook his head slowly and picked up a piece of pizza. "I appreciate you telling me the truth. I don't know why Mason felt it necessary to keep you hidden."

"I think he thought his family wouldn't approve of me."

"I admit I'm surprised and a little envious as well," he confessed with a slight smile.

I nervously picked up a slice of pizza and took a bite. I didn't know how to respond to that remark.

"So, tell me. Where exactly is my son?" He picked up a second piece and bit into it.

"At my house."

"And I'm guessing he was there when I stopped by?" I nodded while chewing. "Where was his car?"

"In my garage."

Hayden laughed aloud.

"I'll be damned. He was probably listening to our entire conversation if I know anything about my son."

"Bingo." I laughed with him.

Hayden and I talked for another hour. It wasn't long before we were laughing at the challenges of raising children, the joys of divorce and various life experiences. I hated to admit it but I was having a wonderful time with him. He was charming, funny, considerate, and extremely good looking. It was also difficult to admit to myself that we had so much in common and if the circumstances were different, I would have been interested in him.

Hayden walked me to my car. We had agreed to keep our dinner a secret as well as my confession pertaining to my relationship with his son. He asked me if it was all right if he waited a good half hour and then returned to my home to have a conversation with his son. I felt it was the least I could do after my earlier betrayal.

Chapter 32

I WISHED I'D HAD more time. It was barely a fifteen-minute drive back to my house, even less if I hit the lights on Main Street. My mind was in a whirlwind, and I wanted desperately to talk with Lisa. But there wasn't enough time. I had to speak to Mason, find some peace there before his father arrived. I knew Hayden wouldn't betray our dinner, but I also didn't want Mason to feel that everyone was attacking him. I felt so torn between the parent side of me and the me that was Mason's lover.

I couldn't imagine what Hayden thought of me for carrying on a sexual relationship with his son. And I still refused to admit what thoughts were running through my head every time I looked at Hayden.

I pulled into the garage and turned off the engine. Mason's car was sitting there quietly. I didn't know what I was going to say when I went inside. It was almost seven o'clock and I had been gone for almost two hours. Hayden was going to arrive shortly, and I was running out of time.

Mason was on the couch reading one of his textbooks while my boys watched *The Big Bang Theory*. They all looked up when I entered the room.

"Hello," I said softly and put my bag down on the corner of my desk. "Did you guys eat dinner yet?"

"Yes, Mason fixed us some spaghetti-o's and grilled cheese." Henry said.

"Thank you." I looked over at Mason.

"Not a problem. Where'd you go? I called Lisa and she hadn't seen you." I sat down beside him.

"I went for a drive. I wanted some fresh air."

"You were gone a long time," he observed.

"Henry, why don't you go jump in the shower? It will be bedtime soon."

"Okay, Momma." He jumped up and ran to the bathroom without hesitation.

"I called my dad," Mason lied. "A couple of times. He never picked up."

Hayden had set his phone on the table beside him throughout our entire dinner. It never made a sound. I recalled him checking it a couple of times and finding nothing. I knew Mason was lying to me, but I couldn't understand why he felt he had to.

"Well, perhaps you'll reach him tomorrow." I got up and closed the drapes on the front window as I did every evening. I flipped on the family room lamp and walked back into my room. Within minutes, Mason followed.

"Alex, I should have told you. My relationship with my real dad is difficult. He's more of a sperm donor with a checkbook than a dad. In fact, I don't even consider him my dad." He sat down on the edge of the bed confessing. "My parents got divorced when I was really young. My stepdad raised me. I rarely saw my real dad. He was always working and never had time for me or my sister."

"I'm sorry, Mason. But you still shouldn't have charged your trip without his permission." I sat down beside him and took his hand.

"I honestly didn't think he'd notice. Besides, he owes me that much. He was never around." Mason had never sounded more like a child to me.

"Seriously?" I rolled my eyes at him. "So, he's not father of the year. Who is? My parents aren't perfect either. That's just life. It doesn't give you a pass for what you did. If you want to be an adult, act like one."

"I am not a child!" He raised his voice a bit.

"And you don't talk to me that way," I said sternly, sounding exactly like a mom.

"I'm sorry." He looked up at me with big sad eyes. "I'll fix this. I promise."

The doorbell rang. I froze. Seconds later, Max knocked on my door.

"Yes?" I replied, and he opened the door slowly and poked his head in.

"There's a man here to see Mason."

"Thank you, Max. Tell him he'll be there in a second and then go to your room to watch TV," I said.

"Okay."

"I guess I have to face him," Mason uttered, sounding like a little boy scared of getting spanked.

"It'll be fine." I pulled him to his feet and followed him into the family room.

Hayden was standing in the foyer looking uncomfortable. "Dad?" Mason stopped short. "I heard you were looking for me."

"Mason . . ." He hushed when I walked into view.

"Mr. Brooks. Nice to see you again." I shook his hand. "Please, won't you come in and sit down." I led him into the family room.

Hayden sat down on the edge of the loveseat. Mason joined me on the couch, keeping a small distance between us.

"I know why you're here." Mason fidgeted with his hands. "I'm sorry and I will pay you back. I promise."

"Thank you, son. And yes, you will. Out of your internship money this summer," Hayden informed him.

"What? But I . . ." Mason started to argue.

"This is not open for discussion. You'll come home this summer and work at my firm to pay off the money you charged to my credit card," Hayden stated firmly.

"Why can't I . . ." Mason tried again.

"What did I say? This is not open for discussion. Do you understand?" Hayden stared at Mason causing his son to look down at his feet.

"Yes, sir," Mason replied in a soft voice still staring at the floor. Hayden took the opportunity to glance over at me and smiled slightly. I had to look away to keep a straight face. "I'm sorry I made you drive all the way down here."

"No problem, it turned out to be unexpectedly pleasant." If Mason picked up any side meaning in his father's words, he didn't show it. "How is everything else going?"

"Fine."

"So, is Alex here? I've been looking forward to meeting her," Hayden probed a little.

Mason looked up quickly. "No. Sorry, you just missed her. She ran to the store to pick up some snacks. We've got a lot of studying to do."

I looked at Mason and then over at Hayden but remained silent. Hayden played his part well.

"Yes, well, that's too bad. I wanted to meet her. Given the hour, I'm going to stay the night. Perhaps we can all have breakfast in the morning before I head back?" Hayden offered.

"Thanks, I'll have to let you know. I'll call you before nine." I could tell Mason was just stalling to appease his father.

"Wonderful." Hayden stood up and we followed suit. "I'll look forward to meeting you both for breakfast." He shook both our hands and walked over to the front door.

"Thank you for stopping by. It was a pleasure to meet you." I smiled at him warmly.

"And you as well, Mrs. Rose. I'm sorry I missed your daughter. I've heard many wonderful things about her. I look forward to seeing her in the morning." Hayden shook my hand one last time, lingering slightly.

"Yes, I know she will be sorry she missed you tonight." I could see the mischievousness in his eyes, and I had to fight the urge to smile.

"Goodnight, Mason. I'll see you in the morning." Hayden opened the door and disappeared into the night.

Mason closed and bolted the door behind his father. His face was tense, and I wasn't sure what he was going to do next.

"I've got to call Jared." He quickly retreated to my room for his phone.

"Jared? Why are you calling Jared?" I followed.

"I need to borrow Emma for breakfast," he gushed, reaching for his phone.

"Are you serious? You're planning to pass Emma off as me? And why do you find it necessary to lie to your dad about me?" I sat down on the side of the bed.

"My dad is difficult. He would never understand or approve of us. And my mom would have a nervous breakdown. Trust me, it's just easier if Emma goes."

For a half second, I considered telling him the truth, but instead I thought I'd let this play out. I was curious to see how far he'd go with this façade.

"Fine, you would know better than I." I got up and walked into the kitchen.

I started cleaning up the mess Mason and the boys had made while I was gone. I could hear Mason on the phone as I started the water. I made a point of not slamming things around even though I was angry enough to do it. I was so insulted. Either he was ashamed of me and our relationship or had decided I wasn't important enough to him to introduce to his family. Whichever the case may be, I could not possibly feel worse than I did at that moment.

*   *   *

Mason left before eight to pick Emma up on campus and make it back in time to meet Hayden for breakfast at nine thirty. I sat on the back porch in my robe nursing my coffee. It was a gorgeous Saturday morning. The dew on the grass was disappearing across the lawn as the sun warmed up the world around me. Winter had finally lost its grip on us and spring was here to stay.

I couldn't believe Mason was going to carry out this charade. A part of me wished I could be a fly on the wall to witness it. I wondered how he had ever talked Emma and Jared into participating in this falsehood. I had gotten to know Emma well since last Labor Day weekend, and I refused to believe she would be happy about deceiving someone's parents in such a manner. She wasn't that type of person.

I finally went back inside and fixed some blueberry waffles and bacon for the boys. I didn't feel like eating. The boys knew something was wrong, but neither knew what it was. And I wasn't about to explain it to them. I knew Max had overheard our conversation in the family room last night with Hayden. He was quiet and kept looking at me in a questioning manner. It was the same look he always gave me after he knew his dad and I had been arguing on the phone.

When the boys finished and decided to practice batting in the backyard, I got dressed and busied myself cleaning up the house. Time seemed to be moving so slowly and I was dying to know how this little breakfast was playing itself out. I think I cleaned the entire house in record time. Restless, I called Lisa to get her thoughts.

"Hello?" She sounded out of breath.

"Hey, what's going on?"

"Oh, I was chasing Logan around the house for the remote." She laughed. "He wants to watch *SpongeBob SquarePants* and Brie doesn't. They did rock, paper, scissors for the remote and Logan lost, but he won't give up the remote. So, we were all chasing him around the house."

"Sounds familiar," I said. Lisa was one of those fun parents that believed in playing with her children and being silly with them. We had that in common.

"What's going on?"

"You wouldn't believe me if I told you." I curled up on the swing on the deck, so I could watch my boys. They were far enough away not to overhear but close enough.

"Really?"

I spent the next fifteen minutes babbling and bringing her up to speed on the last twenty-four hours. I was even honest about my dinner with Hayden and my confession to him.

"So, Mason is making a total fool of himself right now? What an idiot. And you don't think his dad will call him out on it?"

"No. I think this is more of a test of Mason's character than busting him about lying about who he's sleeping with," I said, thinking back on my conversation with Hayden.

"I can't believe you had dinner with his dad. So, what's he like?" Lisa inquired.

"Honestly? And don't you ever repeat this because I will deny it."

"You know better than that."

"I know, but it's horrible," I confessed.

"Spill it."

"If I'd met him under any other circumstances, Hayden is the man I would be dating. Picture Mason twenty years older with green eyes instead of blue, same stature, dimples, features, everything. Mason is damn near a carbon copy of his dad and good Lord, he is charming, gorgeous, successful. Everything I've always dreamed of." It sounded so horrible admitting it aloud.

"Oh my God . . . You've got a serious crush on his dad." She laughed. "You can't date him! I mean never!"

"Don't you think I know that? I'm not stupid. Besides, it's not like they're close or anything. They've both said they hardly know each other. Mason's stepdad raised him, not Hayden."

"Alex, you know me. I'm all for kinky but that is a whole new level of sick and twisted." She continued laughing at me. "I mean, what if you married him. Neither of you would ever be able to get past the fact that you've been sleeping with his son for a year now."

"I know. I know. This whole thing sucks!"

"You could introduce him to me."

"Oh, shut up. You've got Erik."

"And you've got Mason," she countered.

"Yeah, I've got someone who is so ashamed of me he's parading his best friend's girlfriend around to his dad. I can't even begin to tell you how that makes me feel. I must be so important to him. Can't you tell how much he loves me?" I complained.

"Maybe he's afraid his dad would steal you away from him? He damn near has already," Lisa teased.

"I'm so glad you're enjoying this."

"Oh, come on, Alex. If this was anyone else, you'd be laughing too."

"It's not so funny when it's you," I confessed.

My call waiting beeped in on us. I glanced at my phone and saw Hayden Brooks pop up on my screen.

"Crap. Let me call you back. It's Hayden."

"Remember . . . say no to Daddy!"

"Bitch!" I couldn't help but laugh as I switched over. The whole situation was ridiculous.

"Good morning, Hayden."

"Hello Alex, how are you?"

"Honestly, feeling very irritated with your son for his little charade," I admitted.

"So exactly who was the girl with my son this morning?"

"That was Mason's best friend Jared's girlfriend, Emma. Did you call Mason out on it?"

"Nope. I never said a word about his deception. I played it off as if I was happy to finally meet her and told him she was a nice girl. I just couldn't believe Mason would deceive me like this."

"That makes two of us. I don't know whether he's that ashamed of me and our relationship or if I just mean that little to him." I hated confessing that to his father. It made me feel cheap and easy.

"I'm so sorry, Alex. He should be showing you off every chance he gets. He should be so proud to be with a lady like you. I would be." My voice caught in my throat, and I didn't know how to respond.

"Thank you, Hayden." Was all I could manage to squeak out.

"Please keep in mind that Mason is just a child, not a man. A man would never disrespect you like this. This whole thing has shown me that he still has a lot of growing up to do." Hayden tried to comfort me.

"I know you're right. I don't know what I'm going to say to him when he gets back. We barely spoke last night after you left and I pretended to be asleep this morning when he got up."

"I'm sorry I caused this situation," he said with an apologetic tone in his voice.

"You didn't. He did."

"I should have just called him, but I knew he wouldn't answer."

"So, when are you heading back to Chicago?" I attempted to change the subject before it got any more personal.

"I'm on my way there now. I checked out of the hotel before I met them for breakfast. I've got to get back to the office. I left so abruptly yesterday that I've got a lot of paperwork to take care of."

"I understand."

"But I wanted to say thank you to you before I left and tell you that it was really nice meeting you. I had a great time with you last night. I enjoyed getting to know you. My son is a very lucky man and I'm sorry he doesn't seem to realize it. He will someday, trust me, he will and then he'll regret what he's done today."

"It was very nice meeting you also. I wish it were under different circumstances." *I wish that more than anything.* "I had a wonderful time last night also. I hope you have a safe trip home."

"I hope to see you again sometime, Alex. You take care."

"Thanks, you too."

I hung up the phone and set it beside me on the swing. A part of me was a little sad that he was already heading back north, and I wouldn't get the chance to see him again. Boy, if the circumstances were just a little different and I'd met Hayden first, he was exactly everything I was looking for. Men like him were very rare, but I knew Lisa was right. I could never get involved with him.

I put all thoughts of Hayden Brooks out of my head and jumped up off the swing. I jogged out to where my sons were and picked up an extra baseball that they'd tossed aside.

"So, who wants to practice batting? I'll pitch."

Chapter 33

THINGS WERE AWKWARD and tense between Mason and me through the end of the term. He was still sleeping in my bed every night, but I hadn't let him touch me since his breakfast with his father. He knew I was upset with him, disappointed in him and regardless of how many excuses he gave me for his behavior, I couldn't quite get past his deception of his father.

During our last week together after finals and before he left for Chicago, I tried my best to put aside all ill feelings. I didn't want him to leave with things like this between us. At this moment I didn't know what the fall term was going to bring us or if it would bring us back together. I wanted to believe we could survive this and come out stronger on the other side, but I wasn't sure. What I did know was that I couldn't let him leave with this tension between us and all those words left unsaid.

On his last night with us, Mason played with the boys all evening. I kept an ear open to them while they played baseball in the backyard, and I grilled the chicken. They knew Mason was leaving in the morning and neither of them were too thrilled about it. They both wanted him to stay, but he explained to them that he had to go work at his father's firm and learn the business. I noticed that Mason failed to mention the real reason he would be working for his father over the summer, but I respected his choice and never told them otherwise.

I let Mason tuck the boys in without me. He spent time with each of them and talked about what they both had planned during their time apart. I knew the boys were going to miss him and he them, but all three of them tried to put on brave faces. Still, Henry hugged him tightly and told him he loved him before Mason turned off his light and closed his door partway.

I was sitting at my vanity table brushing my hair when Mason finally came to bed. He sat down on the edge of the bed and just watched me without saying a word.

"I washed all your clothes and left them there for you." I pointed to the area behind him on the bed.

"Thanks." He got up and pulled out a couple bags from beneath my bed.

Silently he began packing all his things. It did not escape my attention that he only packed his summer clothes and purposely left all his warmer clothes hanging in my closet or tucked away in the several drawers I had cleared out for him to use over nine months ago. I watched him through the reflection in the mirror and had to smile to myself when I noticed.

Maybe there is hope after all.

"What time are you leaving in the morning?" I inquired, setting the brush down and turning towards him.

"I'd like to be on the road by nine," he said, zipping up the last bag and then sat back down. "Look, Lexie, I know things have been strained between us since my dad showed up here a few weeks ago. You've been looking at me differently."

"How so?" I interrupted.

"You look at me like I'm a child," he stated flatly.

"I have not." I tried to deny it but we both knew it was true.

"I'm not proud of what I've done, but I can't change it now. And I'm going to have to work all summer to pay for the mistake." He fidgeted with his hands.

"Money? You really believe that's what I've been so upset about? The money?" I shook my head in disbelief.

He really doesn't get it!

"Well, I did . . . I don't now." He finally looked up at me. "If it's not the money, then what is it?"

I got up and walked over to him. I stood in between his legs and took his hands in mind. "Mason, do you have any idea how much you hurt my feelings when you introduced Emma to your dad instead of me. You had the perfect opportunity the second time your dad was here to be honest with him, but instead you said your girlfriend ran to the store for snacks. And then you invited Emma to breakfast. Are you that ashamed of me and our relationship, or am I just not important enough to you to introduce to your dad?"

"Wait a minute." He let go of my hands and stood up. "That's what you've been pissed about?"

"Yes."

"I did that for you. You're the one who put me in that position, not me. You have no one to blame for that scenario but yourself," he said hotly.

"How do you figure?"

"When my dad came to the door the first time and mistook you for Alex's mom, you never corrected him. I never did either. What did you want me to do? Call you a liar in front of my dad?"

Damn him!

"You couldn't just let us explain it to him together the second time he was here?" I questioned.

"That would have been lovely timing. I can't even imagine what my dad would have thought of either of us about that one." Mason rolled his eyes and started to laugh.

I hadn't even realized before that I'd backed myself into a corner between the two of them. There was no way I could tell Mason that his dad already knew without confessing that I'd spoken to Hayden behind Mason's back. Either way, I was screwed in this. I could, however, if I ever spoke to Hayden again, tell him Mason's reasoning for the deception . . . that he was trying to make me out not to be a liar in front of his dad. It was rather sweet really, in a childish sort of way.

"So, you lied to save my honor." I wrapped my arms around his neck feeling very foolish.

"Absolutely." He leaned down and kissed me softly. "Lexie, do you honestly believe I would ever be ashamed of you or our relationship?" He kissed me once more. "Never in a million years. I am so proud to be with you. And you'd better know how important you are to me. I love you so much. I thought you knew that."

"I do." I couldn't believe I had been so wrong.

"I hate that I can't be here with you for the summer, especially since you're not taking any classes." He wrapped me fully in his arms. "What are you going to do with all your free time?"

"Honestly, I have no idea." I smiled and reached up kissing him again.

For the first time since our first disastrous encounter, I let Mason take the lead as he laid me down upon my bed. He slowly crawled up my body and kissed me deeply. His hands caressed the side of my face as he looked longingly into my eyes. He brushed my hair away from my face and kissed me once more.

Nothing was hurried, nothing was rushed. Time didn't matter. We had all night. One final perfect night to share. One that had to last each of us a summer long. There was no tomorrow, only now. And we both wanted it to last a lifetime.

*   *   *

I leaned against the side of the loveseat holding my coffee and staring at the two large suitcases waiting in the foyer. I could not believe he was leaving for the summer. Even though Mason never officially moved in with us, he had spent the better part of the last year in my home. I knew he hated leaving us and would have stayed in a heartbeat if I had asked. But I couldn't. As much as I dearly loved him and our relationship, I had always known at some point he was going to leave. I could not deny him this extraordinary opportunity or jeopardize his future because I wanted him to play cabana boy for the summer.

Mason came down the hall carrying his duffle bag, dressed in gym shorts and a t-shirt. His hair was still wet from our shower and rested in small curls. I couldn't believe how much he had changed in the last year alone. He seemed like such an immature boy when I met him. Now, he was growing into the man he would someday become. The naivety and innocence were gone forever from his eyes.

"I think I got everything," he announced as he approached me, setting his duffle bag on the floor beside the rest of his luggage.

"Good," I responded in a low voice.

"Hey?" He took me in his arms and leaned his forehead against mine. "Don't look so sad. I don't have to go you know."

"Yes, you do."

"I'll be back before you have the chance to miss me." His smile did not reach his eyes.

"You'll be so busy you won't have time to miss me," I pointed out.

"Not true." He took me in his arms. "I will miss you terribly."

"I'll be here when you get back."

"I'll be back the first week in August." He kissed me softly.

"I'll be here." I wrapped my arms around his neck and hugged him tightly. "You be careful."

"I will." He let me go and gathered up his luggage.

I walked him out to his car and watched him as he threw his bags in the trunk. He slammed it shut and took me by the hand over to the driver's side door.

"I am going to miss you so much," he whispered, taking me in his arms one last time.

"I will miss you too." I kissed him softly. "I love you."

"I love you too." His eyes glistened with the sadness we both felt. "Tell the boys I will miss them, and I'll be back in time for football season."

"Okay." He opened his car door and gave me one final kiss. "Be careful," I reminded him.

"I'll see you in the fall."

I stood on my porch and watched Mason drive away. It had been a fabulous year. I had survived my first two years of college and we had been together for a little over a year now. The young beanie boy who had started out sleeping next to me in my sociology class had wound up sleeping beside me in my bed. True, he had started out as a fun fling, turned into a psychosexual project, but he also had grown into a lover and a companion.

As his taillights faded away, I walked back into my house thinking of all the possibilities the following year of school was going to bring for us all. I closed the front door behind me and leaned against it, considering what I was going to do with my summer break. The boys were leaving in three weeks to spend a month with Danny, and I was going to be alone for the first time in a long time. And I had no inkling what to do with myself.

My cell phone started ringing in the corner of my desk. I rushed over and picked it up thinking Mason must have forgotten something after all.

"Hello?"

"Hello, Alex. This is Hayden. Are you busy?"

About the Author

Addison Winters is an award-winning author who has a master's in military psychology and is currently completing her doctorate. She is the author of the best-selling With Honors series and the new Heat of Arrest series. When she is not buried in research, reading, or lost in a world of her own creation, she enjoys gardening, hiking, and traveling. Addison resides in East Texas with her husband Eric, their daughters, and three very spoiled puppies.

Making the
Dean's List
ADDISON WINTERS

Award-Winning Conclusion . . .
Transferring Credits
With Honors Series
Book 3

The cards are on the table, and everyone has shown their hand. No one is innocent. No one is coming out without scars. Alexandra, Mason, and Hayden must face the consequences of their actions and deal with the fallout.

But are they ready? Can they handle the reception they are about to receive from their friends and family? When the dust settles, will they be able to look each other in the eye?

In the gripping conclusion of the With Honors series, Alex must decide where her heart truly lies. But will her decision destroy the two families? Will she be able to let go of one of the two men she has grown to love and cherish? And will she be able to live with herself?

Don't Miss the Exciting New Series . . .

Mounting Deuce

Heat of Arrest Series

Book 1

Arya Lucas finally had her life back. After a nasty divorce and moving across the country, freedom was finally hers and she was enjoying it to the fullest. Her small consulting firm was finally offering her the life she had worked so hard to achieve. She had everything or so she thought.

With the urging of her best friend Arya joins a dating site with no desire to start a relationship with anyone, until she meets Detective Deuce. The sexy law enforcement officer was unlike anyone she had ever dated and definitely not her type.

But his enchanting blue eyes and smirky boyish grin drew her to him. His witty sarcasm was undeniably charming. He was compassionate, kind, and sexy. He held a sense of mystery and adventure that she had never experienced before. She never knew handcuffs could be so enticing.

But what she hadn't counted on was his impact on her entire world. How one day she would wake up and find herself in a life she no longer recognized and realize she could not have been happier about it.

Still, is he worth risking her heart for?

Scarlett
Ink
Publishing